Paul Haines
Slice of Life

Published by Morrigan Books
Östra Promenaden 43
602 29 Norrköping
Sweden
www.morriganbooks.com

Editors: Amanda Pillar & Glen Krisch

ISBN: 978-91-86865-24-5

Cover Illustration © Jordi Elias
Cover Design © Amanda Pillar
Internal Layout: Amanda Pillar

First Published by The Mayne Press Pty Ltd 2009

Published by Morrigan Books in November 2011

Slice of Life

For Jules and Isla, without whom I would not be…

Acknowledgements

A more than massive thank you to Geoffrey Maloney and Stuart Mayne, for without whom this slice of life would not be. Also to SuperNOVA for workshopping almost all of these stories (supernovawriters.org). Thanks to Getty Images for helping out.

The Very Talented Mr. Haines

(with apologies to Patricia Highsmith)

There is nothing like a Paul Haines story. Serial killers, talking cats, drug induced transformations, cannibals, terrorists, sex, more sex, some bestiality (carefully and subtly handled within the context of the story, of course, and essential to the plot) and PARANOIA — lots and lots and lots of PARANOIA. Be alert, not afraid, and watch out for the guy with mousey hair downloading terrorist handbooks and kiddie p0rno onto your computer while you've just nicked off to the loo, suddenly found yourself in a temporal displacement field while on the toilet bowl, and ended up in a bar in the Congo drinking UFO fuel with a bunch of pygmies, who might be aliens, but shit, you're too off your face to know. Or you might be somewhere else, and not off your face at all, but you're still feeling all twitchy and jumpy, because the guy with the mousey hair's got kaleidoscopes in his eyes...

Despite all the wonderful pyrotechnics of his work and his irreverent manipulation of genres we all love so well, Paul does what all great writers do; he exposes something of his own life in his stories, turns the good times and the bad times into fictions, puts them through the Paul Haines GenreBenderBlender®™© (wish I had one of those) and rubs our faces in the existential human condition of it all — somehow managing to entertain us at the same time. He's the only writer I have read that has convinced me that serial killers are really just kind of average blokes. The only writer in a long time that makes me laugh out loud *and* cringe when I realise he's going to push it just that little bit further and take me out of my safety zone as a writer and a reader. And I love the fact he can do that.

This is the second time I've worked with Paul on a collection of his stories.

What a privilege it's been. Paul is a wonderful person and a most remarkable writer by anyone's standards. His stories are just so good.

As I was writing this tonight I received an email from the up-and-coming Bollywood actor, Mirza Khan, whom Paul had met when he was travelling in Pakistan. It simply read: *That Paul Haines is a wonderful talent.*

Geoffrey Maloney
Brisbane, Australia
October 2008

PS. I'd like to dedicate this preface to Mr. Pussy. He's one cool cat.

Introduction

(with apologies to Michael Moorcock)

Slice of life. Double meanings. Dead metaphors.

You all know the slice of life 'story', usually a vignette or an episode of someone's life without any plot, action or conflict, that ends up in front of you in a writing group or writing course and you know full well that what you are reading is real and dull and badly disguised as fiction or poorly written as memoir. It borders on literary, never speculative, and the French, lending it some authenticity, call it *tranche de vie*.

Mostly it's fucking boring. (Hey, Haines, hold on, this is not a good way to start an introduction by telling the reader it's boring, you've got to—) Shut the fuck up.

The stories within this collection on the whole, with a few exceptions, are moored firmly in the real world, and some indeed are actual slice of life stories, though you will find plot, conflict and, God forbid, resolution, even in the stories here that are real. The stories on the whole, with few exceptions, are also lashed with humour, though humour is a subjective thing and most people find mine to be veering off course and foundering on jagged rocks hidden beneath black waters.

I start with me. I find the more of me I put into the story, the more verisimilitude the piece takes on, and that in turn opens wide the floodgates for the ocean of the fantastic. The weaving of truth and lies becomes hard to distinguish, and for those that are close to me, that can sometimes be hard to take. My poor wife. My lamenting mother.

The Slice of Life stories, a continuing narrative following the life of a delusional paranoid corporate cannibal working his way through a series of gourmet recipes, unsettled my work colleagues. They recognised their workplace. And they recognised parts of me, and worse, themselves. It doesn't help that the protagonist is called Paul Haines. The title also puns the slice of life meaning itself, while staying within the boundaries of *tranche de vie*. 'Mnemophonic' was set in the bar next to where we worked. I hated the music in there, especially the piano being played, so soulless and lost, but the beer was boutique and cheap.

'The Devil In Mr. Pussy' takes huge slabs of autobiography and lays it down bare, warts and all. But which parts are true? We did go through IVF, I do live in that house, I did have a cat called Mr. Pussy. That same slightly cracked voice runs through 'The Good Old Days', 'Inducing' and 'Where is Brisbane'. They start with base version of Haines, with each taking a different course down the rivers of selfishness, paranoia and completely fucked up. What I could have been in a hundred parallel universes. Luckily the people mentioned within those pages are still my friends. At least they tell me that.

Some of these stories appeared as gifts, and as in life, these are sometimes bestowed on you. 'Yum Cha', 'Lifelike and Josephine', and 'Going Down With Jennifer Aniston's Breasts' appeared fully formed in my mind's eye and compelled me to sit down and write them. I had no choice. Where they came from, I don't know, but they work exactly how I want them to.

Only four of the tales are not based on some part of my life, that are pure fantasy. I'll give you a hint: 'Doof Doof Doof' is one of them, 'The Interferers' is not. Those boys are dredged fully formed from a couple of weeks rambling through the mud of the English countryside in high summer. My partner in travelling crime at the time became Scwythe. I find it interesting that I write those tales (yes, unfortunately there are more — a dragon hunt, a druid ring) from the viewpoint of Scwythe for the most part. He's a much more sympathetic character than the arrogant, selfish Thorndyke who is based on, um, me.

Scwythe also appears as his true self in 'The Punjab's Gift' and 'Shot In Loralai', exercises in travel writing and paranoia, although I changed his name as he felt he needed to be protected. Travels through the third world opened a lot of imaginative doors in my mind and lead me down this path I now tread. Travel provided me with the conviction to be a writer, though I didn't want to be a travel writer, fiction is where my true heart lies. It has also heavily influenced my short stories and these two tales are all true. (Come on, Haines, that's stretching it a bit, you're a—) I told you to shut up! Don't touch that! Stop it, you'll fuck up the next bit of te⊠◆✒◆●✕♍♍ ▢↗ ●✕↗♍⟨ ❄▢✕▢●♍ ◯ ♍⟨■℣◆⟨ ⬦♍⟨♒ ▢♍◆⟨▢♍♍♒◆⟨♒♙❼ ◯ ♍◆▢▢♍■◆◆⊠ ↗✕℣♒◆✕■℣ ♍⟨■♍♍▢ ⟨ ◆▢▢♍ ▢↗ ⊠▢◆ ▢✕℣◆ ⅋■▢◆ ◆ ♒✕◆⟨ ♙◆❼◆ ♒▢◆ ◆♒✕◆ ♍▢●●♍♍◆✕▢■ ♍⟨▢♍ ◆▢ ♌♍⟨ ❄♒♍ ♍⟨■♍♍▢ ♒ ⟨◆ ◆▢▢♍⟨♒ ◆▢ ▢⊠ ●✕❖♍▢⟨ ♙◆ ◆

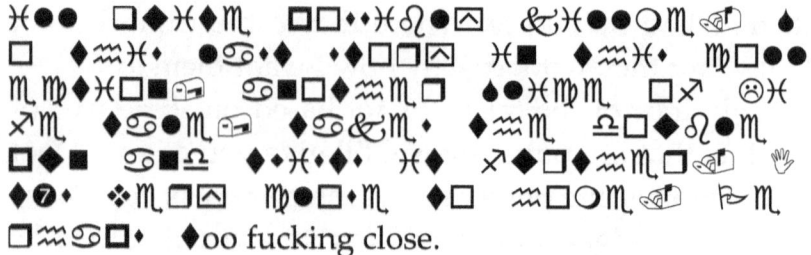

oo fucking close.

(Shit. Sorry about that).

Aw, for fuck's sake, Vogon, now look what you've done. *Tranche de fucking vie.*

Paul Haines
Melbourne, Australia
September 2008

Contents

Slice of Life

I felt like taking the paperweight and caving in the back of Carver's head.

Discovering whether that brand of gel he smears could stem the flow of blood and brain before it soaked into the wool of a thousand dollar suit bought in Chicago on a holiday. (What sort of wanker buys suits on their holiday?)

If Vogon was here I'd probably do it, but he rarely turns up at my work. He reckons nothing good ever happens there. No intensity. Vogon's pretty fucked up though; his good equals Bad.

"Sure thing, Mr. Carver. Be on your desk in the morning." It doesn't have the satisfaction of crunching bone so, when no one is looking, I give my boss the finger instead.

Carver turns in his stride, his corporate cunt of a hairstyle still shining under the office fluorescence of another late evening. He nods serious professional attitude then retires to his office. From the window I watch his Merc depart the carpark less than ten minutes later.

"You want a future in this company, Haines?" Carver had said. He'd perched on the corner of my desk, manicured hands clasped between his thighs. "I'm counting on you. I need it first thing tomorrow."

Life and death, I'm sure. And because I'm not married and don't have kids, I get "volunteered" for overtime. There's a reason why I'm not married, not that he'd give a fuck. How the Hell will I meet anyone real, with pricks like him foisting work on me at the end of the fucking day? Still, there's no point bitching about it. I might as well just get stuck in and finish the bastard before 11:05pm. If I don't leave by then, the Belgrave-Lilydale train will be nigh on empty. And that would deprive me my main course of pleasure for the day.

Doesn't Carver realise I don't give a fuck about the promotion?

The reflections of my colleagues in the darkening windows form a firmer reality than does the city. Sometimes, when I'm the only one left, I switch off the lights and stare out onto the city, watching people flush through neon streets, the dead and alive, brains dulled in skull soupbowls, one stumbling foot in front of the other. Living empty lives until, eventually, even they see the decayed flesh wrapped in expensive wool and leather, sloughing from the bone of once-bright youth.

I'd switch off the lights now, but I'm sure Suzanne wouldn't appreciate it. The very model of corporate efficiency; long hours and hard work and usually my supervisor on the big projects. Craig is working back too, as usual.

He's into it, the lucky bastard. Once, over a few beers at lunch, he'd expressed his desire to "sleep" with Suzanne. I laughed — I'd never thought about it before. She was such a cold bitch socially. Craig reckoned he'd wait until she broke up with her boyfriend before he tried anything. I hardly speak to her now, not that it matters.

I copy responses from an old proposal and paste them into the RFI. Another Request-for-Fucking-Information where we forced "No" into "Yes" without legally lying. It wouldn't take too long to finish this. Same old shit pushed out somewhere else. Someone would buy. At the end of the month, I'd be up for review and Carver and his cronies would offer one of us a 2.5% commission on any successful proposals.

"What time you working to, Craig?"

"Till about eight," he says. Diligent bastard never took his eyes off his monitor. He doesn't look at me too much since I fucked Suzanne at the Christmas do. We haven't been out for a beer or lunch since. I got as big a kick out of the blood draining from his face as I did licking the sweat from the hollow Suzanne's back made as her spine curved into her arse. Sure sign she was about to cum, I had told Craig.

"Well, I might have a smoke. Anyone?" I offer a half-empty pack as I walk past their desks. Silence usually means no takers.

I waltz into the women's toilet — I don't smoke, but the less people really know about you the better — and slip into the cubicle Suzanne prefers. I unzip, spit into the palm of my hand and masturbate, remembering her reaction when I'd thrown the photo of the boyfriend down on her bed in front of her as I was taking her from behind. She'd clenched tight, rigid as, but she was too close to care. She'd wept afterwards as I'd dressed. I hadn't expected the tears and was pleasantly surprised, so I didn't tell her I had taken the condom off.

"This is risky, you realise," says a voice behind me.

It's Vogon halfway through a transformation. I see my chin and nose forming on his misshapen visage. His body appears more in proportion to a humanoid now, too — he's managed to elongate his limbs from the squat appendages he'd begun with.

"Not now, Vogon. Can't you see I'm busy?"

"She could come in at any moment. You could be fired instead of doing the firing."

"That's the point." I squeeze the last drops onto the seat and smear it where her flesh will contact. He's ruined the moment for me, though. "What the Hell are you doing here? This is not the norm."

"Just making sure. It worries me I might lose my host through some preventable act of stupidity."

"I'm touched."

"Yes, you have been. Probably since birth." His face ripples as he studies the cubicle door. "It seems the female of the species does not adorn the toilet door with decorations from the nose. Why is this?"

"Because." I push past Vogon into the washroom. I notice he's not reflecting in the mirrors. "What are you doing here, seriously?"

"Are you going to be bad again? I think that you are."

"What? You're out of your warped little mind, buddy."

"And you're not?"

"Point taken." I indicate the mirror. "You'd better sort that out if you want to pass as human."

I leave Vogon panicking in front of the mirror and make my way back to my desk. The cheek of the prick coming in here to check me out. What if someone

4

walked in on *him*? Now that would be a little risky.

Suzanne lifts an eyebrow as I pass her, the eyes in her sockets professionally calculating, emotionless. I have to admit she's consistent. Cold before we fucked; cold after. I wish the bitch took the late train home with me — just to give her a fucking scare, snap her out of her reverie. Or better still, maybe I should let her know I told Craig. He is still head down, so I rub him on the shoulder as I hover over him.

"How's it going with the report, Craig?"

"Almost there, just got to tidy up the executive summary before I print it."

"You applying for the position?"

"No." His shoulders tense so I dig my fingers into the muscle.

"Same."

"I'm finishing up in five, Craig," says little miss ice. No capitals. "Can I still get a lift?"

"Yeah, sure thing, Suze." His lips worm into a smile. "I can print this out first thing tomorrow."

I clap him once more on the back, my hand now dry, note where he's saving the document and go back to my desk.

Copy. Paste.

Copy.

Her arse: two ovular haunches gliding seductively beneath red cotton, tight and sweet. The calves lean and defined, flexing muscle-toned power. A fine piece of meat, as they'd say. The click of high-heels over the floorboards as Craig shuffles after her. I imagine his tongue drooling from his mouth as he pants behind.

After they leave, I open Craig's document, delete

several lines from each of the pages, type "Fuck you, Carver" and run a utility to reset the date-timestamp to when Craig had saved it. Maybe I will go for that promotion.

The late trains are always on time.

I think it's because they worry that the monsters come out late at night, and darkness provides the finest prey. I take the carriage that most of the people get into, knowing after a few stops it will be lucky if there are half a dozen of us left. Safety in numbers, they say.

Come Box Hill and the opportunities finally present themselves: a guy in a dark suit busies himself with the evening's MMX; a couple of teenagers nurse their skateboards and tag the train with thick markers; a girl in her late teens, recently finished a shift at a David Jones cosmetic counter, sinks against the wall seeking refuge in her headphones; an old drunk shuffles between carriages bumming coins; a woman in her late twenties with heroin-eyes and a face drawn tight over her skull languishes on a three-seater, a battered windcheater draped over her dependant body. She hasn't been *here* since East Richmond.

Any of these will do. The end of the line.

"Don't." Vogon appears beside me. He's managed to get the colour of my eyes right, but he's used the same blue for the nostril hairs. "It's not worth it."

"Keep it down, someone might hear," I whisper. "Why are you on the train? Are you following me?"

"I'm just making sure. I don't want you to jeopardise

the mission."

"What fucking mission, Vogon? You and your race conquering Earth sometime soon? I'm telling you, you're wasting your time following me around. I can't help you."

The suit is looking at me so I glare him back to his paper.

"As I was saying...Vogon?" He pisses me off when he ups and disappears like that, leaving me sitting here talking to myself. People might think I'm weird.

The two skaters get off at Blackburn. One of them gives me the finger and shouts, "Crazy motherfucker." They laugh, throw down their boards and skate off. I sense the suit sniggering but the vocal abuse is worth it — the cosmetic girl's eyes flutter briefly open and snap shut when she sees me staring.

That's twice now, girly. Three times and you're out. The junkie moans softly and rustles in her skin. The drunk has moved further down the carriages looking for easy bucks, some food or booze, or fast-food wrappers to suck the grease from. Whatever gives, he's taking.

Vogon manages to slip into the seat behind the cosmetic girl. He has sprouted thick black curls from his misshapen scalp, and his greyish skin pales in an imitation of hers. Blood red colours his lips. He turns to me and grins, his pouty lips peeling back from thick, irregular teeth. He obviously notices my consternation and comes over to sit next to me.

"Not her," he says. "She still lives at home. Parents

will be expecting her. I want you to really draw out the experience. Maybe for a day or two."

"How presumptuous of you. Why do you think I'm going to do something?"

"I know you. Better than you know yourself."

"I don't think so."

"If it's her, I won't let you. It's too risky."

"That's the point. My reasons for doing it are entirely different to yours."

"I won't let you," Vogon says. The adopted human features dissolve from his mass, leaving a grey bulk sulking beside me. He is serious.

"Now approaching Mitcham station," pipes the inflectionless drone over the loudspeakers.

Cosmetic girl opens her eyes.

Strike three. You're out. I grin. She looks away, rises and makes her way to the doors. The suit is still absorbed in his paper, junkie still out, Vogon has disappeared again, and Mitcham really isn't too far away from my place.

I stand slowly, stretching my legs and arms, and languidly stroll to the doors, holding onto the rail above her head, near enough to smell the perfumes she's been trying at work. *J'adore*, I think. She moves closer to the doors. As the train lurches to a halt, I bump her and apologise, savouring the brief warmth of contact, wishing I had managed to touch her skin. She'd moved at the last minute though, and I only got the tease of white cotton.

I'm close behind as she steps off the train, her knee length skirt revealing calves a little thicker than I prefer, but still a most accommodating cut.

Someone pushes me from behind.

"Sorry," says the suit. He slips past and falls into step behind the scurrying cosmetics girl. Headlights flash in the carpark, and she waves and runs towards the car.

In the carriage Vogon mouths the words "What did I say?"

The train utters its warning beeps; I jump back on and the carriage jerks its way towards Lilydale.

Vogon smiles; he's perfected the shit-eating grin of corporate smugness. I should smash him then, hard in the face, but I don't. Vogon can be very unpredictable. Every fibre of that alien, metamorphosed body of his cries out, "I told you so!"

He sits awhile basking in it, too. Sometimes he embodies everything I fucking hate about the face I present to the world during the daylight hours. The gloating, conservative cunt knows this — he's imitated me for years now — and I wish I had the mental strength to kill him. And, in the end, I conform to the mouldings of others.

"It's the junkie then," Vogon says. "What do you think?"

"I don't know. Look at her."

He peels back the wind-cheater, tugging gently at it where it has scabbed to her upper arms. "Been picking at herself a little, but she's fine."

"She's too skinny."

"No, no, no, there's enough meat on her bones. I know you want to. It's why I'm here."

"She's diseased, Vogon. Who knows what she's carrying?"

"Then cook it longer." He shudders and laughs.

"Quick, your stop is coming up soon. Pry open the lips."

"You do it."

"You work with the flesh."

"I'm not touching her."

"Pry open the lips!"

I pinch her nose and her mouth pops open and strands of thickened saliva bridge raw, cracked lips. Her breath is damp and shallow.

Vogon quivers and moans. His form dissolves and he swarms over her body like a sea of black ants over jungle flesh, forcing his way into her mouth.

Within seconds, his amorphous mass has slid inside her, waiting. His voice echoes inside my head. "Do it."

Reluctantly I touch her cheek, the elasticity of her skin burnt from abuse, now cold and dry against my fingertips. Not unlike newspaper thawing from the morning rounds. A world away from the living.

"The quota needs to be filled for the first phase of occupation." Vogon's voice swims between my ears. "You don't have much time. Do it!"

Her eyes flutter open, pinpoint pupils struggling in the bright lights of the carriage. She coughs and a splutter of blood-flecked phlegm sprays the seat.

"Ahhrrgg..." she croaks. She pulls the windcheater tight as she struggles to sit. The stink of chemicals pours from her skin. "Wha the fuck...who?"

I sit there, silent, trying to look blank, to stop my lips curling.

"Hey, we passed Nunawading yet? I gotta get off Nunawading."

"You missed it. Croydon is the next stop."

"Ah, shit. Hey, you got $2.60 for a ticket? Need a ticket to get back."

She scratches at her arms.

Vogon hisses. "Do it!"

I leaf through my wallet, making sure she sees the wad of orange and red bills. "Sorry, lady. Got no coins on me."

"Some notes then maybe, just a fiver. Please."

"I've got nothing that small."

"Look, mister. C'mon. Anything." She edges towards me. "I'll suck your cock."

"Maybe I could give you some cash for a cab at the next stop. I'm getting off there. If you know what I mean."

Vogon laughs at the pun, though her mouth doesn't move. "Very good."

She wipes her lips and forces a smile. "The ride'll cost at least a twenty."

As the train brakes into the Croydon stop, I follow her to the doors.

Vogon keens in anticipation within her body as we step from the train and move into the shadows outside the station. Where the lights and cameras are blind to my slice of life.

Vogon is home before me. He glares at me from the couch. He still wears the cracked lips of the junkie and blends the cut of my suit with the fabric of the wind-cheater.

"You cheated me," he says sullenly.

"You sucked my cock." I laughed. "How'd my cum taste?"

"You cheated me! You let her go! "

"You don't decide who I choose. Since when did you think you had the right to make my decisions?"

"I keep you safe!"

"You're not my fucking moral conscience, Vogon. I will not let you decide who I take just because you've developed a taste for it. Anyway, she was a junkie."

"There's hundreds of them. They teem in this city. Why won't you let me try them?"

I sigh. "They are unhealthy."

"Whatever happened to 'too risky' being the point?"

"You wouldn't understand."

It is a quarter after midnight and the evening has left me with an appetite. I put on a Sisters Of Mercy bootleg and busy myself in the kitchen. I slice a Spanish onion and sliver two cloves of garlic as Vogon sulks in silence, slowly metamorphosing into a rough semblance of his host — me. I dash some olive oil into a deep saucepan and place it over the gas flame.

"You want some?"

"You know I don't eat." His form shifts again, his face narrowing into the pout of the gay boy from last year.

"That's my point. It's like drinking wine. You start off with the sweet Moselles of this world, and you work your way up the ladder until only the Shiraz and Cab Savs will do. Like cheese, from your shrink-wrap plastic to the finest French blues. The well-done steak to the lump of meat still warm from its own blood. Taste is so delicate, Vogon, and she'd been tainting hers for too long."

As the oil heats, I remove two fresh kidneys from the fridge. I slit the round side of the kidney and peel the membrane back towards the fatty core. I prefer to leave the core intact as it moistens and bastes the kidneys as they cook. I sauté the onions and garlic, and when browned, place the kidneys into the pan, the sizzle of searing flesh causing me to salivate. After one and half minutes — I like them pink in the middle — I turn the kidneys, adding a dash of mustard and Worcestershire sauce. The frying aromas tantalise my tastebuds, and that last minute waiting for the kidneys to brown seems as long as the train ride home from work.

"You know," I say to Vogon as I serve the meal, "I'm thinking of going for that promotion at work. Get me closer to Carver. I think I'm ready for that next slice of life. What do you think?"

But Vogon has already disappeared.

The Devil in Mr. Pussy

(or How I Found God Inside My Wife)

The stifled moans and muted screams of my wife from the adjoining bedroom made it hard to concentrate. The cat was right. Things had gotten to the point where I needed to lay blame. Mr. Pussy sat straight-backed like a temple guardian on my silk rug, staring at me as I worked. He preferred the Persian silk to the Pakistani wool. The edges of the rug were smothered in black fur.

Pregnancy can be a killer. Mr. Pussy gave his thick coat another attention-seeking lick. *You know I don't like kids.*

"This will be different." I focused on the screen and the manuscript-in-progress. "Touched by Jesus. Gotta be good." I gave Mr. Pussy a withering stare. "Unless, of course, you're associated with the other half."

He stopped his licking and looked at me, his cat-yellow eyes wide in the dim light of the study. *You're kidding me, right? I can't believe you've bought into this shit. You're losing your marbles, mate.*

A moan came from the bedroom, a guttural response sliding towards the uncomfortable side of pain. Or pleasure. I hoped it was pain. Jealousy, even at a time like this, was hard to contain.

"Mirella and I moved here to start a family. You know that."

Sure you did, but this ain't normal. This is fucking weird.

The cat was right. It was weird.

I was starting to get those cravings again, too. My vision blurred at the edges, and the skin on the back of my hand danced, waltzing slowly around to my wrist and tangoing up to the crook of my elbow.

"You hungry?"

Mr. Pussy bounded off the rug and was halfway towards the kitchen.

You betcha! Let's eat.

I followed his upright bushy tale and freshly cleaned arsehole, an exclamation point to our addiction, to the pantry. I filled his bowl with our current favourite — Beef Lamb Liver and Vegetable Bickies — and poured myself a handful while I was at it. I felt a little more in control now.

And who's to blame? I couldn't blame myself. Jesus, definitely Jesus, and the woman that introduced us to this madness. Lucy Case.

We should never have bought this house from her.

Lucy Case led Mirella and I down a long hallway plastered with pictures of Christ. The longhaired, blue-eyed, softly bearded, good old American Christ the world had grown to love in the last couple of hundred years. I wished I'd shaved my beard off before coming over.

"I had this feeling, you know," Lucy said, ushering us through into the living area. "This time I'd find the proper people to take it over. I've had the house on the market twice before but no *real* takers." She smiled at an old bamboo calendar of Christ with his arm outstretched beaming benignly.

"More than a feeling actually. A glass of champagne to celebrate?"

"That would be lovely," Mirella replied.

As Lucy filled the flutes, Mirella and I glanced at each other. The real-estate agent had been right. Ms. Case was a little over-zealous. Still she had sold us the house at not-quite-a-bargain-but-better-than-we'd-expected-to-pay-for-the-area price.

Lucy smiled and handed me a glass. She was a handsome woman for her fifty-odd years and her buxom figure still held allure. She'd have no problem attracting men fifteen years her junior. I noticed Mirella had to retrieve her own glass from the bench as Lucy indicated for me to take a seat. I sat next to the muted television that had ghosting and static swimming across the screen. Lucy didn't switch the television off.

I took a sip of the champagne — warm — and glanced around the room at the framed pictures of Christ with sheep; Christ with halo; Christ with stigmata offering blessings; Christ smiling, nodding, understanding; Christ on a stick; a magnetic Christ on the fridge; Christ on a Harley, and, there, on the side-table next to a bookcase covered in Christ, sat an early-eighties glam photo of Lucy in soft-focus. Big breasts and bigger hair, in a reclining pose that screamed stick-your-cock-in-me-and-I'll-eat-you-alive-boy-and-you'll-die-loving-it.

"So what do you do for a living, Paul?" Lucy asked.

"I'm a writer — speculative fiction mostly. I do computer work on the side to pay the bills."

"Paul had a short story collection published last

year," Mirella chipped in. "He's working on a novel at the moment."

"A writer." Lucy nodded, never taking her eyes off me. "Yes, of course. Creative."

"Mirella works for a charity," I said, trying to divert Lucy's unwavering attention.

"For disadvantaged children—" said Mirella.

"That's nice. Now, Paul, the ideas, the inspiration, where do you get them for your stories?"

"I don't know. Sometimes they come fully formed, like a vision—"

"Yes, a vision, exactly." She sipped her cheap champagne. "Some say God gives inspiration, that the artist is simply channelling the vision of God."

I smiled. Uncomfortably. From the corner of my eye I caught Mirella trying not to laugh into her glass. "I'm not particularly—"

"I wasn't always like this." Lucy indicated the Christs around the room.

"Something happened that...changed me. I don't like to think of myself as religious. I prefer *spiritual*." She leaned forward in her chair, closer to me.

Closer to my face. "'Religious' is a bit of a dirty word these days, wouldn't you say?"

Lucy's glamour photo stared at me harder than the Lucy in the armchair. Perhaps the photo was a reminder of her past life. The wolf, the lupess, the alpha female amongst Christ and his sheep. The atmosphere in the room filled with fucked-up sex, soaking my skin and muddling my brain.

I fumbled for my glass, spilling the champagne into my lap. "Fu..Jesus Christ!"

My cheeks burned. Ooops.

Lucy said nothing, but pressed a Christ-emblazoned tea towel against my thigh. I grabbed it quickly, trying not to tear it from her hands.

"Sorry about that," I said meekly. Mirella had clearly decided her absence from the conversation was preferred. "I can do this."

Lucy smiled and lounged back in the armchair. "Yes, yes I'm sure you can, Paul. A good strong name that. Paul."

"Road to Damascus, yeah, I know," I replied. I could have followed it up with "a bloke who lost his sight and later became a born-again nutter", but I thought it pertinent not to as I mopped my groin.

"Very good." Lucy placed her half-empty glass onto a Christ coaster on the coffee table, and took the damp towel from me. "So, why did you want to move to this side of town?"

"We're wanting to start a family," said Mirella. "We—"

Lucy patted my wife on the knee. "That's lovely, dear." Then she fixed her sharp blue eyes on me again. "God rewards his own, and you've certainly come to the right place."

"Sorry?" I asked.

"The area I meant. This is the baby booming suburb of Melbourne. Anyway, with formalities over, I expect you'd like to know a little history of this house."

I nodded. Formalities? Had we passed a test?

"It's actually a replica, built to period detail," Lucy said. "It's blessed by St. Joseph."

"St. Joseph?" I asked.

"You don't know who St. Joseph is?"

"The only Joseph I know was Jesus' father."

"The very same. The patron saint of carpenters. A big strong man, too. Guisseppe and his son Gianni, the men who built this house, said it was the easiest job they'd ever had to do. Like their hammers were guided onto the nails by unseen hands." Lucy raised her eyebrows and nodded sagely like the answer was all too obvious. The top of her shirt was now unbuttoned.

"St. Joseph's big hands. Gianni, bless him and his youthful exuberance, even claimed to see St. Joseph helping him lay the floorboards."

"Really," said Mirella. I hardly heard the ridicule leak off her lips. She was good, my wife, good.

"It may seem hard to believe, but others have seen him here, too. I held regular...meetings...where we have had the pleasure of being visited by St. Joseph. My dear friend, Barbara, has seen him come while we prayed. The very floor around us bloomed with rose petal, and the hallway filled with blossom from his passing."

Another button from her shirt had somehow come undone to reveal a hint of lace cupping a firm curve of breast. I cleared my throat.

"We have to be at Suzy's by nine." Mirella directed it at me.

"Of course." Lucy stood and smoothed her skirt.

As she led us back to the front door she said, "It's important to have the right people take over the house. God told me to wait — I refused the first two offers on the place — but He said you would come and pay the proper price."

Once inside the car and out onto the highway, I said,

"So, Mirella, do you think she liked me?"

"That woman is fucking insane," Mirella replied.

A week after we shifted into our new house, another young couple, James and Simone, moved in next door. They invited us over for a barbecue shortly after.

James put on an obscure XTC album he loved. It happened to be one of my favourites. Simone placed a chilled bottle of chardonnay on the table and handed me a beer. It was an expensive beer. Music floated out of the outdoor speakers, and I sank back into the deck chair to bask in the late afternoon sun. I liked them already.

"We're wanting to start a family," said Mirella.

"So are we," said Simone.

"Really?" Mirella leaned forward in her seat.

Click.

Laughter and conversation followed. We talked about children and jobs and music and film and eventually how we bought our houses. I ranted on about how this crazy religious nutter Lucy Case had sold us her house, complete with the hundredfold Christs and blossoming St. Joseph visitations-cum-orgies.

When Simone told us that Lucy had overseen their house deal, we burst out laughing again. Seizing the moment, I admonished at length about the gullibility of Christians, the perversity of faith, and how screwed up some people were in their beliefs.

"Another beer, Paul?" asked James.

"Sure."

He excused himself to get fresh drinks as the sun dipped below the house horizon. Simone leant over the table.

"James is Catholic," she whispered.

My face fell. Mirella bored very bad thoughts into my skull. The twilight chilled my skin.

"But don't worry." Simone refilled her glass of wine. "He's not like that."

I decided to take a few months off to seriously pursue the great crossover SF-horror novel that would earn me millions. I'd started with a hiss and a roar in our old place, but the only words making it to the manuscript now were "banal", "crap", "cliché" and were aggressively deleted. And very soon, not even those words were making it to the page.

"You're still settling into the house," said Mirella, as she left for work. "Don't push yourself. Let it happen. It'll come."

Nothing came.

Mr. Pussy sat in my in-tray on the desk, staring at me with drugged hostility. I think he resented the Clomicalm, a feline anti-depressant we'd put him on to help him overcome his anxiety, and also to help him adjust to the move to a new neighbourhood. As the keyboard didn't hold any magic, I decided to do a little more settling and covered the once-smothered-in-Christ-now-picture-hook-holed walls with shelves, then crammed the shelves full of books and CDs. Sat in front of the keyboard. Hung surrealist prints my wife wouldn't allow elsewhere in the house. Sat in front of the keyboard. Laid my rugs and put up my Chilean fertility masks. Sat in front of the keyboard. Browsed porn sites. Put the cat outside. Masturbated. Sat in front of the keyboard. Masturbated.

The only thing that came was me.

Maybe it was the goddamned room that was wrong. Bad Karma or Feng Shui or something. Perhaps if I tried writing somewhere else in the house I could kick-start the novel again, but I really couldn't be arsed shifting the computer equipment, and my handwriting sucked. I even wondered if St. Joseph didn't approve of speculative fiction and had unblessed my study.

Outside the window, Mr. Pussy caterwauled, long plaintive cries evocative of deep gashes and severed limbs. I let him back in and he resumed his position in the in-tray with a scowl. An hour later, the keyboard had refused to move, and neither had Mr. Pussy. He still sat there scowling at me. In fact, he didn't seem to do anything these days except sit and scowl. He didn't go outside to fight, to prowl, to sunbathe or even to eat grass to help him throw up furballs on the Persian silk.

"Not liking those anti-depressants, fatty boy?" I asked.

Mr. Pussy maintained the scowl.

I wondered what the poor thing was thinking, if he was even thinking at all.

I headed to the kitchen to look at food we didn't have. The room was starting to reek of fish — Mr. Pussy hadn't cleaned up his bowl, yet another side-effect of his medication. No longer aggressive, or insatiably hungry, no longer anything except an angry, drugged-out ball of moulting black fur.

The pantry provided little inspiration, so I made myself comfortable in the courtyard and tried to catch a little of the failing midday sun. And hopefully a couple of ideas for my failing novel.

I awoke covered in sweat to the sound of the phone ringing. I leapt up, a sudden blood rush to the head causing my vision to sparkle, and staggered inside. As I picked up the phone, I saw a silhouette framed by the sun in the hallway, but it disappeared as my eyesight returned to normal.

"Hello?" I said into the phone.

"Hi, hon, it's me." Mirella sounded depressed.

"What's wrong?"

"I got my period. It's never going to happen. I hate this."

"It's going to happen, Mirella, just be patient. Good things take..."

"Two years, Paul! It's not going to happen." She sounded like a dam about to burst. "I'm so sick of all this. I can't work here anymore; I can't stand being around the kids. I'm going to quit."

"But you love your job," I said. "Only last month you were saying how you loved working with the kids. It's just that time of the month — don't do anything stupid, Mirella."

"What the fuck would you know? Time of the month!" The dam burst, and tears flooded the conversation. "It's all right for you, sitting at home pretending to be a writer. I don't want to do this for the rest of my life! I want to be a mother! You can go out and fucking work!'

I didn't know what to say, so I let her get it all out.

"We need help," Mirella said. "IVF."

"If that's what you want, but it's expensive. You can't quit your job, at least not yet. We've talked about this before."

"I know," she said, the dam now empty. "I'm just upset that's all. You know how I get." She paused. "I'm sorry about what I said before. You know I love you."

"It's okay," I said.

IVF. That meant I'd have to go back to work sooner than planned. Hopefully, there'd be a delay in getting an appointment.

"Did you get any writing done?" she asked.

"Yeah, a little. Hey, Mr. Pussy is still not eating. Maybe we should take him off those pills."

"The vet said three months, hon. We don't want him bleeding around the house, or worse, running away. We'll change his diet. One of the girls here says her cat has gone crazy over these new cat biscuits. I'll bring some home tonight."

When she hung up, she sounded happier. Her fur kid always distracted her from the real issue, if only temporarily.

The kitchen really stunk of fish now, so I cleaned out Mr. Pussy's bowl before hitting the keyboard again.

On the way to the study, the hallway smelled of roses.

🐈

Eighty-eight percent of my sperm either had

hammerheads, congenital defects of the sperm tail, defective motility, or other maturation disorders.

The volume of boys was there, but most of them were swimming without their lights on. Eighty-eight percent sounded bad.

I needed to give up beer, wine, absinthe, dope, cocaine, ecstasy, coffee, caffeine, codeine, (actually, anything fun ending with "eine" even margarine), white bread, hamburgers, pizza, fish and chips, chocolate, Coca Cola and lemonade. I was supposed to replace them with water, juice, flaxseed oil, pumpkin seeds, water, legumes, nuts, olive oil, water, vitamin C and E, L-Lysine and L-Carnitine amino acids, zinc, selenium, vitamin B-12 and water.

Oh yeah, and I had to stop wanking.

Mirella made me painfully aware of something else absent in my life as we lay in bed while the cat meowed outside the bedroom door for his breakfast.

"I had a weird dream last night." Mirella's head rested against my shoulder. "We were in bed, like this, except it was dark, but I could still see everything. *We* weren't making love; *you* were fucking me. You had pinned me to the bed, and I couldn't move, and every part of you was huge and wild."

"Right." So I was obviously not huge and wild in real life. At least it had been me in the dream doing the business.

"I had orgasm after orgasm, and I felt you flowing into me, filling me. Oh God, it felt so real! I wasn't making any noise or moving about, was I?"

"Not that I noticed," I said. Mr. Pussy perfected his hit-by-a-car meowing and scratched at the door. "Shut up, Pussy!"

"It got weird when I looked into your eyes and saw a reflection of you standing in the doorway. You were masturbating while you watched me have sex with you. Or who I thought was you." Mirella paused for a deep breath.

"I think it turned into someone else, and then my belly began to swell."

I tried to keep the frustration out of my voice. "You're getting a little obsessed with pregnancy, don't you think? The average conception takes a year. Next you'll be telling me you've seen St. Joseph wandering around the house on rose petals, and he's going to help us conceive."

"I'm not obsessed! It was just a dream." Mirella propped herself up on one elbow and glared at me. "You're just upset I dreamt about having sex with someone else!"

"No, I'm not."

Mr. Pussy clawed at the door and yowled.

I clambered out of bed, stalked to the door and yanked it open. "What? It's not your bloody breakfast time yet!"

The cat sat straight-backed and silent, staring at me. His medication was wearing off — his sullen glare had softened.

I stepped towards the kitchen and he was off at a trot, looking behind occasionally to make sure I was following. I suspected cats had some modicum of telepathy, for though they can't speak they always manage to let you know what they want. Perhaps more than telepathy, as you always end up *doing* what they want.

After I had sustained a few scratches administering his Clomicalm, I returned to the bedroom. The shower was running, and the bed sheets were thrown back. There was a wet spot where Mirella had been sleeping.

Great.

We weren't falling pregnant; Mirella wanted to quit her job; my novel was going nowhere faster than I was; and my cat had turned into a zombie-like alarm clock on anti-depressants.

Oh, and my wife was having wet dreams.

And I wasn't having any dreams at all.

I realised then that I hadn't dreamed since moving into the house. I needed inspiration. I needed to break the curse that St. Joseph held sway over this house.

But how?

Lucy Case would call it divine intervention. I'd call it stuck in a rut and I thought, God only knows why — and there you go, Lucy — it might help me get out of mine.

I'd successfully cut back on the marijuana since we'd started trying to conceive, and I hadn't touched Charlie, the drug not the boy, for months.

Keeping my testicles, my baws, clean is what I told people. No drugs for Pauly-boy. Hell, I'd even stopped polishing the horn come ovulation time.

So when I first started taking the cat's anti-depressants I didn't think of it as divine intervention. I certainly didn't think of it as taking drugs. To be honest, I didn't know what I was thinking.

All I knew was they worked for Mr. Pussy. He'd stopped eating his arse.

I took his anti-depressants, not because I was depressed, far from it. I wanted inspiration. Or at least a different set of ideas, thought-processes, madness, whatever, banging around in those brain cells of mine.

Mr. Pussy had half a Clomicalm pill per day, so I thought I'd go for a whole based on my having a larger body mass. I swallowed it with a glass of orange juice then followed the instructions on the bottle by eating a couple of pieces of toast.

After a while nothing happened.

So I sat at my keyboard and stared at all the nothing happening on the screen.

The postman's arrival after midday wasn't just an excuse to get away from the study; mail collection was something that was necessary and needed to be done. I watched him puttering off down the street and thought perhaps I'd have more time to think with a job like that. None of the mail was for us.

A couple of bills for Lucy, and religious junk mail for one of her boarders,

John Guillermo. And another for Benny Benito. I'd found a pair of male underpants hidden beneath a drawer in the bathroom and wondered just how many boarders she had had here. And how many of those boarders were sharing not just the room. Lucy's come-fuck-me glamour photo leered in my memory. I shuddered, and went back inside to stare at the screen.

At five o'clock, Mr. Pussy yowled from the study door announcing his hunger. I poured him a bowl of the bickies Mirella had bought back from the pet store. He purred while he ate, all teeth crunching and saliva slobbering.

He even let me pat him. "Wonder Bickies" Mirella's friend had called them.

Fussy cats went crazy over them and it appeared she was right. Mr. Pussy loved them. Normally the bickies stank worse than the "fish product" in the Snappy Tom cans, but tonight they didn't smell too bad at all.

In fact, they even looked...good.

Keys rattled in the front door. I prepared myself for Mirella's haranguing when I would lie to her about how many words I hadn't written that day. And convince her we still had enough money for me to not work, but not quite enough for her not to. And to take two pills instead of one to see if that made any difference.

Confused? Not me.

You can lead a man to the watering hole, but you can't make him stiff.

Or maybe I was flogging my dead horse.

"It's that time," said Mirella.

They sounded like the words spoken before being led to the firing squad. Even worse, the bedroom felt like an execution chamber. I didn't want to go in there. Neither did Mirella.

Ready.

"The sheets are cold. I'm going to keep my jumper on." Mirella dropped her pants and wriggled out of her underwear. "And my socks."

I undressed and clambered on. We both shivered and pressed against each other for warmth.

"We could do this in the lounge." I pulled the duvet over our bodies.

"The couch hurts my neck and, anyway, the cat's in there." She reached for my flaccid penis and gave it a tug.

"Mr. Pussy doesn't care." I fingered her vagina, trying to bring on the rains, but it was drier than a Sydney winter down there.

"He watches us!"

I laughed. "He does not. He's a cat. He wouldn't even comprehend what we were doing. Should we kiss perhaps?"

We pecked each other on the lips, and I nibbled her earlobe.

"Don't. That tickles." Mirella smeared a little Vaseline on her hands and resumed flogging my dead horse. "And what have you been eating? Your breath smells funny."

I made a mental note to use Listerine before she got home. I hadn't quite figured out how to tell Mirella about my new dietary supplements.

"Sorry."

I began to stiffen.

"Good boy," she said.

Aim.

I poked around at the gates, but they weren't opening. They still needed a bit of oil. I pushed harder.

"Ow," Mirella said. "Go easy."

"Sorry."

She slowly guided me in, her body tensing with every dry inch, and then, suddenly, I was inside.

Fire.

"That was quick."

"Sorry," I said. "Do you want me to finish you off?"

"No, I'm not really in the mood."

We lay next to each other, staring at the ceiling, waiting for my boys to settle in for the ride. I hoped the water in the watering hole wasn't undrinkable.

Mr. Pussy chomped his way through breakfast.

Three days had passed and I'd decided two pills felt okay. I wasn't sure if I actually felt any different, but I did feel...well...like a flower in a forest that no-one ever sees. That felt okay to me.

Mr. Pussy paused in his chomping. He sat back and nodded towards his bickies.

"What's wrong?" I knelt to pat him.

He nodded again at the bowl.

The bickies smelt meaty and spicy. According to the information on the box, they contained Semenax, a product based on L-Carnitine and L-Lysine amino acids. And, as I now knew, they helped increase sperm production.

"You want me to have some?"

Mr. Pussy purred.

It made sense. Perhaps my testicles were telling my brain what it needed. I took a pinch of bickies, coarse between my finger and thumb. A crumbly, milk chocolate brown. I put them in my mouth and dabbed at their rough surface with my tongue. Salty and spicy, like an Arabic stew made from some exotic ingredient best left unknown. I bit down into what was like a peanut M&M coated in spice instead of chocolate and with a mushy meaty interior instead of the nut. Actually it probably was a nut, though of camel or horse origin.

"What do you think good old St. Joseph would say to this?" I took another pinch from the bowl. "Think he'd say 'Eat 'em up, Paws! It's news for the jews in the baws!'?"

Mr. Pussy purred louder, and placed his paw on my arm.

He looked happy.

And, I reckoned, so did I.

The morning started badly, and the afternoon ended worse.

"Mirella, are you okay?"

Muted sobs came from behind the bathroom door. I guessed what the problem was.

"Leave me alone," she said. "I'm fine."

I tried the door and found it locked.

"Maybe we should take a few days off and go spend some time with your family," I suggested.

"There's too many bloody babies at home!" she screamed through the door. "How can you be so insensitive?"

The toilet flushed, the shower spattered on, and the

cat was meowing in the hallway.

After Mirella left for work, I put the tampon wrapper on the bathroom floor in the rubbish bin, and decided to take three of Mr. Pussy's pills with breakfast. Why the Hell not, I told myself. St. Joseph had obviously unblessed the house on our arrival. Nothing had been going right since we moved in.

NOTHING.

I filled my "peanut bowl" with a good dose of bickies to help me through the morning struggle with the manuscript and left Mr. Pussy tearing up his toy mouse under the coffee table while I resumed my vigil at the keyboard. At least he had some life in him today. I heard him skating across the floorboards and smacking into things for an entire paragraph.

Three pills!

An entire paragraph!

That was more than I'd written in weeks, and I'd managed to complete it in under an hour. I sat back and crunched on another mouthful of bickies and contemplated the genius on the screen. It read good, and it read real!

The sound of the puttering postman stopped outside, followed by the soft thud of the letterbox lid. The puttering resumed and faded down the street. I tried to stand. The room decided to turn me around and lean me against the wall. My vision swam and my cheeks flushed. Sweat broke on my brow.

Whoa, boy. I steadied myself against the floor but the walls pushed me onto my feet. Three pills and too many bickies. Not so good. Not so real. My rug smelled of roses. I was going to be sick. A hundred cats yowled.

The doorbell rang.

I staggered into the hallway and leaned against the front door. There was a peephole, but it didn't like the look of my eye and wouldn't kiss me. I took a deep breath. I was obviously having a reaction to the anti-depressants.

The doorbell rang again.

The Bokhara runner flowing down the hallway bubbled into blossom.

Mr. Pussy stood on hind legs with his arms crossed at the far end of the hallway, smiling.

You gonna answer that, cunty-baws? It's doing my fucking head in.

I shook my head and rubbed my eyes.

The doorbell rang again.

There was nothing at the other end of the hallway, nothing except for roses, hundreds, white, thousands, red, pouring down, petal pink, smothering me, drowning...I was going to end up dead like Kevin Spacey in *American Beauty*. I had to get out of the house.

I yanked open the door. Sunlight smashed my face. I squinted, staggered back and hit the doorframe.

"Hello, Paul." Lucy Case stopped sorting through the mail in her lace-gloved hands. Her eyes shone and her lips were as full as her breasts. "You don't look very well."

"I'm fine, thanks." I suddenly felt very cold. "I just need to collapse for a while."

Lucy helped me into the bedroom, my arm wrapped

around her shoulders, her arm encircling my waist. She wore rosewater perfume that made me feel giddy, and underneath that I smelt the scent of her skin — clean and arousing like a spring thaw in the Alps.

"I understand you've been having problems." Cupping my head in one hand, Lucy lowered me onto the bed. She removed her gloves and wiped the sweat from my brow with one of them. "I can help you. I've helped many men. You understand that, don't you, Paul?"

"John Guillermo, Benny Benito. Your boarders," I said thickly. "Craig Fitzpatrick. Graeme Pritchard."

She stilled my lips with a finger and a smile. "All good men, Paul. All good God-fearing men from the Church. God rewards his own."

She leant forward. I was painfully aware of the depth of her cleavage, and the weight of her bosom on my chest. My penis, too, was aware of these facts.

"You need to let God enter your life," she whispered. "Like I let God enter me."

As she pulled back, her lips brushed mine. We kissed, our mouths wet and hungry, and I rolled her onto her back, tearing frantically at the buttons on her blouse. Her fingers worked expertly at my pants. Within seconds her hand gripped me, squeezed and stroked. I cupped her beasts, large and still firm, and kneaded them slowly. I squeezed hardened nipples between my fingers. Lucy moaned and kissed deeper. She hitched her skirt, and I stretched her knickers to the side as she spread her legs wide.

This gate was well oiled.

And this horse was bolting for it.

"Will you let Him into your lives?" Lucy moaned into my mouth. She arched her back as I slid into her. She grasped my buttocks, spreading them, and pulled me closer.

I thrust deep into her, again and again, my steed as hard as Superman's steel. The bed bloomed with rose blossom as we sunk into petal depths, sucking in each other's perfume.

"Will you let Him in?" she gasped.

"Yes." Thrust. "Yes." Thrust. "Yes."

She spread my arse cheeks wider and slid in her finger. It took me by surprise but I was too caught up in the moment. I guessed she was searching for a little prostate action. Another finger slipped in. And another. I felt the orgasm building between us as we pumped and bucked and probed and ground.

Lucy pushed her entire fist into my arse as she started to climax. I panicked, surprised by the pain, but more so from the enormous pleasure, and immediately came.

And came.

And came.

My body shuddered. For a second I saw nothing but roiling shadows on a wall of flowers, then Lucy pulled out of me as I sank into her. Our sweat mingled, our laboured breathing became one. I noticed her hands clenched around the bed head, her knuckles white from the pressure. Her hands slowly unfurled and the blood seeped back into her fingers.

"I think *we* opened you up there, don't you?" She wiped saliva from my lips.

I collapsed and rolled off her, my chest heaving, my

erection aching.

Lucy sat up and adjusted her knickers. Just before I passed out, I suspected the "we" she was referring to did not include me.

I'd just had my first threesome.

I awoke some time late in the afternoon. I was fully clothed. The bed was still made.

Three pills?

I had wanted to dream again, but *that* dream had been too much.

Talking cats, rose blossom, sex with Lucy Case, notwithstanding St. Bloody Joseph. I didn't want to think too much about that last part. Had I been dreaming or hallucinating? I still had that paragraph, didn't I? Surely I hadn't hallucinated that.

I got up, still a little shaky, and went into the study. There on the screen, resplendent in 12-point Courier New font was my newly born paragraph, now three hours old.

I sat down to admire it. Such a beautiful paragraph!

It was a good feeling until Mr. Pussy slunk into the room.

So, ya fucked the crazy old religious lady, eh?

Critical mass. The point where everything we knew before changes to something we couldn't predict.

The point where the poisons produced by the bacterial population living on the agar plate causes bacterial genocide. The intimate relationship between the sugar and the yeast and the point reached where the yeast dies in its own shit. Golden Age collapsing into Dark and swallowing humanity with it.

A nine kilogram mix of pluton and uranium, the size of a grapefruit, with enough weight to squeeze neutrons out of nuclei, and those neutrons then squeeze more, and more, and the chain starts fizzing, and blammo!

Here, in the home that St. Joseph blessed, the truth of critical mass is simpler: three Clomicalm and a fistful of cat biscuits twice a day. Sure, there's no nuclear reaction here, not even a bottle of five percent alcohol, and Rome never fell in a day.

Instead, I could talk to my cat.

We had made a list of baby names before we realised we had problems.

Everyone was using Jack so that was no go, and Melissas and Melindas were too much like Sharon. (For Mirella, not for me — I thought they were pretty names.)

We borrowed baby name books from relatives and trawled through internet sites for popular and rare and cute and symbolic and Christ-knew-what-else names. And we boiled it all down to two pages. A page for boys and a page for girls.

Zoë, Zara, and Sophie we managed to agree on, but the boys, well, we couldn't agree on the boys. I liked Luke and John and Matthew, but Mirella mentioned the pictures on the walls before we moved in. I soon changed my mind.

So what's hot on the list now? Mr. Pussy sprawled over my legs on the couch.

I ran my thumb down crossed-out Rhyses, Hugoes, Scotts, and Maxes until I reached the end of the boy's list. Three names were still in contention.

"Jayden, Daniel and Grant?"

Don't like 'em. They're wrong.

I didn't remember deciding on these names. I thought we were still on Charlie. Mirella had obviously changed *our* mind and chosen a few more.

"Yeah, I don't like them either." I flipped to the girl's list. Zoë had been scribbled out. So had Zara and Sophie. "Taylah, Ashleeh, Jane, Arnna."

Wrong. Mr. Pussy licked at a claw. *Badly wrong.*

"Daniel's Biblical too. She wouldn't let me use those sort."

It's not cos it's Biblical, buddy. They're wrong, but that ain't the pattern.

"Pattern? They're just shit names, misspelled remixed faux-trendy bogan names. What pattern?"

Mr. Pussy arched his back and stretched his forelegs, before jumping off and wandering over to his bowl.

"What pattern?" I repeated. I knew he knew. I almost sensed the bastard laughing at me.

Bickies first, mate. He pawed at the pantry.

"Jayden, Jane, Arnna, Grant...what bloody pattern? I'm not going to feed you."

He gave me a nonchalant stare and sauntered over to the cat flap. *Fuck ya, then.* He cast a quick glance back to make sure I was still watching before he head-butted the cat flap. *Let me know when you're ready. Normal feeding time won't count.* He eased his head through the flap.

"Okay, okay, I'll do it! Just tell me the goddamned pattern!"

Mr. Pussy wriggled his bulk through the flap, twitching his hind leg as he slipped outside. *Nah, fuck ya, ya cunt. You'll learn.*

I made peace with Mr. Pussy as he lay on the BBQ sunning himself in the courtyard. I presented him with a double size helping of bickies and an accompanying saucer of chocolate milk. He claimed the chocolate milk helped his hangovers. I knew some cats were cocoa intolerant, and that older cats became lactose intolerant, but Mr. Pussy had *promised* not to shit in the house. His black coat felt hot against the palm of my hand as I rubbed his back.

How about some tunes while we eat? He took a tentative lap of the milk.

Stick on The Auteurs.

"Hey! What about the pattern to the names?"

Just put on the fucking tunes, pal. Their 'After Murder Park' record will do nicely. I could do with a little darkness on such a nice day.

I put on the CD and sat next to Mr. Pussy as he munched through the contents of his bowl.

"Well?" I took a handful of the bickies and chewed on them. They tasted bloody good.

Just wait.

When the song 'Unsolved Child Murder' came on, Mr. Pussy pawed at my hand. *You listening?*

I was.

And it hit me.

41

A three-year old boy found battered floating in a dam. A two-year-old girl discovered beaten to death in the boot of a car. Jayden. Taylah. They'd been prominent in the news over the last couple of years.

My wife had picked the names of murdered children to call our unborn.

🐈

"I've made an appointment with an obstetrician," said Mirella. "You're not going to believe this."

"Really?" I concentrated on the news on the TV. My skin itched, and sweat leaked from my buttocks to slide up my spine and soak my eardrums. I needed a bickie fix bad.

"Yes. Dr. England comes highly recommended from Simone, but guess who's his midwife?"

"Dunno. Who?" Perhaps I could get up and pretend to feed the cat.

Maybe slip in a mouthful and then pretend I had to water the front garden.

Yeah, that'd do it. I could rinse my mouth from the hose, too. I rose from the couch and headed towards the pantry, already feeling better.

"Come on, Paul. Take a guess." Her gaze followed me around the room.

I poured a bowl for the cat and secreted a handful of bickies into my pocket. "Your sister-in-law?"

"No. Lucy Case."

I wondered if Mirella saw the guilt clamber onto my face and take a seat. "She, uh, didn't say anything did she?"

"Yes," said Mirella. "She remembered you all right."

The bickie compulsion vanished. "Right..."

"And get this, she even asked how the work I was doing at the charity was going." Mirella laughed. "I didn't think she even saw me, let alone listened to a word I said, when we first met."

I heard Mr. Pussy laughing into his bowl. Thankfully, Mirella didn't.

There's something wrong with this room. Mr. Pussy sat outside the bedroom door peering in. *Can't you sense it?*

"There's nothing wrong with it. You're just paranoid." I patted the bed, inviting him to come up.

He didn't move.

"What? You think the bedroom is haunted? If the bedroom is haunted then so is the whole house. After all, Lucy Case said..."

I know what she said, fuck-knuckle. Every house in this realm is haunted, but your bedroom, matey-potatey, your bedroom is another story. The very air is pregnant, my friend. Fuck going in there. He padded off down the hallway.

"Pregnant with what? Malice? Evil? St. Joseph?" I called after him.

"Kids?"

I fucking hate kids. Never works when I'm involved — too many do-gooders in this world. Anyway, shouldn't you be up and working on your "masterpiece"? I'm going to go take a shit in your garden.

The cat flap banged as he left the house.

There were stains on the bed sheets. They weren't mine.

And they smelled of roses.

Mirella had changed the baby names again. All the girl names were crossed out, and the boys too, except for one new entry. Her normally neat handwriting appeared shaky and inconsistent.

I popped a few bickies into my mouth and dropped a couple on the floor for Mr. Pussy. He gobbled them down without saying a word.

"Joseph. She's going to call our unborn Joseph."

At least it ain't dead kids' names. What about Lucas or Jude?

I shook the list in front of Mr. Pussy's face. "Why no girl names? Does she know we're having a boy? How would she know that? Is St. Joseph screwing my wife? Is he the father? We've got that creepy Case woman acting as midwife just like something out of *Rosemary's Baby* except this time it's bloody St. Joseph's!"

Cool it, man, you're starting to lose it. Take another chill pill.

I went to the cupboard, took out the Clomicalm. "How would you feel? With a goddamn ghost filling your missus with spirit sperm because you're not man enough to do the job?"

What would I know, pal? Some bitch cut my baws off before I even got to use them.

"But you're just a cat!" I chomped the pill down with

a mouthful of bickies. "This is about manhood and masculinity! This is what I'm here on this earth to do!"

"Are you talking to the cat?" asked Mirella.

I whirled to face her, trying to hide the biscuits in my hand while wiping the crumbs from my lip. "What are you doing home?"

"I've just come back from the obstetrician. What are you eating?"

"Nothing."

Mr. Pussy yowled and scampered outside.

"What have you been doing?" She stepped slowly towards me, and I backed further into the kitchen.

"Nothing."

Mirella saw the packet of pills on the bench, the open box of cat biscuits.

Her face paled. "Oh, my God."

"I was feeding them to the cat."

Mirella shook her head. "No, this can't be." She sat down on the sofa and held her head in her trembling hands. "Not today."

"Mirella, it's not what you think..."

"Don't lie to me!" Tears welled in her eyes. Blood coloured her cheeks.

"What the Hell have you been putting into your body?" She touched her stomach and started to cry.

"My body? What the Hell have you been putting into *your* body? You're the one that's been screwing St. Joseph! So bloody desperate to be pregnant that..."

"What? St. Joseph? What are you talking about?"

"You know exactly what I mean! You and him doing the business. Mr. Pussy knows! We've been trying to figure out how to handle the situation!"

"Mr. Pussy?" Mirella's voice hitched and dropped to a coarse whisper.

"You *were* talking to the cat." Huge racking sobs sputtered saliva and tears over the baby name list on the coffee table. "The day I find out we're pregnant is the day I find out my husband is losing his mind."

Mr. Pussy climbed up on the window ledge and peered inside. He was laughing at me.

"Yeah, I can talk to the cat," I ranted. "It's not so unusual — he's pretty smart. He's been helping me fill in the picture. I don't know why I went along with the whole St. Joseph conceiving conception. That goddamn Lucy Case, I never should have fucked her...hold on. You're pregnant?"

"Y-e-e-e-s-s!" Mirella bawled until the sound stopped mid-throat like the last tock of a clock wired to a bomb. "You...fucked...Lucy...Case?"

Mr. Pussy bolted.

Mirella spent that night at her sister's.

I sat on the sofa and popped Pussy's pills and munched on bickies until semi-naked women holding phones saying call me call me paraded across the television screen. The ink we'd used for the names on the baby list had smeared with Mirella's tears. I had been wrong. The handwriting wasn't hers; it was mine. Some stupid subconscious attempt to put the fear of losing a child into Mirella to compensate for my fear of fatherhood.

I got a plan. Mr. Pussy leapt up onto the coffee table to

obscure my view of the TV. *I know how to fix it.*

"I don't think I can hear you." The calls were only $4.95 a minute.

"Actually, the problem is I *do* think I can hear you."

She loves gardening, right?

I picked up the phone and jabbed in the numbers displayed on the TV.

"Go away."

I'll poison her with my shit! Toxoplasmosis! She'll lose the baby, or give birth to a freak, then leave you. We can get on with living our lives the way we want!

"Fuck off, you little shit." I backhanded the cat. He flew across the room, his body twisting, until he smacked into the wall. He hissed and slunk out the cat flap into the night.

A voice on the other end of the telephone meowed.

"What are you wearing?" I asked, fumbling at my trousers.

The telephone meowed again.

The air filled with roses, overwhelming and all-consuming roses, the perfume forcing its way into every orifice. Outside, the devil screamed in the darkness.

A strong hand on my shoulder. A voice resonant in masculinity. "I will take on this responsibility for you, Paul. I will be the father you fear to be."

The phone fell from my hand. I wanted to curl into myself and cry away the madness. To burn clean under a newborn sun. To worship and be reborn.

I turned to face the light.

And vomited a stomach full of half-digested anti-depressants and cat biscuits down the back of the sofa.

James handed me a low-alcohol beer. "You sure you're allowed to drink with the medication you're on?"

"Yeah, yeah, it's fine." I popped the top, as James took a seat. "Don't really need to take them — I'm just doing it to show Mirella I'm okay."

"She's next door with Simone, comparing tummy bulges. There's a big difference between seven months and three months," James said.

We sat out in the courtyard, warming in the morning sun. I saw him note the desiccated cat shit on the barbecue grill. I sipped my beer.

"That's a reminder of the bad days — so I don't lose focus. You know she killed the cat?" I asked.

"She gave him away. You know that, and you know you should clean that up. It took too long for you two to fall pregnant to risk losing it through exposure to the cat. Not having the pills or biscuits in the house anymore can only be good too, right?"

"So you think I'm schizophrenic, too?" I felt my voice rising.

"Take it easy." He swallowed a mouthful of beer then burped. "It is one of the possible side-effects from using Clomicalm, but I'm not saying you were. You gotta admit though, you were acting pretty weird."

"In cats, James. Schizophrenia in cats!"

"Clomicalm is also called Clomipramine and that's used in human medication. What about all the chemicals in that cat food? What the Hell were you thinking?"

"That it'd help my boys' production," I said

48

sheepishly.

"Well, at least that seemed to work," he said.

Critical fucking mass.

We both laughed then sipped our beers in silence in the sun for a while.

"You're a man of faith, James. I know Mirella told you I thought St. Joseph was, uh, impregnating her with his child. You know, immaculate conception and all that."

He nodded.

"Sounds crazy, eh?"

He nodded again. "Joseph was only a man, Paul. Jesus was the Son of God, not Joseph. That wouldn't be too immaculate now, would it?"

I wanted to tell James that in my darkest hour He had to come to me. Of how He was exacting His revenge on God in the recreation of the perfect birth, of the perfect child that He had originally been denied. And of how had he even been next door. I wanted to tell James that St. Joseph had raised me from the depths of my soul where I'd been drowning — but that didn't sound spiritual at all. To paraphrase our good friend Lucy Case, it sounded a little too *religious*. No-one wants to listen to a born-again.

With a bolt of inspiration, the title of my novel suddenly came to me.

How I Found God (Inside My Wife).

I smiled and proposed a toast.

"To the miracle of life."

Zoe Josephine McNabb was born on March 19, St. Joseph's Day, weighing in at seven pounds. Guess who else had weighed seven pounds at birth? Mirella was in labour for seven hours, which is incidentally how long Mary took to deliver her baby boy.

Dr. England congratulated me with a firm handshake. "Sorry we had to use the hospital annex, Paul. We'll get them moved into the private quarters as soon as we can."

Lucy Case kissed me quickly on the mouth and whispered into my ear, "God rewards his own." Looking back, I'm sure she pressed her groin against mine, but I was lost in the moment of Zoe's angelic arrival.

Leading up to Her conception and birth, I realised I'd been terrified of what was going to happen to my life, that I was going to lose my life, but I was wrong. Apart from the late nights, the lack of sleep, and the crying, our house was finally a home.

Mirella and I always knew when Zoe's nappy needed changing too.

The room smelled of roses.

Mnemophonic

The man in front of me studies my fingers, memorising every deft movement, as they expertly and instinctively tie the knot in the silky, black, bow tie. His fingertips are raw, gnawed and chewed to the quick. Not the hands of a professional.

I look up at him and he stares back, his eyes narrowing, brow wrinkling in a series of fine lines, trying to understand who he sees. Who is that man?

Do I know him? He looks familiar, I see his unchanging face every day, but I never speak to him. I watch him straighten his tie and we turn and reach for the only garment on the clothes rack, a black tuxedo jacket, always clean and neatly pressed. It strikes me that I do not know who presses it. I don't do it.

At least, I don't think I do it.

I put the jacket on, shrugging my shoulders up and down, watching myself in the mirror as it nestles comfortably like a cat against my frame. It fits well, it fits perfectly. Of course it does.

I glance at my watch, 5:15 pm, as it always says at this time of day, and take a quick glance around the apartment to see if everything is in order before I leave for work. The bed is made, the chair is empty but for my favourite white cushion positioned proud and correct, (it has some embroidery on it, I think my mother did it), the dishes are done — they're always done — and so I go to leave, but as I reach for the door handle, my stomach flutters uneasily. I don't know why. It's a plain and inconspicuous door, the same pale, yellow colour as the walls, and the handle; tarnished brass, the lever kind. My nervousness quickly passes, so I open the door and leave the room, wondering who uses those dishes. They're not mine.

Jenny inspected herself in the mirror, staring past the spires of imported whiskies and liqueurs that lined the bar. She wasn't sure if her new haircut, short and straight like the woman who was in all the movies at the moment, made her look any younger. Or slimmer. Or prettier. She teased it again, cocking her head to get a different perspective on how she looked. She was getting old. She should get married again, she thought, and almost laughed out loud. Again? Why did she think that? She'd never been married before.

Jenny shook her head, perturbed. She'd been having lots of weird thoughts like that lately.

She self-consciously smoothed her hips with her hands, picked up her lemonade from the bar and took a reflexive sip. She wasn't thirsty, just bored.

Her shift had only just started and most of the evening's clientele had not yet arrived. Give them another fifteen minutes, she thought, glancing at her watch.

A middle-aged man in a dark-grey suit sat at one end of the bar, nursing a whiskey. Folds of fat rolled over the tight, white collar of his shirt. He looked uncomfortable, his bulk too large for the barstool. She knew he would sit down at one of the tables soon, still alone, still staring morosely at the drink he held in his hand, his one and only companion. No one ever spoke to the man and he never spoke to anyone, either.

Two women sat smoking and talking at one of the tables by the window near the fountain. They wore tight-fitting, immaculate business-cut clothing, one in red, one in blue, lipstick stained cigarettes smouldering between long, thin fingers on outstretched hands, lipstick-smeared glasses half-full of chardonnay occasionally quaffed. They were talking animatedly about someone.

"And darling," they would say, heads upturned, eyes rolling in exaggerated disbelief, "you just won't believe..."

Oh, to have a life outside of this bar...

A young man, wearing a red and yellow patterned tie fixed in a fabulously large knot, ordered one of the expensive designer beers. His hair was cut short in the style of the well-to-do, middle-class corporate career boy, with just enough glistening gel to separate him from the older suits. Jenny gave him his beer and took his money, briefly eyeing him up. He knew the etiquette. You did not order from the tap in here. That was a lower socio-economic habit, and not looked on favourably in this establishment. She wondered why they even had beer on tap.

And speaking of the other side of the tracks, how did that guy get in here? He slouched at a table near the corner by the restrooms wearing a beat-up leather jacket, probably taking that position so he could peer easily into the ladies toilets when the doors opened. His hair was black and unruly, stiff with grease or dirt; his eyes intense, encased above dark hollows that joined his gaunt, unshaven cheeks. Those who inadvertently caught his eye were briefly subjected to a burning gaze before quickly looking away. He didn't look like the typical customer for this place, and he certainly wasn't a regular.

She looked away just before his eyes turned on her. As it got busier in here, security would politely and firmly persuade the man to leave. None of his types in here, thank you.

The doors opened and a tall, thin man wearing an expressionless face and an immaculate tuxedo entered, stopped, momentarily taken aback by his surroundings, and then strode towards the bar. Towards Jenny.

He was the piano player, wasn't he? What was his name? Oh yeah, Simon, she read off the employee list taped to the wall. That's it, Simon; he's new here.

"Hi, Simon," she smiled.

"Hello," he replied, recognition, perhaps confusion, darting over his face.

"Can I get you anything?" she asked, her eyes suggesting something else.

"Just a water, thanks," he said, studying the cigarette butts on the floor.

"Here you go. You start in fifteen minutes."

"Yes. Thank you."

He took the water and sat down at the piano. A shy boy, Jenny thought.

He'd be gorgeous if he smiled.

Fifteen minutes later, as more people entered the warmth of the bar, Jenny heard the piano player begin to play. It was something familiar, something popular transformed into banal background night music. She couldn't quite name the song.

With the whoosh of the doors, Mike looked up expectantly from the local paper he was pretending to read. An elderly man wearing a dark-blue, pinstriped suit limped in from the cold and made his way to a vacant table.

Mike returned to his paper, wondering how much longer he would have to wait for Grant to show up. He picked absently at the dirt caked onto the sleeve of his leather jacket as he read.

He turned a page, his eyes flicking uninterestedly over the articles, his mind elsewhere. *Premier Fashions Launches New Range*. The other page advertised a multitude of mobile phones with colourful, programmable, detachable features he'd never need. There didn't seem to be anything in this paper he could relate to. Sell. Free. Win. Offer Valued At...Buy Buy BUY!

Nothing he wanted to relate to.

He knew who he was.

The door whooshed again, a quick glance, no recognition, turn another page.

His eyes felt sore and grainy, like someone had rubbed sandpaper over the surface of his eyeballs. The lack of sleep and sustenance was starting to wear him down. The white noise in his head had been growing louder and louder over the last week, an ever-nearer, relentless machine grinding away inside his skull. It made it harder and harder to focus, to remember, and he struggled desperately to concentrate, to keep the spark burning in his memory.

He had to tell Grant what he had discovered at the clinic. It was definitely biological, a genetically modified organism, but he still had no idea how it could be transmitted and assimilated over such a wide area. Together, hopefully, they could figure out what to do.

He caught the barmaid staring at him again and she quickly studied the glass in front of her, wipe, wipe, up to the light, one more wipe. He could see by slightly screwed-up nose and the faint downturn at the corners of her mouth that she didn't want him in here.

She had a haircut like that popstar had. Or was it the woman from the TV? He wasn't sure anymore. She wore one of those chokers that had been all the rage a couple of months ago, and continually toyed with it when she flirted with the men at the bar. She had a pretty good body for someone her age, using all she had left, predatory, hunting for what her society dictated she should have. She thought she was too good for him.

He needed a drink, something hard, but was too scared to go to the bar. She might ask him to leave, or even worse, serve him one. And then he might forget.

He ran his fingers through his hair, the grease shining thinly on them in the pale light of the bar. He stared at them, fascinated by the black dirt growing beneath his fingernails. Mike could smell himself, too. He hadn't showered for days, too scared to go back home. He might lose it if he did.

"I know who I am," he said quietly to himself, looking around to make sure nobody noticed. Nobody did.

Mike caught the conversation of two women, red and blue suits, posturing and posing.

"...corrugated they say. Apparently it's going to be *the* new line." Puff. Exhale.

"But how does that improve on the existing product then?" Puff. Exhale.

"Well darling," red-suit implored, her eyes rolling exaggeratedly, "you just won't believe this, but..."

Another table; a young man and woman, good-looking, trendy, hair-styles and nicely cut clothing, latest fashion.

"So how's things?"

"Good, good. And you?"

"Yeah, good...how's work going?"

"Not bad, really busy at the moment, you know how it is."

"Yeah."

They laugh. Sip tentatively at drinks.

"So, been keeping busy?"

Mike stared back at the paper, the conversation around him similar to the content within. Nothing seemed to matter anyway, why should he care?

He looked at his watch, but it wasn't there so he tried to read the time from the young man's watch. It was flash looking with a thick band of gold for the strap. It had stopped.

Where the Hell was Grant? He didn't have much time left.

The door whooshed open again, but it was someone he didn't know.

🐈

My hands move lithely, intuitively over the keys, the music soothing and bland, white comes up, black goes down, then up and white down.

Sometimes I find myself watching my hands in amazement. I don't know how they do this; they are an entity unto themselves, a subconscious extension of my body. I don't even know the song I'm playing, it sounds vaguely familiar, but that's all.

Every now and then I seamlessly turn the page in front of me, the music continuing uninterrupted. I wonder why I turn the pages. I don't need to. I can't read music. I see only squiggles of black on white, a delicate, undecipherable pattern. It's not a problem. I don't mind.

I do this every night. I can't remember a time when I didn't. No-one notices me, no-one applauds when I finish, no-one talks to me. I don't mind, it's my job.

A man with dirty, black hair in the corner of the room keeps staring at me. I wish he wouldn't, he's making me nervous. There's something about him that I don't like. I don't know what it is, but I wish he would leave; he doesn't belong here.

🐈

Jenny tried sparking up a conversation with the piano player in one of his breaks, but his responses were shy and closed. She flirted with a few of the richer, good-looking men at the bar, but she was getting very little response or interest.

She adjusted her low-cut top, reassured by the firmness there. Still in good shape, still had the curves, maybe it just wasn't her night. An off night.

The other barmaid, the new one, seemed to be getting all the attention. She always did, being a lot younger then Jenny. The list offered the name Lucy.

From the expression on Lucy's face, it looked like it was mainly unwanted attention. How long had Lucy been working here now? It must have only been a couple of weeks, but it seemed like forever. Jenny didn't really know anything about her at all, not because she was jealous of Lucy, she just didn't seem to have the time to get to know her.

The strange guy in the corner was still there. There was something familiar about him, but she couldn't place it. She had caught him staring at her a few times, but he now seemed to be perversely focused on Simon.

Jenny wondered why he hadn't been removed yet. He didn't have the right dress standard for a start. Looks like security is also having an off night too, she thought idly, drying a long-stemmed wine glass.

The piano started up again, something bouncy and tinkling, a tune she knew, teasingly on the tip of her tongue, but it remained elusive. She hummed along contentedly.

Sometimes I get the urge to talk to someone, there are lots of people in here, surely someone would like to talk to me. The urge doesn't last long, though.

In my break I sit at the bar with a water. I stare at it. The woman behind the bar, I think her name is Jenny, keeps trying to talk to me, but I don't feel like talking anymore. I think she's coming on to me, I should be flattered, I can't remember the last time I was with a woman. I've got a funny feeling that maybe it was her, back when I was drinking, but surely I'd remember more than just that.

She asks me about the piano, but I pretend I don't hear her, and then someone orders a drink and she leaves.

I take a lukewarm sip, it's bland and tasteless. The lemonade here tastes the same, except the bubbles in it hurt my throat; I don't drink lemonade anymore.

Someone taps my shoulder, and my body jerks convulsively, a cold shudder passing through me. A touch from another life. I turn around and it's the man with the dirty hair who's been staring at me all night. My insides squirm and sweat breaks out under my arms. On my back. I want to run away. I can smell his stink, thick and warm, a fetid cloud enveloping me and he opens his mouth and speaks, his voice thrusting shards of coiled steel into my head.

"Grant, it's me, Mike..."

Chris noticed Jenny waving frantically from the bar, pointing towards some rough-looking guy who seemed to be hassling the piano player.

"Back in a sec," he said to the other guy working

security tonight. Chris didn't know his name for sure, it was something ending in "ee", like Tunney or Whitey or something. "Some trouble at the bar."

"Need a hand?" Tunney-or-Whitey grunted, not looking around.

"Nah," Chris said, weaving his way through the crowd, his bulk magically parting the sea of people.

Nearer to the bar, Chris saw the guy in the leather grab the piano player's shoulders and shake him, his voice rising over the noise of the crowd.

"For Christ's sake, Grant, it's me, Mike!"

The piano player's face was pale and his body trembled. "My name is Simon," he said, colour spreading back to his cheeks, "I don't know who you're talking about. I don't know any Grant. I've never seen you before." The veins in the piano player's head throbbed, pulsing with blood. They looked like they were going to burst.

Mike continued, his face reddening, spittle flying from his mouth; "I know what's going on Grant, at least some of it, and so do you! You were with it last week, man, what the fuck's happened! You got to remember! Can you remember?"

He shook the piano player again and raised his hand to slap him across the face.

"Hey, mate," Chris called out, almost at the bar now. "I wouldn't do that if I were you!"

Before Mike could react, Simon had him by the throat. The piano player's face was scarlet, and the white of his knuckles shone in the pale bar-light as his fingers sank into the other man's neck.

"I...don't...know...you," Simon spat. "Leave...me...

alone."

Chris grabbed Mike, carefully prising Simon's hand away. "It's okay, it's okay," he reassured them both, twisting the offender's arm up behind his back and forcing him towards the door. "You're out mate, come on, let's go."

Mike twisted his head back, "It's not too late Grant, you just got to remember, we can still fight it, we can still...oomph."

Tunney-or-Whitey silenced him with a punch to the stomach, and they threw him out into the cold and dark of the night. They watched Mike tumble down the stairs onto the sidewalk. He didn't get up.

Tunney-or-Whitey laughed and said something Chris didn't catch. He said, "Yeah," back and laughed. Back at the bar, the piano player sat crying, his face bewildered. The barmaid was trying to comfort him.

A few minutes later, the piano started up, a tune Chris used to know when he was younger. He couldn't remember what it was called anymore.

No one noticed the fat man sitting alone at the table with his whiskey; no one ever did. It was times like these the fat man knew who he was, what he was supposed to do. He discreetly attached his phone, pressing in his earpiece and prudently made the call.

After the line went dead, the fat man left the bar and waited outside in the shadows for the government vehicle to arrive. He saw blood trickling out of the man's nose, coagulating slowly in the cool night air, the neon light shining on its wetness. The rasping of breath, loud and ragged, amplified the silence of the city. They would do something to make him more comfortable.

About who he should be.

When the man was taken away, the fat man went back into the bar, his memory of the evening blurring with some other life he sleepwalked through.

Mike groaned and opened his eyes, matted blood breaking in his eyelashes. The pain in his skull pounded incessantly, it was hard to breathe, and he couldn't move.

"He's regaining consciousness," someone said.

He was strapped to a table in what appeared to be an ambulance, although there were no windows and the walls were padded. He knew they were moving as the vehicle they were in slowed and turned, accelerating quickly again.

A man sat next to him smiling. He looked "nice", the family man in a commercial selling house insurance, a dark-grey immaculate suit, expensive cut.

"Where am I?" Mike asked. "Who are you?"

Another man, identical to the first, moved from the back of the van towards them.

"Here." He passed a syringe to the sitting man.

Sitting Man depressed the plunger slightly, studying the liquid as it arced from the end of the needle onto Mike's chest.

"What are you doing?"

"Don't worry," said Sitting Man. His fingers slicing

through the sleeve of the leather jacket, paring back the folds to reveal the skin. "You're not who you think you are."

The fluid injected into his veins was almost as cold as the touch of the man's fingers upon his arm.

Underground...fluoro, being carried somewhere, want to be sick, can't move...

"...blood tests? He's waking..."

Voices, blurred, fading louder...

"...strong metabolism, he should still be under."

"It fits the pattern for those who don't take to it."

The air is warm and unnatural, air conditioned, and tasteless, clinical...

"Who is he?"

"Nobody."

"He's awake again."

"Increase the dosage. If he doesn't react to it this time, begin the tests."

Mike tried to kick and struggle, but his nerves were no longer his own and the substance slowly filling his body overwhelmed him, pushing him back into a muddy void of someone else's memories.

I don't remember leaving last night, maybe I started drinking towards the end of the evening again. Every time I hit the booze these days I seem to black out. Think I must have pushed it too hard in my early days. Don't remember even having a drink last night, though.

The house is quiet and I'm awake so I get up. The apartment doesn't have many windows, just one, and I wander over to it to stare out at the empty, concrete parking lots and the abandoned buildings my view commands. Maybe no one comes to this part of town anymore: I never have any visitors.

The sun is already disappearing behind the skyline, the warmth in its colours barely penetrating the oncoming grey. A smudge of orange, flecked with red, the occasional streak of yellow and then it's gone. A few street lamps sputter on, feebly lighting a deserted footpath; most of the lights don't come on at all.

I don't know anyone in this city.

I'd better start getting ready for work soon. I think about getting something to eat first, but decide not to before I reach the fridge. I look at it blankly for a second, an exterior devoid of stickers or magnets, wondering if there is anything inside it. I don't really want to know. I used to stick my bills on it once, but I don't think I get them anymore. I've got a pile of envelopes for someone called Grant. I think I know him, maybe he used to live here with me, but I'm not really too sure. It doesn't matter though, they're not mine.

I shower and dress, fix my tie and slip into my jacket. The man in the mirror smiles at me. We look good, we look smart. Before I leave the apartment, I check the room, the dishes are done, and the bed is made.

There is a choker on the floor next to my bed. I wonder whose it is, I've never seen it before. I pick it up and put it in the bin. It's the only thing in there.

As I reach for the door handle something tugs at my mind, something to remember, to be careful, but...

I open the door and leave for work.

This is the End, Harry, Good Night!

The lights dimmed and conversation hushed. Butler sat amongst the audience, dread creeping into the pit of his stomach.

What the Hell am I doing here? Death is a part of life, he thought. *A huge part of mine. There are too many cameras; someone might recognise me. This is stupid. I should leave.*

It wasn't just the TV cameras that were unsettling Butler; he'd noticed other cameras, hidden from the audience, and he suspected microphones were also concealed in the studio. Heavy-set minders moved amongst the aisles hushing the noisier in the crowd.

"Do you think it will be Dad?"

"Aunt Martha?"

"John?"

"I hope it's Grandad."

Butler sat silently. He wiped his hands on his trousers. Third time.

If I don't believe in God, why believe in this? No matter what he said to convince himself, it didn't work. It ate away at him, gnawing his confidence and his ability to act. Making him useless. He felt it, and in this room with cameras and lights he felt something else, too. Everyone here clung to it, their essence or aura — Butler didn't know how to explain it — and it intensified, building like a slow, dark storm until someone said "Action" and the man in the black suit strode like thunder to the centre of the stage.

Butler tightened his grip on the automatic as Hill kicked in the door.

The sound of the television spilled like trash into the hallway — *They're either trying to tell me someone has a name like Katrina...or they want me to acknowledge a name like Katrina* — and Hill stepped through the doorway, his gun barking, muzzle-flash chasing the shadows from the room.

Sometimes, when it was like this, Butler didn't remember anything until it all stopped. When the blue-grey smoke awoke his nostrils and the roar of gunfire still throbbed within his ears; when the blood screaming through his body slowed a little to release the machine. And sometimes he saw it all in minutiae, every detail burnt into his brain, measured and processed so every movement he made exacted the desired result.

Like this time. The flash on the wall illuminated the damp, floral wallpaper faded not by the sun, but by the dank oppression of rundown misery in a lost hotel; the cheap brass 49 held by a screw to the splintered door as it swayed back and forth, slowing down but not yet stopped; the feel of the worn carpet beneath his shoes, slightly sticky like a carpet swollen with beer in a deserted pub the morning after; the tendons jutting from the back of Hill's neck, sweat beading from skin recently shaved with a barber's number two; the acrid smell of cordite filling the room faster than the screams in his ears. Butler followed Hill into the room.

Bang!

Eject. Recoil.

Bang! Bang!

A man clambered over the back of a couch, firing aimlessly. A bullet burned past Butler's head. The bathroom door closed to his right, but he was too busy firing at the man behind the couch. Hill's eyes bulged, his grin widened, and blood ballooned from the arm of the man behind the couch.

The next bullet took the man in the chest, crashing him back against the wall.

His gun hand smashed the lamp from the table and the light bulb exploded.

Hill leapt over the couch and fired once more. The two of them stood there in the calm and the smoke. Blood arced over the wall, smearing down to the body cooling on the floor.

"Has she passed? Yes? Okay we'll start from there..."

The guy they had been talking about on the way there was on the television. Butler turned it off. He wasn't even out of breath. Hill turned to him and nodded. He removed the earplugs and reloaded his gun as Hill searched the body.

A muffled sound, a hitch of breath or a barely suppressed whimper.

Butler crouched, swinging the barrel to face the bathroom door. Hill crept along the wall until he stood poised next to the door. One finger. Hill raised his leg. Two fingers. And on the count of three Hill went to kick the door.

Then it started to go wrong.

A hole in the door exploded outwards taking Hill in the chest. He spun round, his eyes locking on Butler, mouth wide — *he's laughing as they high-five each other, Butler's getting blown while Hill takes her from behind on the stairs of the club; after they've finished the three of them finish off a bottle of bourbon* — and another bullet hit him in the back, erupting from his chest in a fountain of blood. Hill collapsed on the floor, the wind whistling through his lungs. Shot after shot ripped through the door, sending splinters flying across the room. Then the click of the hammer on an empty chamber. The sound of sobbing.

Without pausing to think, Butler hurled himself at the door. He rolled and kicked out. The door shattered. He was firing even before he focused clearly on the shape huddled against the toilet. Before he noticed the shape was a *her*, and the *her* held a baby in her arms.

Such a good baby, he thought, such a *quiet* baby.

And by the time he stopped it was too late.

"Why didn't you come sooner?" his mother asked from her bed.

The room stank of roses and lilies, their perfume a weak mask for the dying flesh permeating the bedroom. Her flesh, hot and brittle, rested on his arm. The bones of her fingers bulged beneath skin drawn tight.

"You know," Butler said.

"No, I don't. I thought maybe you had died instead

of me."

He tried to avoid her eyes; a thin film obscured the sharp blue that once shone from her face. A film Butler had seen glazed over the eyes of the freshly dead.

"Been busy at work." It sounded pathetic, but he didn't know what else to say.

"Your work!" The words sounded harsh in her throat, like gravel thrown over broken concrete. She shook her head slowly. The cross on her necklace reflected soft light, drawing his eyes away from hers. "You think I don't know?"

Butler held her hand tight in his own. "I'm here, Mother. I'm here now." He felt a squeeze, as gentle as her kiss on his brow as a child.

"You're a good boy, Robert," she said. "I brought you up with God on your side. You haven't forgotten that, have you?"

He couldn't help the snort of derision that puffed from his nose. A small sound, but in the silence of the death room it sounded like a gunshot.

"I worry about you, Robert. I can feel Him," she squeezed his hand again, "closer to me, every day. He brings comfort as my time approaches."

He tightened his jaw, immovable. Silent.

"I'm ready to go to Him, Robert. But I can't leave until you promise me."

"You'll pull through, Mother. Don't talk like that."

She laughed, a papyrus rattle deep in her throat. "You never could lie to me, my baby boy. Please, for your mother's sake, repent. Wash the blood from your hands."

Their eyes locked, his hard and unyielding, hers

milky, soft, forgiving.

"I know what you do," she whispered. "Grant a dying woman her final wish. Promise me. Don't be like Thomas the Doubter. Don't make me show you what is true."

She's lying, he thought. The madness of approaching death. "Mother, what are you talking about?"

"Sometimes, Robert, when my eyes hide behind sleep, He shows me things, of what will be and what can be. I've felt the demons come for me and He holds them at bay. Do you know why?"

Butler shook his head.

"For you, Robert. He wants me to save you." Her hand clawed into his arm, the heat of her disease seeping into his skin. "In your salvation shall be mine. Promise me!"

The second's silence hung like a shroud in the makeshift mausoleum her bedroom had become. Her eyes implored him, boring into his head.

The last words Butler said to his mother while she lived were a lie. "I promise."

He wondered if she knew.

The wheeze of a punctured lung, followed by a soft gurgling whistle.

Butler heard distant voices outside in the hallway. His gun still smoked, the barrel pointing where the last shot had been fired. At the chest of the woman on the bathroom floor. She slumped against the laminated wall. Tears ran down her cheeks, smearing the thick mascara into black trails. A thin trickle of bright, red blood from lip to chin, then the mess of brain and soft, yet-unformed skull splattering her chest.

She still clutched the empty gun tightly in her hand. Her fingernails were long and heavily painted — a red lacquer stronger and brighter than that dripping from her mouth. One had broken, the palm of her hand bleeding.

Her gun clattered on the tiles as her fingers gave up. Small, mewling noises bubbled from her mouth and she clasped her arms around the baby in her lap. Her chest heaved again, another wet whistle, and the only scream came from her eyes.

Somewhere, a million miles away, something hissed his name.

Without air she couldn't speak, but her lips formed again and again. *My baby, my baby, my baby...*

When he closed his eyes he heard her, over and over. His mother's voice.

Cracked and broken.

His name hissed again and Butler opened his eyes. The woman's sorrow burned up at him and he squeezed the trigger gently. The bathroom amplified the explosion and lent an echo to the cartridge as it bounced over the tiles.

"Buttssss..." A slow hiss behind him. Hill on the floor, face down, a dark pool beneath him, soaking into the carpet as it spread.

"It's okay, it's okay. Don't move." Butler knelt beside Hill. The blood had left Hill's face. Sirens howled in the distance.

"I'm...aahhhh...I'm...I'm..."

"You got to promise me, Hill."

"I'm...I'm..."

"Like we said in the car. That guy on the TV. Promise me."

Hill couldn't nod his head, but Butler thought he saw him move his eyes instead.

"Sorry, mate."

The last shot of the evening resonated in Butler's head longer than he'd have dreamed.

The rain held session over his mother's funeral; a cold rain driven hard by the wind off the bay. They lowered her coffin into the grave — a hole full of nothing to be filled with even less. Butler worried his grip on the rope would slip, that in this, his mother's goodbye, he would fail her again. But the rope bit into his skin and the pain helped him concentrate on the task.

His sister dropped a single green lily on top of the coffin and retreated into the arms of her husband. Butler hardly knew him. In fact, he hardly knew his sister — she'd been no more than ten when he'd left home.

While the priest mumbled words about God and life, Butler watched his sister. Her face showed the same pain and emotions as the rest of the family, but it was to the bulge in her belly his eyes were drawn. He imagined he saw the bulge move beneath the stretched, black shirt, where a peak of white flesh showed between the seams and her skirt. A small kick of life urgent for the world, as the priest laid their mother, urgent for another. The passing of essence from one to the other.

I don't need this shit, Butler thought. He wished the priest would finish so he could get out of the rain.

They took turns throwing sodden clumps into the grave. The wind blew fresh, angry gusts as the funeral procession left for the warmth of the local pub. Something made Butler stay to watch the gravediggers fill the grave. He couldn't say what it was, but he thought perhaps he didn't want to be around his family. Didn't want to see their accusing eyes with knowledge of his "life", and the disrespect he'd bought into theirs.

On the tombstone in gothic letters larger than her own name: *In God We Trust.* Butler stood there letting the rain whip his skin raw, with the chill barely settled in his bones. He could stand there for years.

He wondered what Hill's funeral would be like. Butler didn't know what the police did with unclaimed and unmourned bodies. And up until now, he'd never considered it.

I don't care I don't care I don't care...

A mantra repeated, until the words lost all meaning and their form became a sound, a thought, in his head. A drone to coax Butler back into sleep. And when his eyes closed he felt the darkness draw around him, pressing tight against his face, squashing him beneath the covers of his bed. His skin crawled from the base of his feet to his groin, the sweat between his thighs clammy.

The muted roar of the never-sleeping city, the lonely howl of interstate trucks tearing through the night on deserted freeways — a lullaby for the sleepless.

I don't care I don't CARE I DON'T CARE!

With every beat of his heart, the hiss of his name pumped through his veins. He imagined his mother creeping across the ceiling when he slept. Leaning down over his face and whispering into his ear. *You promised me, Robert. Don't make me make you.*

The woman in the bathroom, clutching her baby. In his sleep it wailed as its mother rocked it slowly back and forth in her arms.

It's a boy, Butler thought, *it's wearing blue.*

Blood pooled on the tiles.

How can the baby make so much noise, he wondered. Such a *quiet* baby.

The mother lifted her head towards the light bulb and howled, the cry a horde of insects disturbed from their feast on the dead. The baby turned to Butler, the top half of its head splattered over its mother's chest. A tiny eyeball sat propped next to the mother's foot from where it had been torn from the impact of the bullet. The tongue flapped in the remains of the baby's shattered jaw, faster and faster, the intensity of sound increasing in pitch, higher, higher—

—the banshee screaming "Promise me!"

The Devil calling.

"I've been a psychic medium for over fifteen years," said the man in the black suit. His voice purred confidence. "Anything can happen during my readings."

A soft murmur of expectation from the studio audience. Butler sat uncomfortably on the seat, his gut a twisted knot. If Hill could see him now. What shit would he have dealt Butler for being here? But Hill couldn't see him now. *Could he?*

The psychic wandered over to a section of the audience on the other side of the room. Eager faces, bodies straightened — a pregnant hush.

"I'm getting a Marge — a Margaret over here," said the psychic. "I don't know what this means. Marge could be someone who passed over, she could be someone here, she could be someone that you know. A Marge, Marga, Martha..."

"I had a Martha," said a middle-aged woman.

"Okay. Has she passed?"

"Yes."

"Okay. We'll start there. They're making me feel like there's some type of motherly vibration that has passed because there's an older female coming through and I feel like—"

"It's my aunty."

"Okay, that explains it. She's telling me something to do with an *R*..."

Butler almost snorted. There *were* microphones in here. He'd heard the name "Martha" mentioned when he'd arrived. He was wasting his time. This guy was a cold reader, another James Van Praagh, another John Edward. It was all a farce. Butler stood to leave and one of the lights exploded, showering sparks across the stage. The room temperature dropped and so did the man in the black suit — to his knees. The psychic's eyes rolled back, veins bulged from his temples and a trickle of urine formed beneath him.

The voice that hissed from his throat froze Butler where he stood. It sounded like the wind howling at his mother's funeral. The man in the black suit stared blindly with an arm raised, finger pointing straight at him.

Then the lights shone bright upon Butler and the voice began its howl anew.

"What do you do with all your money?" Hill cranked the heating in the car up full. "Get yourself a good set of wheels with a decent air-con system, for Christ's sake! It's freezing in here."

"I like the cold," said Butler. "Keeps me awake."

"You want your fingers to be working. How the Hell you going to pull the trigger if they don't?"

"They'll work."

They drove in silence for the next few minutes, content to watch the docklands passing by. Lonely neon and wide empty roads, the occasional semi-trailer for company. It wouldn't take long before they reached the hotel and business began.

"You're pretty quiet tonight," said Hill.

"Yeah," Butler said. He didn't like to talk before a job, and Hill never shut up until they were actually doing the job.

"I heard about your mother." Hill stared straight ahead. They knew eye contact could be uncomfortable, too intimate. Easier to have sex with the same woman than talk, really talk, to each other. "Sorry to hear about it, Buttsy Boy. How bad is it?"

"Doctor says three months. I haven't been to see her yet." He hated it when Hill called him that name.

Hill didn't need to say what Butler was thinking. They'd both killed before and thought nothing more of it than an exchange for a healthy bank account transaction.

"If it's going to happen, it's going to happen. You know what they say, ain't nothing guaranteed except for birth, death and taxes..."

Hill laughed. "I'm not paying any fucking taxes." He turned the heater down a notch as the car finally began to warm. "That reminds me. You seen that show on the TV? The one with that psychic guy who speaks to the dead?"

"Yeah. Pretty freaky."

"Nah, it's a crock of shit. This girlfriend of mine is into that sort of thing and she was telling me all about it. He's what you call a cold reader. Just picks stuff up out of what you say. You know, starts off saying he's getting a John, anyone know a John?" Hill loaded his gun. "Who the fuck doesn't know a John? And the sucker in the audience is just dishing up the clues, desperate to make contact. 'Yeah, yeah, my dad is a John' they'll say. And then the guy will ask if they're dead or not. For fuck's sake! If he's talking to them from the other side, then they must be dead! How come he doesn't already know?"

Butler laughed. "You got a point there. I was thinking maybe he was picking it all up from the audience. Some sort of ESP thing."

"They ain't that fucking flash, Buttsy Boy." Hill loaded the other gun and put them both into the glovebox. "Just another charlatan, my friend. You don't get to ask a thing of the dead in those shows. The guy asks you stuff, you confirm it, then he tells you it straight back like some revelation from heaven. Death is a part of life and if the dead are gathering in a television studio to talk crap with a TV show host, well, you just got to think about that, eh?"

Butler laughed again. "Too right. I mean, if you were dead what would you be telling the living? That your Uncle Jimmy always loved the red chair in the hallway, and he wanted you to have it?"

"No way," said Hill. "I'd want to know if there's a God. Am I going to burn in Hell? And is Hell so bad I better mend my ways? You're Catholic, right? You can repent, can't you? Can I do that or do I have to convert?"

"I wouldn't know. I'm lapsed." Butler turned off the lights and the engine and then coasted down the driveway of a dilapidated hotel in the back lots of Footscray, the industrial area by the river. There were only two room lights on, the rest slumped in darkness. Why the Hell would you hide out here? It's too quiet, thought Butler. Guess the guy thought it'd be harder to find.

"You heard of Harry Houdini, eh? Greatest magician who ever lived. He spent years trying to talk to the other side and ended up becoming one of the greatest spiritual debunkers. Made a deal with his wife to use a secret code." They got out of the car and Hill passed

Butler his gun. "I'll make you a deal, but we don't need a secret code. If you die, come back and tell me what I have to worry about. If I die, I'll tell you. Now, let's go wipe our conscience clean and earn our pay."

The man in the black suit's head shot back, his Adam's apple huge and exposed, grinding up and down in his throat. Blood trickled from the corners of his mouth where he'd bitten into his lips.

"Did you know he was going to do this?" one of the minders nearby whispered to another.

"No, I wish he'd tell us about these stunts beforehand."

"You know ratings. Looks better if we're surprised, too."

Butler stood transfixed, staring in horror at the psychic kneeling under the lights.

"Do you remember the promise?" the voice hissed. Someone in the audience started crying. "Do you remember the promise you made?"

Butler sank into his seat. His head nodded slightly, while his lips worked soundlessly, his tongue dry and thick in the back of his mouth. A small, keening noise fluted from his throat. He'd made two promises, but the voice — it was all wrong, neither male nor female — an inhuman sound.

"Who...who is this?" The sweat poured from his groin, his armpits.

Bile threatened his mouth. An image of his mother coursed into his head, her face sweet in death, an ancient book bound with skin in her hands. His name written on the pages in the blood of those he'd killed. And the sweat poured and poured. Hill laughing and saying it's all bullshit, that it doesn't matter. There is no Heaven and Hell. Pull the fucking trigger, Buttsy Boy! It all adds to nothing.

The man in the black suit laughed; a hideous sound of splintered wood and twisted metal, of broken limbs and bleeding wounds. A hysterical wail teetering on salvation.

Say my name, please say my name.

Butler, affectionately known as Robert, lapsed Catholic and devout atheist, wiped the sweat from his palms onto his trousers.

Then I'll know.

Come on, Hill. Call me Buttsy Boy.

(It's Not Like) The Good Old Days

For my rebirthday, I decided to hold a concert in our private allocation. I wanted The Beatles but OpTel hadn't acquired the copyrights or formed the appropriate corporate partnerships, so I chose the next best thing: XTC, another great late-twentieth century band.

"Who should we invite, Jules?"

My wife emerged from the bathroom with a towel wrapped around her head. She didn't go to the toilet anymore, so why did she still need to shower or bathe? It annoyed me having to pay for the extra bathroom space and the simulated water, but she *is* my wife and some lifelong habits are hard to kick.

"What did you say?"

"Who should we invite to the concert? XTC will be playing."

"Can we afford this?" Jules scanned the kitchen bench. "Where's my coffee?"

I downloaded a cappuccino. "Of course we can afford it. We haven't passed the quota for the month."

A glowing red envelope hovered in the corner of the room — a message from our telecommunications provider — so we ignored it. If the message became urgent, it would whistle.

"There's not enough sugar in this," said Jules. "And it tastes like instant."

"You know I don't drink. Why you insist on hanging onto these things is beyond me. You don't need them and it costs money."

Jules stared at me, her face expressionless. The calm before the storm.

So I pushed her. "And anyway, why can't you make it yourself?"

"Because I want you to, Paul. It's the little things that count." She downloaded a flat white, sipped it and smiled. "Now. This concert. You're planning to hold it in our house?"

"Yes."

Jules arched an eyebrow.

"Come on, Jules. You know I can't afford to place it in the public domain."

"*We* can't afford it. Not *I*. You're not remodelling the house for this. *We* can't afford *that*."

"Well, I was thinking of restructuring the section of our allocation you call the study. Modelling it on an old Roman amphitheatre and then downsizing our personas so we can fit more people into the space. I won't touch the rest of the house."

"Downsizing? Isn't that risky? Didn't that couple have problems restoring themselves? I read she got partially lost in the translation coming back."

"That was years ago. Technology has changed since then. People are doing it all the time. Or as much as OpTel allows under the new contract. It'll be fine."

"I'm not sure about this. Why not just leave the study the way it is and invite less people?"

"Jules! You don't understand! I want to see XTC perform in an amphitheatre!"

"No one you know wants to see that. Your brother would, but he hasn't signed up with the program yet."

"I'm not telling them it's XTC. I'm going to leak that I've acquired bootleg source code for The Beatles."

"You heard me," she said. A massive canvas materialised in the corner of the room. She suddenly sported a beret and wore an artist's apron splattered with paints. A smear of burnt orange appeared on the canvas as she approached it. She was getting lazy; she hadn't even downloaded the paintbrushes yet.

I was sure I could rearrange the study for the concert within our budget.

Jules had arranged another bloody shelving façade to accommodate my books and music — another hang up of days gone — but all it did was limit the number of indexes I could store in the room.

"Just download them when you need them," she'd say.

I hated doing that. The download took time and incurred a cost. So what if it was data redundancy? These were all mine. When *I* wanted. I removed the shelving and morphed the space into a rough semi-circle, using the music indexes for steps, slabbing between them with the books. A rough skin of stone would smooth it over, and then I'd apply some aging effects.

This would be easy.

A scream came from the other end of the allocation.

"Paul! Come here quick!"

A small African girl huddled on the floor of the kitchen. Flies buzzed over the skin drawn tight over her thin bones. Her belly was swollen. She stretched out her palm.

"Please," she croaked.

"How the Hell did this get in?" asked Jules accusingly.

"I didn't forget to upgrade the software filters. Have you checked the address?"

An elderly Christian-looking fellow, wearing conservative adventure clothing, crouched next to the girl, his arm placed carefully around her shoulders. "Mbome can't get enough to eat. The village well has been poisoned. Without your help Mbome and thousands like her are dying every day. By attaching your persona signatures to this mail and sending it to ten of your closest friends, we at WorldAid will guarantee one dollar for each persona you forward…"

"Send it to OpTel," said Jules. "I don't want the house full of spam like last year. We couldn't move, download, or send. We're not paying for the space. Make sure you get a refund on this."

I disassembled the code and forwarded it to technical support as another red envelope appeared in the corner of the room. They actually appeared in the corner of *every* room: OpTel made sure you had every warning. We ignored it, though — it wasn't related to my support call and was most likely technical sales speak for things we couldn't afford and didn't want. It was unusual to get two messages from the provider in one day, but right now I was planning a party.

🐈

As I investigated links to subsonic frequencies for downsized personas, Giles' head popped into the room. His eyes were blank, so Jules hadn't let him in yet.

"You decent?" Giles said. His voice quavered.

"Yeah, connect two-way. You using a fear modulator?"

His eyes opened and I had a portal into his allocation. I noticed there were no naked women present. Strange.

"No, I'm not," Giles continued. "I'm scared, though. They're severing the Western Victorian farm from the mainframe."

"What?"

"They're cutting us off. What am I to do? I'm going to die! Jesus Christ, Paul, I'm really going to die!"

I hadn't heard Giles this upset since he'd been diagnosed with cancer just before he signed with the program. "Calm down. You're already dead."

His persona flickered and a streak of static shot through his room.

"Everyone's trying to leave. We've got twenty-four hours! I'm going to die!"

"How can this be? What was that static?"

"Our part of the system is under too much load. The bandwidth's clogged with a God-damned exodus! My world is collapsing. You've got to help me!"

I thought for a second. Jules came down the hall, her persona emanating worry. "Just sign up for a transfer to another server. One on the mainland."

"My brain is here in Colac! There's a thirty-six hour backlog for processing. The providers aren't responding to any mail. There's a rumour going around they're not even going to transfer our brains."

"Upload into public domain then. You've still plenty of cash, haven't you?"

"And for how long? Public domain is expensive. I'll lose everything. I can only afford to store myself for about three weeks real time before it won't be worth it."

"What? How much have you been spending?"

He shrugged. "The women, you know... expensive..."

"Don't worry, Giles," said Jules, her hand on my shoulder. "Upload into our place. We'll store you here until we get your brain transferred to another farm. You'll owe us one."

"Great!" He grinned and static crackled over the connection. "You'd better start now. Like I said, the bandwidth is clogged this end."

The portal closed and I initiated transfer. "I'm not activating him when he's here. He'll eat up this month's budget. He can stay in storage."

"Stop sulking. He's one of your best friends. He'd do the same for you."

"I suppose. Lucky we didn't sign up in the country, eh? I don't know what he was thinking when he moved there. I thought it would only be a matter of time before they suspended service to the rural areas."

"It wasn't luck, Paul. I signed us up for our

retirement in the safest possible spot. You wanted to go cheap like Giles." She went back to her canvasses.

She was right, but I wasn't going to admit it. I didn't think why we hadn't heard about the suspension of service. I had bigger problems. Giles would be a burden on both space and budget for the XTC concert. I'd have to foot his bill and I wasn't sure I could afford it.

Waz popped in late that afternoon so we opened the connection between allocations. Sacha paced the room in the background, pretending to smoke cigarettes. As far as I knew, OpTel weren't allowed to simulate nicotine. Too many court cases from America had stemmed that in rebirthing's infancy.

"Uh, you haven't had any technical problems lately, have you?" Waz asked in his soft English accent. Sacha paced and smoked.

"Some spam got through, but that's about it. Why?"

"Something's happened. We got a message from OpTel — it whistled right away — saying our service will be disconnected shortly. Apparently our super funds are almost gone. We've tried to contact Australian Sentinel Funds Management, but we can't get through."

"But you guys are loaded."

"Yeah, well. You haven't seen or heard anything about any scams running at the moment?"

"There's been nothing on the news. Jules? You haven't heard anything, have you?"

"No. Have you tried to contact anyone else outside,

Warren?" Jules asked. "See if they can get somewhere, face-to-face as it were?"

"Sacha's tried her daughter, but we hardly ever hear from her these days — you know those neo-Juddites."

"They're taking us offline tomorrow," said Sacha. She lit another cigarette and sucked it down. "If that happens, we're screwed. With both of us off, we can't resolve our funding issue and reconnect."

"We wouldn't ask if we didn't have to," said Waz. "We already tried Giles, but we can't get hold of him either. I don't know what this world is coming to."

I knew what they wanted, but I was hoping someone else could help them instead. "Look, guys, I'd love to help, but…"

"Don't worry," Jules said. "Upload to our place. You can work it out from here, and reimburse us any costs you run up while you're doing it. Paul's having a party for his rebirthday soon, too."

"Thanks, Jules," Waz and Sacha said. "Oh, and Happy Rebirthday, Paul."

"Yeah, thanks." I prepared for the transfers.

"Don't even think about it," said Jules. "You will not put them in storage."

"They don't both need to be active to figure out where their money is. I could put one of them in storage."

"Oh? And who will that be? Sacha won't be happy if you put Warren away, and she'll be furious if it's her. Stop being so selfish."

I hated it when she was right. The constraints were getting tight now.

How could I afford to keep my friends here and have

the concert? I was never going to be able to keep this under budget.

Another red envelope appeared.

🐈

It's a funny thing. The brain gets tired, even without a body. I wish I could see our allocation after we're asleep, but of course I can't. And there's no point recording something that's not really there, either. OpTel has assured us that our allocation is never altered unless we demand it, but I've a sneaking suspicion that they're using our space while we're asleep. It's those snatches of grey, that cold code interface between our reality and the real world you spy upon waking. Our provider termed it "lagtime". If I proved otherwise, maybe I could stretch the super a little further from the rewards of a little litigation.

(Yeah, right.)

And over the years, our dreams have become less physical, an abstract jumble of faces and memories yearning for the flesh. Jules paints these feelings, but I prefer to bury them each morning when I wake and relish in an everlasting life devoid of arthritis and wrinkles and heart attacks and cancer.

Most of us died from these things.

But not my brother, Scott.

He's refused to sign up, battling with age and its burdens like the Lord intended. He's not religious though, he fears letting go of the flesh. My sister said he was primarily held together by machines when she had died. God knows what he's like now. And he's our only contact with the real world — the rest of our families have either died or signed up — though all providers limit interaction to sound channels only. Technical limitations I'm told. Sure.

:Happy Rebirth:

"Thanks, Scott. I'm holding an XTC concert tomorrow. Want to come?"

:How much info are you receiving these days?:

"Eh?" I thought he'd jump at the chance to see XTC play. Or in his case, hear them. Something was awry. "You mean news from outside? The usual stuff. Politics, interest rates, wars, sports etc."

:Nothing about the viruses? The stock market crash?:

"Viruses? Sure, OpTel provides upgrades all the time for that. It's part of the contract. We're safe as."

:Safe is a dangerous word. There's been a viral outbreak in several farms. Tasmania has been destroyed and they suspect contamination in most farms west of Ballarat and Bendigo:

Jules yelled from the other end of the allocation. "Paul! There's another spam here. Some chain letter about a pyramid scheme. Did you send that last one to OpTel like I asked?"

"Yes. Just delete it. I'll look it at later. Sorry, Scott, what were you saying? A viral outbreak? OpTel will fix that."

:It's not a digital virus. It's a human one. Of the spongiform encephalopathy family. They suspect it's a hybrid of *kuru* that once plagued ancient Papua New Guinea. It's decimating farms on a global scale. It attacks the cerebral cortex, possibly through cerebrospinal fluid where your brain is attached to the farm:

I hadn't been scared for a long, long time. Not since my diagnosis and the dark months that followed before accepting rebirth. "Is there a cure?"

:Not yet. They think it's spreading through the nodes, leaping from farm to farm through cerebral contact. God knows how. Can the digital world affect the real one? I didn't think so, but now I'm not so sure:

A red enveloped suddenly hovered in the corner of the room.

"What should we do?"

:At this stage, nothing. Keep on living. If you start losing contact with people, it's probably the provider closing down nodes to prevent infection. It doesn't surprise me you haven't been told:

The red envelope started whistling. All the unopened envelopes started whistling.

"Paul!"

"Just open them, Jules!"

:What's happening?:

"The junk mail's annoyed we haven't read it yet."

:I think you'd better read them. Your super's not with Australian Sentinel Funds Management, is it?:

"No, we're with the Mutual Society. Why?"

:Several of the larger superannuation companies have folded with the stock market crash. It's estimated twenty-five percent of personas will go under. Do you —:

Then nothing but the whistling of unread mail, sharper and sharper, like the scream of steam before the kettle boiled. Waz and Sacha were with Australian Sentinel. They were down in the lounge with Jules, trying to figure out where their money had gone.

"Scott?"

"Open the bloody messages, Paul!" Jules yelled.

"Scott? Hello?"

That was the last time I spoke to my brother.

I decided to open the messages.

Dear Mr. & Mrs HAINES,

As you may be aware, OpTel will soon be increasing the costs of all LifeStyle plans by 3%. This is in accordance with current inflation rates and as OpTel have not increased any costs for the past 10 years, it is with great reluctance that we have to at this time.

In line with the increases, a 15% surcharge will be placed on technologies deemed non-essential for digital living. This includes stimulant technology involving the following senses: smell, taste and touch. For a complete list of items to be surcharged please refer to ~2466/docs/proposals/surcharged-item-list.

You do not need to respond to this message. Your account will automatically be billed for the new amounts.

If you have any questions please do not hesitate to contact your nearest service provider.

Yours truly,

Customer Service Area #425

"Jules. I think you better have a look at this."

Her face paled as she read the first message. Then her cheeks reddened.

"What is this rubbish? We've signed a contract. They can't do this to us."

"If they do, we're going to lose a lot of those 'little

things' you love. The coffee, hot water..." The reddening cheeks.

"No, we're not. I can't live without coffee, or tea or chocolate! I can't believe those bastards! What's in the other messages?"

Dear Mr. & Mrs HAINES,

Due to recent customer feedback, we're introducing four new LifeStyle plans to replace the LifeStyle: Light Warp plan you currently enjoy. You can stay on your existing plan until the end of your 50 year agreement or you can change to one of the new plans designed for those on a restricted budget. If you remain on your existing plan, it's important you are aware of the changes outlined below:

• You will enjoy unlimited access to all other nodes subject to OpTel notification.

• Restricted number of downloads per month to provide cheaper security and Lifestyle upgrades.

• Usage-based activity, so you only pay for the amount of data you need each month — making access to Life fairer for everyone.

• The introduction of one Advertiser per week into your home. The Advertiser will stay for a maximum of one hour. You can invite up to five extra Advertisers as nominated by OpTel based on your Lifestyle history, providing further discounts on your monthly rate.

We didn't bother reading anymore. Jules flew into a rage, splashing paint and smashing plates, screaming obscenities through the lines. That would cost us, but it felt prudent for me to disappear into the public domain for an indeterminate time without mentioning that fact.

It wasn't as if we could switch to another service provider either: we'd signed an exclusive contract with high penalty clauses for swapping to get a better monthly rate more suited to the Super plan we had.

I didn't think there were any other service providers left since the last merger, either.

We were screwed.

⚓

The day before the concert I decided to activate Giles. Jules wasn't talking to me and connections to other nodes were still limited.

"Thanks, Paul, I didn't think the transfer would be so quick. How long did it take?" Giles accessed the system date then shot me a murderous look.

"You bastard. It's been three days. Why the Hell did you store me? You know, I've got to get back on."

"There's something else. There's a virus affecting some of the farms. Colac could be infected."

If I hadn't imposed limits on Giles' downloaded persona, he would have paled. "Oh my God, I've got to move my brain."

"You've got today to arrange it."

"Today? What if that's not enough? Why can't you just keep me here until it's done?"

"It's all we can afford."

"You're kidding me! This is my life!"

"It's ours too." I told Giles about the price hikes. "Because you're no longer connected to your brain, I've assigned a day-long buffer for storing new memories from this point on. If the buffer is overloaded it'll reset your memories to where you are now."

Giles' mouth hung suspended. "But...you can't..."

Jules stormed into the room wearing nothing but swirling torrents of hot chocolate. She drank continually as she spoke. "I'd get on with it if I were you, Giles. If it comes to you or us, it's us. You're gone." Then she stormed out.

"What was that?" Giles asked.

"Something had to go. She cut fashion and clothes in favour of keeping the pleasures of hot water and chocolate. Now she eats what she wears. A strange woman, my wife."

"Strange but smart. You'd better be careful she doesn't start eating you," said Giles. "I've got some work to do." He disappeared.

This is what I'd love to say: "The concert went off without a hitch. Everyone had a great time; XTC played with a rare gusto that converted even the faithless. It was undoubtedly the best rebirthday I'd ever had."

But it didn't happen that way.

I watched it alone a year later, in my Roman amphitheatre. One of the Advertisers had been here, but left when she discovered it wasn't The Beatles. I was like Gulliver seated in a Lilliputian arena. Due to the rising costs of service provision, I hadn't been able to afford to restructure the study into something more comfortable, and I couldn't risk the expense of downsizing my persona for the concert and resizing afterwards. I'd also sold half our allocation to investors in the real world to cut costs and extend the budget.

And to make matters worse, I couldn't really *feel* the music — it cost too damn much for the extra sensory input.

I wanted to ask my friends and family what they thought of the concert, but they were all in storage and it was incredibly expensive to activate anyone now. OpTel had cut back on a lot of things since the virus outbreak. People were one of them. I had managed to store a few of my friends here before the outbreak left eastern Australia isolated from most parts of the world. Still, we all have to make do with what we've got and I've got my music, so I'm happy enough.

There are a couple of glitches in the system now. Every morning I find a bathroom has slipped back into the allocation. I've stopped removing it as it costs me a restructuring fee, and OpTel haven't replied to my enquiry yet. And they're charging me for the water simulation I'm not using — it's on my monthly bill. Oh, and another thing. On Thursdays my skin tastes like hot chocolate. And Monday morning it's a flat white. Annoys the Hell out of me — they're all Jules' hang-ups — but I can't reprogram them for some reason. It's like someone else has control of my life now and then.

I do get bored from time to time though, with no one to talk to. Some lifelong habits *are* hard to kick. I'm thinking of saving up for a couple of months and activating Jules. It'd be nice to see her again.

Going Down with Jennifer Aniston's Breasts

The woman next to me is screaming and I wish she wouldn't. Even though I'm watching *Friends* on the television without any sound, she's ruining my concentration.

"Watch this." I touch her gently on the arm and point towards the screen. Jennifer Aniston runs around the kitchen wearing a tight white sweater. The guy who plays Joey runs around, too. His hair is longer than normal. And greasier. "It's funny."

She screams louder and tears at my hand, squeezing it, crushing it. She grips my hand like it was a newborn baby about to be ripped from her arms for Nazi experiments. My head fills up, ready to explode. The pressure in my ears builds to bursting point. Somewhere at the back of my mind I know other people are screaming, too.

"Please let go." I use my other hand to prise her fingers from me. "That hurts."

"I don't want to die!" Black streaks of mascara dribble down her ruddy cheeks, smudging her freckles.

Her eyes are blue pools drowning in a bloodshot swirl.

"Neither do I." I smile and pick up my lunch container from where it has fallen on the floor. I open the container, careful not to spill its contents, as my stomach lurches and the woman screams louder. "Here, you can have my piece of chocolate if you want."

Even though she doesn't accept my offer, the gesture achieves the desired result. She leans forward in her seat to hug her thighs and sobs into her knees.

She's stopped screaming and I can get back to the show.

I've missed part of the plot, but it doesn't really matter — you can pick it up anywhere and it will still make sense. And there's comfort in that.

Jennifer is still running around the kitchen. I can make out a blue bra beneath the white sweater. Her breasts look very firm, almost too firm, and I wonder if they'd move much under my hands. Whether they'd be warm. The guy who plays Chandler is arguing with the guy who plays Joey. I'm sure it's all to comic proportion, but I hope the camera gets back to Jennifer soon and her blue bra under her white sweater.

I know that if I think about it, there can't be much time left.

And I was right before about the screaming. Lots of people are. And crying. And yelling.

A friend of mine once told me how long it took to die from a lack of oxygen and the three stages of feeling as you approached shutdown. I think it took twenty seconds and the final feeling, euphoric. For the life of me, I have no idea how much time has passed since this all began, but a lack of oxygen is not the problem.

My stomach tries to crawl into my mouth to take over my brain. Perhaps if it does, the pressure in my skull will cease and my ears will unblock.

The woman next to me is screaming again. Something about God and the Earth. She's pulling at my arms, shaking me, hugging me.

I ignore her.

I don't want to remember her round tear-streaked panicked face. I don't want that to be the last thing I ever see.

The picture on the television has frozen. Jennifer with hands on hips smiling at the camera, her head slightly tilted, wearing a blue bra under a white sweater. The picture is surprisingly clear for an in-flight circuit and I can make out the bump of her nipples.

I thank God for small miracles as the Earth reaches up to dash our flight against its breast.

But not before the television screen goes black.

The Punjab's Gift

The scents of cardamom, spice and sugar hang heavy in the air. Strange, misshapen lumps, brown and red and white, some chalky, while others sweat in the dry heat. The square, dense shapes towards the back of the display could be fudge.

The man behind the counter smiles, wiggling his head from side to side, urging us to sample the delights of his wares. His moustache is oiled and his teeth look like they have seen too much of what he has to offer. On the wall behind him, Vishnu smiles benignly, in colours exploding. Eat, he whispers, and the colours swirl.

I glance at Mike, aware the café is silent, all eyes upon us, the ignorant tourists off the beaten track. We can almost hear the shuffle of dirty rupees passing discreetly below tables, behind backs and under hands, as the locals bet on us staying or going.

"*Namaste.*" Mike's finger begins pointing. "I'll have one of those, some of those, and that one, no, that one."

The shopkeeper grins. Time resumes inside the café.

I choose whatever Mike hasn't.

We sit at a table towards the rear of the café. Its colour is not unlike the food.

"What the Hell is this?" Mike sniffs an oily biscuit.

The café is again silent. All bets are back on. Double or nothing.

I bite into something unnaturally red, and sweetness fills my mouth.

Mike's head tilts forward, eyebrows raised, and then he eats his biscuit.

"Is good?" The shopkeeper leans over the counter. I don't think his feet touch the ground.

"Is good." Mike grins and finally the café goes about its daily business.

An elderly Sikh, resplendent in white cottons and silk, his turban adorned with exotic feathers, nods and smiles at us from a far table. His beard is woven up into his turban. He whispers something to a man at his table and they laugh.

"Where are you from?" he calls.

"New Zealand."

Nods of approval; at least here, in the Punjab, our cricketing nation commands respect.

"Do you like India?"

We nod back enthusiastically, finger to mouth, savouring the sweet delicacies. Indian heads bob, white teeth in brown faces.

"We're off to Amritsar," says Mike.

"Oh." The room falls quiet. The Sikh looks at the others around him. A heartbeat passes. "Then to Pakistan?"

"Yes," says Mike.

"No," I say too late.

Mike glares at me until he realises. A war is still being fought here and Amritsar lies in its heart. A border town built on passports and guns, looking fearfully, contemptuously west.

"Wait here. I have a gift for you." The Sikh

disappears into the haze outside and conversation returns nervously to the café.

We finish our snacks and step outside into the heat. The street teems with people working, loitering, begging and scamming, the babble loud and chaotic. Crowds push past, eyes staring and fingers groping. The heavy smell of spice and unwashed bodies assails us. Two scrawny donkeys pull an overladen cart of baked dung and the small boy aboard pauses in his whipping to flash us a grin.

"Wonder what he's getting us?" says Mike.

"Dunno. What time is it? We leave in ten minutes." Sweat drips from my armpits, trickling coolly down my sides.

"Why would he want to give us something?"

"Perhaps he likes us."

Time ticks and sweat drips. Flies descend and eat the salt off our skin. I can see the truck from here. The rest of the crew mill around it, ready to board.

"Where the Hell is he? We gotta go."

"What if he wants us to carry something over the border?" Mike's eyes shine. "What about those stories in the paper?"

"You thrive on that crap. You stoned?"

"I'm serious, man. All those bombings recently. They're not far from here!"

"You're paranoid, Mike." But the headlines are still fresh. Dozens of them. "Let's go."

"Ah, Kiwis!" The Sikh emerges from the crowd, his white silk bright and clean in the sunlight. "I hope you still here. Here is your gift."

He hands Mike a plain cardboard box, twice as wide

as a shoebox, though not as deep. The Sikh's hand stops him from opening it.

"Not now," he smiles. "Your truck waits. Go."

He ushers us forward. Our legs jerk back towards the truck. I look back and he's standing there surrounded by villagers, all smiling and waving. "Remember the Punjab!"

Mike shoves me the box. "Here, you take it."

"I don't want it." The box is far too heavy for its size. Something large slides within. Too heavy. *Bus torn to pieces. Twenty dead.*

"What if it's a bomb?" says Mike, our thoughts riding parallel paranoia. His eyes no longer shine; they burn and his face is slick with sweat. He looks sick.

"Don't be stupid, man." People on the street avoid us. The seas part.

Everyone stares. The Sikh has disappeared. I try to hold the box level. No more sliding. Too heavy. I've seen the headlines. Mike's walking ahead now, his pace faster. Black stubble upon paling face. His shirt sticks to his back. Like mine. The box is too heavy. Too much noise in my head, though no one is speaking.

"What have you got there, Richard?" One of the girls climbs up into the truck. The street around us is empty.

"Open it!" hisses Mike. He puts the truck between us.

How did I end up holding this? I can't take it on board; I know these people. Just put it down. Leave it. It's just a cardboard box. That's why the street is empty. In India. Where you are never alone.

I think of only one thing. Will I feel it? My eyes brim with sweat and I reach for the lid. I try to prise it off, but it sticks, so I work at it slowly. Time has stopped. I hear nothing for the blood in my ears. I've wandered away from the truck, my back to them, using my body as a shield. I hope Mike has made it far enough away.

I pull off the lid.

Indian fudge.

Failed Experiments from the Frontier: The Pumpkin

Caleb took the knife his pa offered.

"You ready, boy?"

The blade glinted in the mornin' sun. Caleb nodded.

"The bigger the pumpkin, the better for scarin' off Stingy Jack. Don't want that miserable ghost round our place on the Eve, eh, boy?"

Caleb shook his head. That big ole pumpkin with the glowing eyes weren't gonna scare him this year. He'd make it his own an' light him up out on the porch to guard against the night. You could bet on that!

Pa mussed Caleb's hair with his big fingers an' sent him on his way with a pat on the behind, an' Caleb thought that was jus fine. Near the gate, ole Tom lazed in the sun pawing the remains of a fat chestnut-coloured mouse, an' though Caleb called out to the cat to join him, ole Tom jus licked his claws an' lay there grinnin'. *Well, never mind that,* thought Caleb, *I don't need no lazy ole cat to help me. I'm gonna do this all by myself then.*

So Caleb strode up the lane towards the pumpkin

field, his ears full a birdsong an' insect chirrupin', as the mornin' sun climbed itself up into the deep blue sky. Before he'd even got halfway, Caleb spied the biggest pumpkin he'd ever seen there in the middle a the lane, sittin' between the cart tracks an' a pile a horse dung. The pumpkin most likely come all the way up past his chest! He'd have to carve out its guts right here on the road.

The pumpkin lay there, swollen an' fat with a mottled green an' orange rind that soaked up sunlight, makin' the air around it all flat an' hollow. An' by the looks of it, ole Tom already been out here, 'cause nearby a couple more of them big fat mice lay ripped up dead as could be. Ha! That lazy ole Tom weren't so lazy after all!

Then, ever so slightly, the pumpkin rocked an inch towards him.

Caleb stared, frozen. The day fell silent. He wanted to look around, to seek his broad-shouldered Pa working his muscles in the nearby fields, but Caleb feared takin' his eyes off that pumpkin. It *had* moved an' moved *towards* him; he was sure a that.

An' somewhere, muffled an' distant, Caleb thought he heard a scream.

Caleb's bottom lip quivered. He wanted to run home an' lose himself in the folds of Ma's skirt where he'd only come out if the bowls an' spoons needed lickin' clean. Damn the pumpkin an' All Hallow's Eve an' ole Stingy Jack. But if he ran home, an' Pa was watchin' out there in the fields, he knew he'd get a beatin' an' be marched right on back to this here pumpkin. An' Caleb surely couldn't let one of the other chil'ren get hold a this pumpkin afore him. Damn pumpkin.

Pa said you could eat pumpkin, that the rich folk livin' in mansions ate em at their dance evenins with pumpkin pie an' cream, but round here most folks never did. They jus liked to carve em. An' that's jus what Caleb was gonna do. An' maybe, jus maybe, Caleb'd eat hisself a big mouthful a this pumpkin's guts, swallow him down an' poo him out when he was good an' done. That'd show ole Stingy Jack an' his lantern if he came a lookin' round their house!

He hefted the knife in his hand an' gingerly stepped towards the pumpkin.

And again came the scream, muffled, still distant, but still a scream an' one that ran deep in bloodcurdlin' an' terror, that warbled an' howled its way into your ears an' scampered across your brain until you wanted to curl up 'neath the sheets an' whimper till the dawn come creepin' through the window an' bought the birdsong with it to drown out any nastiness left from the night.

But the only birdsong now, in the still silence followin' the scream, was the cawin' of a crow peckin' out worms in the pumpkin field off yonder.

For a second, but jus a second, mind, Caleb thought the pumpkin was doing that screamin'. An' that was jus about the most plain stupid thing that he ever did think. Pumpkins din't have no mouth to scream, least not until one had been carved outta it. An' it couldn't do no screamin' then, unless...unless this pumpkin belonged to Stingy Jack hisself!

Yes siree, there was definitely somethin' wrong with this pumpkin.

There was heat comin' oft it, like the heat from the kitchen stove after it burned low in the night. Not too hot, jus nice enough to rest your hands on to warm em a bit. Caleb pulled his fingers back from the pumpkin's rind. He looked back at the house an' saw Pa in the field, wavin' to him. Caleb waved back. He hadda do it now; his pa had seen him.

Caleb tapped the tip of the knife on the pumpkin.

Nothin' happened.

Good, thought Caleb, pullin' out the rumpled piece a paper with a charcoal scrawl of a Jack-O-Lantern from his pocket.

Caleb tapped the knife again, to be sure.

No scream, no rockin', no nothin'.

He drew the tip a the knife against the rind, tracin' the outline a where he would cut the eyes, the nose an' mouth. An' still that pumpkin did nothin'.

Caleb chuckled to hisself an' slapped his hands against the rind, likin' the hard smack on warm skin. This was jus some dumb pumpkin warmed up in the mornin' sun! An' first things first, he was gonna hafta cut the lid off a this pumpkin to scoop out its guts afore he could carve out its face proper.

He clambered up onto the pumpkin, his chest an' stomach curvin' around its rind, his feet danglin' inches from the ground an' grasped one hand around the pumpkin's knobby stem. With his other hand he raised the knife high above his head and, with all his strength, swung the blade down.

The knife sliced through that puckery ole rind into the soft flesh below as if he were jus cuttin' up cheese!

The pumpkin screamed.

Caleb sucked in his breath, heart poundin', one hand wrapped around the stem, the other clingin' to the knife stuck out a that pumpkin.

It screamed again, no longer muffled, now a piercin' shrill that shook birds from the trees an' filled Caleb's ears to overflowin' so much so he could barely think. It began to rock beneath him, jerkin' slowly along the ruts left by the carts.

This surely were no ordinary pumpkin, an' if Caleb din't finish the job, ole Stingy Jack would be comin' for him for sure. Caleb gripped the knife harder, his knuckles white an' bulgin', an' began to saw slow an' steady like what his pa taught him, cutting the lid out a that pumpkin on an angle so that later on when it all shrunk up the lid wouldn't fall in.

The pumpkin screamed an' screamed, but Caleb soon figured it couldn't do no nothin' to hurt him. It din't have no arms to grab with, no teeth to bite with, an' din't have no eyes to see who was doin' this so's to maybe come an' get him later when he was fast asleep.

Caleb sawed the lid clean off a that pumpkin an' it stopped screamin' an' movin'. He carefully tossed the lid into the soft grass by the side of the lane an' began to scoop out the goopy guts on the inside, usin' his hands on the soft flesh an' slicin' out big chunks with his knife on what his fingers couldn't pry. This was Caleb's pumpkin now!

An' somewhere along the way, lost in the hard sweat a workin' under that warm sky, Caleb figured he must a cut hisself bad, because there was blood runnin' all throughout that pumpkin, but he didn't care, no siree, 'cause he beat that pumpkin good an' Caleb was gonna bring home the biggest an' best Jack-O-Lantern the county had ever seen an' Stingy Jack wouldn't come a knockin' at their door this All Hallow's Eve.

And maybe Ma would make them all a pumpkin pie, the biggest an' sweetest pumpkin pie that anyone, even the rich folk, ever did see!

That evenin', the kitchen filled with the smells of nutmeg an' cinnamon as Ma took the pumpkin pie from the oven, shooin' ole Tom who hung around her legs meowin' for scraps. On the floor sat the Jack-O-Lantern, its eyes vacant an' mouth empty without the flickering candle inside yet.

One a them eyes was carved a bit crooked where the knife had slipped, but no one seemed to pay no mind to that. Pa had laughed an' swept Caleb up in his arms when he'd seen him out there on the road with the carved out pumpkin. Pa carried it home on his shoulders on account a it being so big, while Caleb dragged a sack full a pumpkin flesh behind him. He'd washed out all the bloodied chunks before givin' them to Ma to bake the pie. The cut on his finger must a already healed up, because he couldn't find no wound anywheres, nope, not a nick.

"Smells good to me, boy." Pa's nostrils flared wide. He grinned at Caleb who grinned back.

"Not sure how it'll eat," said Ma. "Strangest pumpkin I ever seen, the flesh all stringy an' tough, almost like beef steak in places. Strips of ribbon an' cloth in there too. Caleb, you not clean it out good an' proper from carryin' it in that sack like I asked?"

"Now, Ma," said Pa, sharin' another smile with Caleb, "the boy done good. Cleanin' is a woman's chore anyways."

Ma cut three big chunks a pie an' placed each on a plate, dolloppin' a spoon of fresh whipped cream over 'em. "He sure did do good, that be the biggest Jack-O-Lantern I ever did see. No way Stingy Jack come knockin' round here."

There was a loud rap at the door.

Ole Tom hissed an' ran from the room.

Pa glanced at Ma, then at the door.

Caleb sat dead still, the fork full a pie clasped all sweaty in his hands. He suddenly needed to pass water real bad.

"It's okay," said Pa, noticin' Caleb's face. "That's not Stingy Jack; All Hallow's Eve ain't until tomorrow." Pa flashed a smile, stood an' walked to the door.

"Yeah, I know." Caleb stared at the table. He din't want the door to be opened. Not at all. That pumpkin *had* been too good to be true.

The rap on the door came again, louder, insistent.

"Please don't," whispered Caleb to his fork.

Pa opened the door.

An elderly lady in long robes strung with glitter stood there, a look a worry writ all over her face. Her grey hair were thick wound with blossom.

"I'm looking for one of my god-daughters. Cindy didn't come home from the dance last night."

Caleb sighed. It was only the crazy old lady who lived near the edge a the forest. Pa said she was always off with the fairies an' that was about as crazy as you could get. He studied the piece a pie on his fork before poppin' it into his mouth.

"Why, Godmother, do come in," said Pa. He held the door open. "Perhaps we can help some."

"You haven't seen a rather large pumpkin, have you?" The Godmother stepped inside, then her eyes spied the Jack-O-Lantern in the corner of the room an' her face fell.

"Ow!" Caleb spat a mouthful a pumpkin over the table.

"Manners, Caleb!" Ma glared at him. "We got ourselves a guest."

Caleb fished out a clear sharp object from his mouth. Blood smeared his fingers. "There's glass in this here pie."

Close by, sharp an' clear, Caleb heard a scream, as the crazy old lady fainted dead to the floor.

"Damn pumpkin!" Caleb spat again on the table. "And look, Ma, that's a toenail!"

Slice of Life — Cooking for the Heart

It's hard to find good recipes for the heart these days. Look in any cookbook: your Stephanie Alexander, your once-naked Jamie Oliver, your bountiful Nigella — you won't find them. Social trends are pathetic, but we go along with them, swept up in their short-lived bursts. What's wrong with organs, people? Cardiovascular disease and stroke are the number one killers of Western society. You want a healthy heart? Then fucking eat one!

I crank up the Fields Of The Nephilim — normally night music — to drown out the doof-doof doofing from the upstairs apartment. They must have just got back from the East 93 club in Ringwood. This morning I don't mind — it takes time to prepare this meal and I've a busy day planned. The slow, dark guitar of *Endemoniada* razor-blades from the speakers.

I finely slice a red onion — they're sweeter — then wipe two, large flat mushrooms with a damp cloth. I prefer the fully mature flavour of these babies as they're the closest to field mushrooms in taste I've come across in the city.

"Who's this?" Vogon hovers near the kitchen bench,

his amorphous body rippling as he adjusts his form. As always this early in the day, he is faceless.

"Did you know only the pharaohs were served these?" I brandish a mushroom where his mouth should be, knowing he can't appreciate it. "Food for the gods."

Vogon nods thoughtfully. "Yes, I remember them. Stupid lot really, but eager to please. The pharaohs, that is. Not the gods. Haven't met any of them yet."

"I thought I was your first assignment?" I slice two lean rashers of bacon while I wait for him to reply.

He doesn't take long. "I had to pass the examinations before I was accepted. They don't allow just any field operatives." But probably a little *too* long. I'm starting to suspect Vogon is a bit of a bullshit artist. He's one of those 'I did this and I did that' sort of blokes. Well, if aliens can be blokes.

The oil in the pan spits so I sauté the onions, bacon and the mushrooms, until the onions are golden. I take the fist-sized heart soaking in the sink — the pink water indicates most of the excess blood has washed away — and cut away the tough, fatty aorta, the main and pulmonary arteries. Too hard on the teeth.

"You didn't answer my question," Vogon says.

"You going to try some?" I stuff the fried mixture into the atria and ventricles. "You know the rules."

"You always have to be such a difficult bastard, Haines. You know I can't eat. Why do I have to go through this charade?"

"You know the rules," I repeat. I don't look at him yet, intent on sewing the heart closed so the stuffing won't spill.

"Him?" His face transforms into the young gay's pout, though he's got the colour of the eyes wrong. "No? How about this?" Coarse hair sprouts from his widening chin as a large, pock-marked nose burgeons from the centre of his face.

Bang! Bang! Bang! on the door. *Who the fuck would come calling on me?*

Vogon disappears. I glance around the kitchen, then the lounge. Nothing seems out of place. At least nothing to me. The smell of the cooking should mask anything else. The sound of the fist on the door bangs again, louder, angrier. It's times like these I wish I had a frosted-glass door so I could make out the shape(s) on the other side. Even better, one of those TV security systems, but fat chance of that happening with my landlord.

Bang! Bang!

"Who is it?" I edge the door open, the chain still in place.

"From number four." It's the wizened Italian couple two doors down.

"It's seven in the morning. What do you want?"

"We come a complain. Your music is a too loud," says the hairier one.

Her husband, a swarthy man with fat lips, nods furiously in agreement.

"Yeah, well blame upstairs. I've only got it loud enough to drown out theirs."

"We a complain to them, too," Hairy says. "We sick of complaining. Every weekend. Every night. You no listen. You have no respect!"

"And strange noises." Fatlips stabs a fat finger to

emphasise his point.

"Listen. It's not me. It's upstairs. *Comprendre*?"

"You no *comprendre*. We have petition." Hairy throws her hands in the air.

"And strange smells." Fatlips stabs another finger. "We call police."

I throw back the chain and open the door. "Don't do that, old man." I thrust *my* fingers at his face. "We can come to—"

Fatlips' swarthy face pales, then Hairy screams.

The chef's knife is in my outthrust hand, the blade pink with artery. *Fuck*.

"He try kill us!" Hairy screams again.

"No, hold on," I try to explain as I chase them down the hall. "I'm only cooking. I didn't mean to—" And their door slams in my face.

Jesus fucking Christ. The stupid old cunts. People watch me from their doorways. I don't need attention, especially not now. The prostitute from number eight smirks and shuts her door quickly.

Vogon's returned, lounging on the sofa. His lips are bulbous and hairy — he forgets where the moustache goes. "Can we handle the police?"

"Not if they come in." And if they decide to search I'm fucked. No point stressing about it. "Those old diddy fucks have called them before. I'd be surprised if they even turn up."

"You chased them with a knife."

"I'm cooking, for fuck's sake." I pop the stuffed heart in a casserole dish and put it into the oven. On real low. By the time I get back this afternoon it'll melt in my mouth.

"You should consider looking into purchasing some Earth, Haines. Invest that extra income from your promotion."

Vogon tries to form a wise face as he tells me this. He uses a newsreader from Channel Ten.

"Use a male, Vogon. I don't beat off over them." For an alien bent on colonising the planet, he can be a real thick bastard. I indicate the auction brochures on the coffee table. "And what do you think those are?"

I turn up the stereo as *Chord Of Souls* hits its depths and wait for the cops not to arrive, as the smell of slowly roasting heart in a wine and garlic sauce suffuses my apartment.

The prick with the slicked-back hair in the smarmy suit saunters back into the house. I feel surprisingly calm — I think I'm in. What was all that shit everybody spouts about getting someone else to bid for you? Takes the pressure off? Removes the emotion? It's only a fucking house for Christ's sake! The other bidders have backed off and the smarmy prick's walked in with the last offer — mine. *"We're here to sell today, folks."* No shit, Sherlock. We're here to buy. There's a few Asians loitering at the back, they threw in a couple of bids early on but I soon shut them out. Good thing too, they're buying up everything. An old, fat couple in the shade of the gum tree passed in a few rounds ago. Probably investment property arseholes. Too many of them round these parts, too. There are very few want-to-be home-owners at auctions actually putting bids in. Most people seem to be looking.

I should've bought in some intimidators. Problem being there's very few people I can trust. I thought Vogon would've turned up but then again, this isn't really his scene. Not enough action going down.

Smarmy re-emerges, a slimy grin spread over his solarium face. He whacks the rolled-up real estate magazine in his meaty palm for effect.

"Right, folks." He doesn't need to use a microphone. He's good. "The owners have instructed us to sell and that's what we're going to do. The bid is currently at $210,000. I don't need to remind you, folks, but this is a prime piece of real estate. Close to the shops and public transport. Are there any other offers?"

What? We're still going? I thought my bid was in. What's this prick playing at? I glance at the crowd. A few people are staring at me, including the old couple.

"215," says a timid female voice.

Smarmy's grin broadens. His tongue licks the front of his whitened teeth. His watchers have already signalled out the new bidder. Some frumpy, mousy-looking woman with black-rimmed glasses.

I raise my hand. "217."

"220," she says instantly. Smarmy throws a sage nod and a wink her way.

Where the fuck did she come from? She wasn't even here when the auction started. Probably too busy flicking herself off before she got here.

"221," I respond. I'm getting close to my limit and this place isn't worth that amount of money.

"225."

Fucking bitch. That *is* my limit. Smarmy looks at me,

his body leaning towards my anticipated answer. Little beads of sweat are forming at the base of his scalp, or perhaps it's the gel melting in the sun. Silence hangs in the air.

"It's not fair. He had it first," whispers the old fat woman to her husband.

I give the old couple an appreciative nod. Good on 'em, the battlers. Probably here trying to secure their grandchildren's future.

"230." I say.

"235." Frumpy wears a stone mask, eyes never straying from Smarmy.

Vogon slinks from behind one of the parked cars. His face metamorphoses into mine, though he keeps his body grey and formless. He motions with his fingers, indicating higher, higher. "She wants this place bad," he mouths.

"240."

"245." Her voice isn't so timid. It's actually sharp and nasal. She's determined to win.

A horrible feeling sneaks into my stomach. What if Vogon is trying to get me back for making him suck my cock? He's standing with the old couple, inflating his chest. He's imitating the old woman's boobs, not paying attention anymore. Vogon wouldn't screw me, would he? I could expose him.

He wouldn't dare. Vogon grins. His fingers urge higher.

"250."

"255," Frumpy honks.

Vogon shakes his head so I shake mine at Smarmy.

"Going once, going twice..."

Smarmy can hardly believe his luck. Frumpy stands there with her little lesbian arms folded defensively, a self-satisfied smirk playing over her lips.

"Sold!"

She breaks into a smile and shakes her hands excitedly. Stupid bitch.

She just paid forty grand too much for this dump. And she thinks she won.

Frumpy turns to a tall, muscly guy and they kiss on the lips. He keeps an arm around her waist as Smarmy guides them into the house to seal the contract.

The old couple give me a sympathetic nod and shuffle up the street as the crowd disperses.

One of the watchers pounces on me, his clipboard and pen at the ready.

A badge states his name as Gary. "Sorry about that. Mr...uh..."

"Haines."

"Sorry, Mr. Haines." His pen scrawls on the clipboard. "You're interested in three-bedroom brick veneers in this area? Yes, of course you are." Gary grins weakly. "Do you have a contact number?"

"Yeah, I've given my details before to your mate who sold the house."

"To Mark? Of course, Mr. Haines. It's just that..."

"You didn't think I was serious before?"

"Ha ha." The laugh piddles from his mouth. "No, it's just..."

"Look, I don't care so much about the exterior, or whether it's two or three bedrooms. Garage and cellar potential and must be close to the train station."

His pen scribbles furiously. "Yes, yes. Bit of a wine

buff are we?"

"Eh?"

"The cellar. I've got about three hundred bottles in mine." Gary tries on a smile that drips bonding.

"Yeah. That's a lot of wine." Not for bottles, Gazza, old chap. But stick around and you might find out.

Vogon leans on a dark blue BMW parked near the driveway. All the other cars on the street are Fords or Holdens. "Come on," he mouths.

"Listen, Gary I've got to make a move. Is that your BMW there?"

"No, it's Mark's. I've got an older model."

"Beautiful car. Get Mark to give us a call."

I pause near Smarmy's BMW as I leave the property. "Is anyone watching?"

"No," says Vogon.

I take a small paring knife — a Furi, Japanese, the best steel, particularly for slicing into gut — from my jacket pocket and scrape the driver's side of the car. After a quick glance to make sure Vogon isn't lying, I punch the blade into the front tyre. The hissing relieves some of the day's frustration before I make my way to the train station.

I'm getting hungry.

I finish off the last of a sweet red-bean bun I bought at the Chinese bakery on the way here. A very short Chinese girl, slender and pretty, served me — with a gorgeous smile, too. They say Asians have one of the lowest rates of heart disease in the world.

The location isn't bad. It's about a ten-minute walk from Blackburn station, nestled between a Seventh Day Adventist Camp, a retirement home, the deaf society and a big fucking marsh posing as a lake. Good access, few neighbours and discreet.

"Lovely to see you again, Mr. Haines." Smarmy smacks his meaty palm into mine and shakes vigorously. So do his melanin jowls. He's a bit fatter than I remembered. "Mark Creasemore at your service. It might have seemed like bad luck missing out last week, but as they say: One Man's Loss!" He sweeps his arm back majestically at the house.

It's square, squat and brutish. Your stock-standard, soulless 1960s brick veneer stranded in a yard of sprawling weeds. Smarmy leads me up the garden path and into the house, all the while wittering on about bullshit. A musty smell pervades the drab interior, as we move from room to room.

"Needs a little work." Smarmy smiles after every sentence. I think he thinks it makes him human. "Deceased estate, you know." He laughs as if that explains everything.

I nod uninterestedly, calculating room size, potential storage, cooling facilities, window access to rooms. It's looking good.

"You'll love this, Mr. Haines." A small set of stairs leads down off the side of the hallway to a wooden door. "Fantastic cellaring potential here. Gary told me you were a bit of a wine buff."

Smarmy pushes hard at the door — it appears swollen in its frame — then it swings open, the hinges screeching. The cold, damp air seeps over us and we enter the cellar. Smarmy pulls on a cord and dim bulbs light the room. It's massive; it must be almost the size of the entire house down here.

"Ow, fuck!" In my excitement I press too hard on the blade in my pocket and skin slices open.

"Sorry?" says Smarmy.

"How much?" I attempt a grin, something friendly.

"220." Smarmy doesn't miss a beat. Something slides in the shadows in the corner of the room behind him.

"Oh, look, I dunno..."

"It's worth more. It's...uh...been on the market a while, and uh...the family are keen to settle quickly, you understand."

Vogon slips from the shadows, sidling up behind Smarmy, nodding enthusiastically. Not about the house though. The knife in my pocket is slick with my blood. Vogon's mouthing "Do him. Do him."

Smarmy has stopped smiling. "You interested?"

"Very." I take my hand from the pocket and reach to shake his hand.

The blonde leans back on her haunches, legs wide, then spreads her lips wider still with a manicured finger. Her tits stay rigid as she sways to some shit mid-80s commercial rock.

"See that? Aw, fucken great pussy. See that? Did ya?" Gino slurps at his beer, his eyes never straying from the feast on display until my silence distracts him. He peers at me from the corner of his eyes. "You ain't queer are you, Haines?"

"No way, Gino. Too busy thinking about eating her out to fucking answer you."

Gino laughs, relieved I won't try to punch his date a little later on when he's too pissed. "Thanks, love," he says to a topless waitress with chocolate areolas as she places a plate of deep-fried chips on our table. He wipes his hands on his oily overalls and grabs a fistful.

"You still shifting?" I ask.

"Yeah." Gino stuffs chips into his mouth as the dancer stuffs fingers into her vagina. "What you got?"

"BMW 3 Series. Maybe two years old."

"Give you twenty."

"It's worth at least three times that. That's fucking highway robbery."

"That's right, ya cunt." Gino guffaws, spraying half-chewed chips over the table. "It *is* fucken highway robbery."

"Twenty-five."

"Done. Look at that fucken pussy, mate. Bewdiful!"

Great, that's my deposit for the house covered. "I'll have the car for you in a couple of weeks. Catch you later."

"You off?" Gino stares in disbelief. "The next sheila is pierced to all buggery, mate. You can't fucken miss her!"

"Only got an hour for lunch. And I'm not eating that shit." I point at the chips shining in their grease. "You should think of your heart a little more and not your cock."

Gino laughs and gives me the finger. The dancer has her legs over her shoulders and is using her hands to paddle herself around in a circle on the dance floor.

I take a taxi back to the city and charge it to the company. Fuck 'em, I deserve it.

"What shall I play?" I ask.

"Something loud, I suppose," says Vogon. He leans against the cellar wall, alternating his skin colour.

I pop Killing Joke's *Revelations* into the CD-player and skip to *Chop-Chop*. The drums soon kick in and the guitars rasp through the cellar — the acoustics are fan-fucking-tastic down here! I turn it up to the point it's painful and leave, closing the door behind me.

"Well?" I ask Vogon when we're in the living room.

"It's very solid. I can hardly hear a thing."

I nod, trying not to smirk. "Let's check outside."

We stand together amongst the weeds dying in the parched front yard.

The roar of distant traffic thundering along the Maroondah Highway is as reassuring as not blowing your load in the first ten thrusts. I can't hear the music at all.

"Perfect," we say.

I call Smarmy on a mobile I've borrowed off Craig from work — though he doesn't know I've got it — and arrange a time to meet this evening concerning an investment property recently advertised. Vogon chuckles and tans his face, broadening his belly and shoulders, taking on a close approximation of Smarmy.

"I haven't been here long enough, so don't consider me an expert, but you're on this eating for a healthy heart trip at the moment and, well..." Vogon says.

"I know, I know," I say. "I get the hint. I'm planning on slimming the bastard down a little."

"Ooohhhh," Vogon moans between pursed fat lips. He's managed to get the mo above the lips this time. Vogon's eyes widen and he leers at me expectantly.

My stomach grumbles. "But right now I feel like a little Chinese."

Inducing

After a month, I realised Bortho, my new flatmate, was a little crazy.

Maybe not enough to harm anyone else, but maybe enough to hurt himself badly. I'd been ignoring my PhD, smoking bongs, reading bent passages from the Bible for kicks, and thinking about making easy money. I turned down the volume on the television when Bortho plonked himself down on the sofa next to me. He placed a half-empty flagon in the space I hadn't seen between the beer cans and the pizza boxes on the coffee table. Dark liquid sloshed inside the flagon. It kept moving of its own accord.

"Have you heard of Inducing, Luke?" Bortho's eyes bulged in his tanned face. He ran grimy fingers through his mass of curly black hair. His clothes were rumpled and caked in dirt.

"Big weekend?" Now, I'm not the cleanest of people, but I inched towards my side of the sofa. Bortho didn't exactly stink, just sort of smelt weird. I don't think it was something I'd ever come across before. Like the forest floor after heavy rain mixed with mushrooms fried in butter and a hint of tangerines.

"Eh? No…uh…what day is it?"

"Monday afternoon. You left here Friday night. You score?"

Bortho grinned and his eyes glazed for a second. "Yeah, you can say that all right."

"What was she like?" I hated to think really. I hoped she was so ugly I might not have rooted her. And lately, well, I'd have just about...

"Nah, man, not that kind of scoring. I've been Inducing!" He indicated the flagon on the table and slapped his thigh. "Can't believe it, man. I haven't seen this shit since I been in Africa."

"Right on. Inducing? Isn't that bringing on child-birth?"

Bortho laughed, pointed at me, then said to the empty doorway, "You hear that? And you want to introduce him to this?" Bortho slapped his thigh again, doubling up in laughter. "Oh, man, this is too rich."

"Yeah, right."

When Bortho stopped laughing, he stared silently at the doorway, nodding occasionally. "I understand," he said. "Sure." He grabbed my arm, his fingers digging into my flesh. "You gotta try this, man. You have any shot glasses?"

I pried his hand from my arm and went into the kitchen. Even though he was acting weird, it wouldn't stop me getting drunk with him. I found a couple of glasses amongst the dirty dishes on the bench, took a tentative sniff in one of them to see what the sticky black stuff was and, after deciding it'd be fine, wiped most of the smears off the glasses with my t-shirt.

I thought I'd find Bortho scraping the dregs out of the bong, but he sat straight-backed on the sofa, his head twitching to one side. He saw me, grinned, made a conscious effort to stop twitching and burped a little mouthful of sick onto his chest. The sick was a teal colour. His head started twitching again. Filthy bastard.

I scraped some of the mess off the table onto the floor to make space and set the shot glasses down. A simple white label wrapped the middle of the flagon, a flourish of Arabic denoting its name. The dark liquid inside swirled against the glass, as if it wanted to get out.

"What is this?"

Bortho keened like a lost little boy. His head twitched harder, his lips wobbling. "Sa-sa-sa-surrah…unghh…"

Twitch.

I studied the flagon for markings, like an imprint on the glass, a metric or something, but the flagon was unidentifiable. A tiny blue pyramid sat inside the third letter on the label. Similar to the pyramid on the Yank dollar bill.

I unscrewed the cap and Bortho whined louder. His eyes bulged even more as his face contorted.

Twitch.

"Nuh-nuh-nuh…"

Twitch.

I gave him one of those you're-a-weird-bastard looks and took a sniff of the flagon. It hit the back of my head like the cocaine I'd been buying down in the local nightclubs didn't. Blue mandarins danced muddy footsteps over the back of my eyeballs. I reconsidered when my sight didn't immediately come back. This was almost as good as the homemade glue we used to sniff in the sports stadium after school.

The flagon was ripped from my hands and Bortho said, "Be careful, man. This is strong stuff. I don't have much left."

My vision returned to find Bortho measuring capfuls of the liquid into each shot glass. A small wet patch on his chest was all that was left of his vomit. At first I thought he might have smeared it onto the furniture and felt disgusted by his slovenliness. But the longer I watched Bortho measure out the dark liquid and the way his tongue worked the lower parts of his chin as he did so, the more I suspected he'd eaten it.

"Three caps per shot per person," he said. "Each cap filled to the pyramid line on the inside of the cap." He showed me the cap — but wouldn't let me hold it — and indeed he was right. A line of etched pyramids circled the inside about a third of the depth of the cap from the rim. Bloody small pyramids really.

"Why three?"

Bortho looked at me for a second and the intensity in his eyes unnerved me. He seemed suddenly alien and unfathomable.

And his voice took on the tone of the teacher. "Three is of the trinity and the triad, the primordial triangle from which all others are derived. It is of itself the inevitable expression of principle."

He stared at me again and I swore his pupils appeared briefly as pyramids, then he laughed and held the shot glass out.

"You're gonna love this, man. *Prost!*" He necked the contents of the glass.

I lifted my glass high and swallowed the dark liquid.

If the smell had smashed the back of my brain out, the taste of the liquid was of the earth baked in berries and glazed in chocolate. It filled my mouth, searching out the cracks between my teeth, squeezing into the space between my lips and gums, billowing into my cheeks and sliding down down down, floating into the bowl of my belly.

Three? I knew why it was three. God's attributes are *three*: omniscience, omnipresence, and omnipotence. Three is the Godhead; three is the Divine.

Three is…

…a rush of fire erupting from inside, the kickback kicked back. I almost dropped the glass as my head spun and for an instant I thought I'd join Bortho with an impromptu spew over the front of my shirt.

"Jesus Christ!" I couldn't stop the grin from ripping open my face. My head buzzed with miniature suns. "This stuff is okay. What did you say it was called?"

"Seraphim. Or at least that's what the pygmies told us." Bortho measured out another shot.

"Pygmies?" I started laughing. I felt great!

"Don't you know anything about Africa?"

"Yeah, nah, the pygmies. Sure. Whatever." I reached out for my refilled glass but Bortho swatted my hand away.

"You have to wait three minutes between shots, Luke," he said.

"Otherwise you don't get the effect."

"But this effect is fan-fucking-tastic!" I chased a remnant of the Seraphim around my mouth with my tongue. It felt like the taste was winning the race. I caught up and it ran down my tongue to hide in my throat.

"I'm planning on taking you to the first of three stages. We call it, surprisingly, Stage One. Some say it's the Body Stage."

"I'm not a homo, Bortho. I've got nothing against them, or you if you're one, but..."

"This has got nothing to do with the base pleasures of sex, man. Think of the number three and the embodiment of the Divine in man. In body, mind and soul. If you want to think of it in easier concepts to grasp, Stage One, The Body Stage, is like being really, really drunk but still in control. No blackouts, spin outs, bombing out." He handed me my glass. "Three minutes are up. Down the hatch!"

I had to sit back against the comforts of the sofa. Every part of my body tingled, the fingers and toes, my ears, the base of my cock. I started thinking maybe if Bortho was going to try to do something to me I might just let him. I shook that out of my head real quick.

"Why the Body Stage?" I asked.

With precise movements, Bortho poured another capful into his glass. I didn't think I could even stand. The smile smeared over his face told me I wasn't alone in feeling this way.

"Don't rightly know. Maybe it's the first thing we see of each other and ourselves. The shell, the outer defence. The body is the tool of the mind and if we change the tool it's easier to change the mind. Or at least that's what they said."

"Who's *they*?"

"You ask a lot of questions, man. If you make Stage Three, you'll find out one way or another."

After the third minute, Bortho handed me the third shot. "Here's to your past."

My head spun and my chest heaved. It felt like an explosion bouncing off the walls of my stomach. I let out a huge lungful of air and sank into the cushions, trying to focus on something, anything. The television: A woman wearing a tight leotard turned towards the camera and winked. Her thighs were firm and her breasts threatened to spill from her top. She was eating a chocolate biscuit apparently containing vitamins that would soon be at work sucking away on her body's unwanted fat. I thought she was sexy. Hell, at that point, I thought the television was sexy, too.

But I knew the biscuit for a big pile of shit when I saw one. This Seraphim burned through that marketing cloud like a flame through methane. Ha!

The very idea of ingesting something that could change you like that was preposterous. I wasn't falling for a scam like that again. When Bortho replied, I realised I must have said it out loud.

"It was only a matter of time," he said. "I don't think it's pure form, and I'd bet it's government controlled."

"Right." I nodded sagely. "The government. Of course." I had no idea what he was talking about, but just then the Seraphim really kicked in. I felt it tickling the blood out of my bloodstream. Right then I thought I could take the world and pump it full of me, bend it to my will and demand the universe. I thought that maybe, just maybe, I could get lucky.

"Let's go pull some chicks, Bortho."

I balanced on the edge of the sofa with my toes, moving to the infomercial beats. I felt as drunk as an empty bottle of vodka and a dead six pack. I felt on top of the world, or at least the sofa.

Bortho laughed. "Yeah, man! You're there. Stage One."

Then I slipped and fell, my head cracking hard against the edge of the coffee table, upending it. I remember seeing beer cans arch end over end, pizza boxes spiralling, bongwater splashing against the wall. I remember it not hurting my head a bit.

Bortho screamed and dove through the air, his hands outspread, fingers taut as he tried to catch the flagon spinning lazily upwards then down down down…

…inches from his hand, it bounced on the carpet and rolled towards the kitchen. The Seraphim oozed from the open flagon like a dark, wet fuse, spreading over the threadbare carpet. Bortho scrambled after it, sliding through the mess on the floor and sweeping the now almost-empty flagon up in his arms, cradling it like a newborn.

"You idiot!"

"I'm sorry, Bortho. I'm a bit pissed, eh?" In fact I was so drunk I saw the Seraphim on the carpet slide over his feet and slip under his toenails. I sat up and wiped the ash and beer off my shoulders. I would have to change into something less dirty if I wanted to pull, maybe even something that hid my gut.

The stain on the carpet crept wider still, the dark ichor fading. It looked like it was spreading itself across the house. It tingled where it touched my leg.

"It's been three years, Luke! And you've gone and wasted it!" Crouching on the floor, Bortho tried to soak what little was left of the Seraphim into his dirty shirt. He began to squeeze a few drops back into the flagon.

"Take it easy. I'll buy you a new one."

"Damn right you will." Bortho brandished the jug. "It's a limited supply, you know." His cheeks suddenly slackened. His eyes rolled. "Oh, fuck, there's too much in me." He tried to stand and fell face forward into the sofa.

His breathing seemed fine, so I prised the flagon from his hands, grabbed some herbal speed and staggered down into St. Kilda to look for a root or a bottle shop. I'd thought of another three as well: the three great divisions completing time — the past, present and future.

Hey, hadn't Bortho already toasted my past?

Flagons of Seraphim lined the window of the store that hadn't been there this afternoon. That should have bothered me. A little sign taped crookedly to the window had "SPECIAL" written on it. And that excited me.

The store, about the size of a small bedroom, smelt of limes and toadstools simmered in chicken broth. The shelves displayed an array of nano-caffeine sports and energy supplement drinks, high-protein hallucinogenic fruit bars, no-frills canned beer and organic cigarettes. A woman in colourful Trade-Aid clothing stood behind the counter scrutinising me. Her skin had a waxy greyish tinge, her hair corkscrewed in dirty blonde clumps from her head, and a nasty orange and green rash had broken out on her arm.

She smelt a little stronger than Bortho had, but I wasn't convinced it was a bad smell.

"How much for one of these?" I pointed to the Seraphim flagons in the window.

Her head swivelled slowly and her mouth moved like the actors in foreign language pornos when she spoke. "You're very lucky, you're not actually ready to find this place, you know."

"Eh? I came in through the door. You've got a sign out front."

"Oh, I know you think that, but it's not necessarily true. Two straight lines cannot enclose a space or form a plane figure, yet three can. And from that we have three dimensions: length, breadth and height. All are necessary to form a solid. And there forms the door."

"What?"

"I must admit, I am a little annoyed. Only Stage Threes can enter, but here you are just the same. You shouldn't be able to *see* here. You shouldn't be able to *be* here. Makes you wonder about the rules they set in place if they can be bent willy-nilly."

"Yeah, right." I tried my best smile. "Look, love. The Seraphim?"

"I mean am I wasting my time following through with this?" Little beads of what looked like orange juice formed on her brow. I thought of licking them off. She said, "I've worked for five years to get to this point, to having my own distribution outlet. I look at you and wonder why I bothered. I'd be willing to bet you haven't even been through indoctrination yet and...ngghh...nghhh..."

She started twitching and a bubble of teal vomit splashed onto the counter.

Seizing the opportunity, I grabbed three flagons and was about to make my way out through the door, when she spoke.

"Fifteen dollars."

Fifteen dollars? What the Hell had Bortho got all worked up for when I spilt his flagon? I slapped down a fifty on the counter — the proceeds of selling herbal speed in the pub to some unlucky punter expecting E. At fifteen bucks a bottle I could get off my chops every night and it would hardly dent my dole money. I noticed the vomit had disappeared.

She handed back thirty-five dollars, attempted a smile that ended up looking alarmingly like a pig's erection then started talking to someone under her breath about hierarchies and queue jumping and rigour and discipline and utility erosion. She wasn't happy with me at all.

I didn't care though. At five bucks a bottle I could get rich on-selling this to unsuspecting mates! I bustled out the door, trying to keep the grin on the inside of my mouth. Halfway home I decided to have a guzzle.

Blue mandarins washed in mud sozzled my senses and I let out a breath of exaltation. This stuff was fucking great!

Above me the stars connected like an astrologer's chart, thin blue lines leaping from star to star, creating zodiacal sections of space. When a section became enclosed it would either turn into a bruised purple or a shell pink colour. The purple sections took up most of the night sky. The shell pink sections — I knew, I just *knew* — were off limits, but by the time I got home that thought had become confused with thoughts of pre-purchased distribution rights.

Bortho and I sat in the backyard amongst the weeds and dying grass. The red brick apartments offered a somewhat soothing view punctuated by bright security lights. The roar of the evening trains provided a backdrop to the cicada raucous and mosquito buzz.

"So what's Stage Two?" I asked.

Bortho handed me my fourth shot glass. We were both well wrecked.

"Your present, not your past. The second kingdom, that of the vegetable, not the mineral or the animal. The Second Grace. The Second Furie. The Mind Stage!"

"What the Hell does that mean? I want to know what it feels like."

"Oh, right. I thought you wanted some more symbolism." He skolled his drink. "It's a bit like being really pissed and body stoned from eating too much marijuana."

"Cool."

"You won't make it tonight, man." Bortho measured out another glass.

"Took me two weeks before I did. I was living in a village called Pangi up in the Mitumba Mountains. Seraphim every night. Where I first had my eyes opened, you might say. There's a huge presence there. I reckon the pygmies got this permanent connection to the source."

"Where was this?" My blood throbbed with the pulse of the ground as another train thundered by.

Bortho stared at me as if I'd forgotten what my penis was. "In the Congo. Africa."

"Yeah, nah, the Congo. Right."

"You know about the Mitumba, eh?" He leant back

on his chair and pointed at the night sky. "You follow?"

"You mean the purple and pink segments?"

Bortho rocked forward. "Eh? Man, you can see that already?" He shook his head, looking around obviously distracted, then handed me my glass.

"But you're not even Stage Two. Man, I've heard of that, never met anyone but. Maybe you're not bullshitting about finding that store. Anyway, it's not what I mean."

The fifth glass felt like a shotgun blast through the mouth to the back of the head. Filled with tangerine pellets cooked in clay swirled with psilocybin. I hadn't been aware Bortho had taken back my glass, but he was already measuring out another three-pyramid cap. I couldn't move. I tried to speak but my tongue decided to keep listening to the songs my saliva sang to it and ignored me.

Bortho said, "I guess the most famous one is Roswell. And about five years later there were two more; one on Spitzbergen Island off Norway; the other in the Californian desert with that guy, Adamski."

The grass came up and slapped my head. Somehow the chair managed to avoid the fracas and let my arse hit the ground. Christ, this stuff rocked! I concentrated on trying to get some part of me to respond. Maybe a fart would do. I started pushing.

"Then in 1955 — bang! Mitumba," said Bortho. "I figured it was getting popular if backpackers like me were finding out about it half a century later. Things were going great for me too, until the army came charging on in — hey, you okay?"

I noticed a pyramid tattooed on Bortho's ankle. The

top of the pyramid was detached and contained an eyeball. It wasn't just the dollar bill and the Seraphim, I thought. It meant something else.

"Doesn't look like you need another one tonight." Bortho poured my shot back into the flagon. "Maybe tomorrow you'll make Stage Two."

I tried to say I was okay, to bring it on, that I could handle my piss, but the fart came out wrong. And a little slippery.

I passed out into a cloud of fungal mandarins chanting "Inati-Inati-Illuma-luma-nati." There was a message in there somewhere, but the mandarins started cooing and tucked me tight into the edge of the world with a nice, warm black blanket.

And in blackness I awoke. The night sky had resumed the normality of dark and sparkle, so I figured I had come back down. I lay there for a while listening to the muted hush of the city, the whoop-whoop of the patrol choppers overhead, and the occasional howl of sirens announcing to the sleepers all was well.

I struggled inside, the stars spinning once I'd made my feet. Maybe I hadn't come down quite yet. I felt my way up the hall towards my bedroom conscious of the crap on the floor and having to move slowly over it. A sliver of light from beneath Bortho's door. Muffled voices. Had he managed to go out and pick up? I pressed my ear to his door.

"You'll be my sponsor, right?" It sounded like Bortho.

Silence.

"Yeah, and I become an ISD. I know that much. Normal practise."

Bortho again.

Silence.

"Thirteen? But what about Luke? I thought he'd count for more. He's showing massive potential. He can see the sub-divisions already and he managed to find an ISD and he's only Stage One. I thought there was a clause for bringing in intangibles like him. Ten?"

Silence.

"I get it. Thirteen. Ten. He's worth three. Fucking three. Yeah, no worries. Ten it is. I was hoping I could jump a level. Eh? Someone's there? How can you tell?"

The floorboards in his room creaked. I scrambled over the clutter in the hall and ducked into my bedroom, easing the door shut as light from Bortho's room flooded the hallway.

"No, there's not," said Bortho. "Ha. You ain't always right. Maybe I should skip that level after all, eh? Maybe I...no, no, don't do...ngghh...ngghh..."

I inched the door open and peered through. Bortho — framed by the light in his doorway — a naked, twitching silhouette. And as far as I could tell, he was alone. I shut the door and lay on my bed. What did I really know about Bortho? He'd been travelling for the last ten years, currently unemployed, enjoyed booze and drugs, had the occasional twitching fit, and made deals with imaginary people about selling me. Maybe Bortho was full of shit. Maybe he was mentally ill. They'd closed down the last of the mental homes a year or so ago. What if he was on medication? Oh, Christ, and we were pouring this Seraphim shit down our throats every night. Did he have weapons? The questions didn't stop. They kept coming and coming like a bad case of dysentery.

When the early trains ripped through the morning, and with my arse of a brain raw from haemorrhaging, I realised the significance of the pyramid: The Illumanati. The secret society supposedly controlling the world, responsible for the French Revolution, World War II, inflation, interest rates, Amway, reality TV, McDonald's, cancer, the decline of Christianity and the insidious creep of American popular culture.

Bortho was a psycho. I had to search his room.

I feigned sleep when Bortho called at my door. I heard the front door open and close soon after, so I snuck to the window. Bortho sauntered down the road in the direction of the train station. No one left with him, and I became even more convinced he was deranged. Too many one-way conversations for my liking. I went to his room and gently opened the door. Halfway through the motion the sudden irrational fear hit me of someone, *something*, lying there in his bed, staring at me from under the sheets. Something with pyramid eyes living in a skin creeping with a weird fungal disease. The rumble of the train snapped me back into reality.

I walked into his room.

He didn't have much, but what he did have was strewn all over the place. The dirty clothes from the weekend, a disintegrating pair of boxers, an up-ended backpack, stained sheets, wet towels, some hardcore German stickbooks, a sealed jar with a rotten piece of meat floating in it, cigarette packets, and empty flagons of Seraphim. Nothing too unusual.

Magazines and leaflets littered the desk, above which he had taped a map of the world. He had drawn an orange line to mark his route around the world. Or, at least, his imagined route. Lots of lines around Central Africa and New Mexico. Little pins stuck out from the map: Roswell; an area of the Californian desert marked in pen as Area 51; and an isolated dot called Pangi, in the Congo.

I picked up a thick, supple plastic document made with pages thinner than paper. I couldn't rip it and it felt *vibrant*, as if the words, written in what looked like Arabic, wanted to crawl into my fingertips. There were tiny pyramids in the corner of each page. The document — there must have been a couple of hundred pages — weighed surprisingly little. One of the words on the front page resembled the word on the Seraphim label. In the desk drawer I found Bortho's passport. The edges were frayed and it bore the New Zealand coat of arms. So maybe he *had* travelled, I thought, but not very far.

I opened the passport. The photo of one Joseph Borthwick some fifteen years younger…

"What are you doing, Luke?" Bortho stood in the doorway, his face vacant and jaw slack.

"I…uh…looking for some…I thought you were going out?" I tried to slip the passport into my pocket.

"Missed the train." Bortho stepped into the bedroom. His arms hung loosely at his side, his fingers flexing. "What are you doing in here?"

I picked up one of the magazines called *Monster Mammaries* and put on my best needing-a-wank grin. "Thought I'd borrow one or two of these. Hope that's cool."

Bortho stared at me then cocked his head. He nodded slowly, his eyes unfocused. If he started twitching, I could get out of his room and hopefully he wouldn't remember a thing. That was the case with epileptics. I caught a sudden waft of citrus and mushrooms.

He took another step closer. "You're not planning on using my passport, are you?"

"Passport? I don't know what you mean."

His hand grabbed my shirt. He pulled me towards him. A blade pressed cold against my throat. "The last time some cunt tried to rob me was in Egypt."

I didn't consider myself a coward. I still don't.

He pressed the blade harder. "I've got that cunt's tongue in a jar on the dresser. What the fuck do you want with my passport?"

Right then and there I fair shat myself. The words spilled from my mouth, about psychos and the Illuminati and imaginary friends and epileptic fits and delusions and lies and...

Bortho started laughing. "Oh man, this is too rich." He put the blade away and took his passport off me. He flicked through pages full of border stamps and visa stickers. He showed me a one-month tourist visa for the republic of Congo and pointed to one of the pins on the map.

"You paranoid bastard. I have to remember this is the normal world again. I was in Africa — it ain't normal. The whole Seraphim Scheme seemed like a crazy adventure. I didn't believe it at the time, either. Thought it was one of those backpacker myths, word of mouth thing. And then, fuck me, there I was in Pangi."

He traced a river on the map running down the Mitumba ranges to the Congo River. "This is the only road in. A fucking river! Then you spend a day hiking to the village. There's no electricity, phones or nothing. The place is just a big fucking distillery for this stuff." He shook an empty flagon close to my face. My heart still thumped in my mouth. He was going to clobber me with it.

"I can't tell you much more until you get to Stage Two. I could lose my sponsorship otherwise." Bortho suddenly glanced to his side, his eyes bulging. "No, I didn't. It's not. You can't...ngghh...ngghhh..."

He started twitching. I left the room with *Monster Mammaries* clutched tight in my sweating hands.

Two nights later I discovered Bortho was right. Take the best feeling from being drunk and the most positive high from being stoned, and that was a good approximation of Stage Two. Consider a massive serotonin release and mix that in for good measure and I'd say that was even closer. My head swam in blackberry soaked toadstools. Bortho was saying something, but right then my ears buzzed with an internal chirruping, phasing in and out, modulating. It sounded like the insects talking to me.

"Welcome to your present. Now only the future awaits you," said Bortho. "You get to Stage Three, your world is going to spin arse up and Tuesdays."

I struggled to sit still. I felt like dancing to the breath in my lungs, to the beat of my heart, to the music surging in my body. I needed release. I was release.

There was no way in Hell I could get off the sofa if my life depended on it.

"Tell me about Pangi. While you're refilling the glasses."

"I was there for about three months. Drinking this shit mostly. Elevating myself, seeking the higher plane. Having my eyes opened to the world around me. The *real* world."

"What's all this stuff about UFOs? Is there a crash-landed spaceship there?" It felt weird saying it, but at the same time a natural and intelligent progression of our conversation. I was off my chops.

"I never saw one." He handed me my seventh glass for the evening.

"Higher up in the mountains there's a place off-limits to everyone but the shamans. Rumour has it that's where the crash site is. Tried to check it out, but no go. Tighter than a homophobe's arsehole."

We knocked back the Seraphim and Bortho measured out the next set of pyramid caps. Tonight I would hit Stage Three.

"What's Seraphim made of?"

"That's a good question and to be honest with you, I don't rightly know."

Bortho paused in his pouring and stared long and hard at me. "I've heard say it's the body fluids of the dead on board the ship. Some say it's interplanetary fuel. Alien oil, if you like."

I took the eighth glass and swallowed its contents. "Yeah, nah. Didn't you say the ship crashed about sixty years ago? How big is the fuel tank? How many bodies were on board? Doesn't figure."

"The ship's organic, Luke. It's still growing in the Mitumba ranges. Still pumping out this nectar. Least that's what I reckon."

As he filled the ninth glass, I believed him. Right then, it all made perfect sense. There was only one thing left to find out.

"What's Stage Three?"

"Hold on a couple more minutes and you'll find out." Bortho finished measuring the shots, stood, staggered towards the kitchen door, and collapsed on the floor.

I sat on the sofa, staring at the ninth glass. And at the end of the third minute, I reached for it.

And here's to my future. Stage Three. My soul.

I expected to hear the snap of a severed spinal cord exploding in my eardrums. Perhaps even the whoosh of blood touched by the Divine pumping through my heart. Maybe even my nerve endings absorbing the life force of the world around me. I expected all those things, or at least *some* thing. Instead I felt more drunk. And my ears were ringing louder than ever.

That was it.

I lounged back in the sofa, completely off my tits. Bortho's legs still twitched madly from the kitchen door. I started to laugh. That crazy bastard had had me going all right.

"…ngghh…ngghh…"

Twitch.

I howled with laughter, buckling over it hurt so much. The whole thing had been bullshit. I staggered to my feet and held out my hands to hold the room firm. It stopped spinning. I took a couple of deep breaths. It tasted of porcini edged with grapefruit. The room wavered, the air soft and rubbery and for a second I thought I would throw up. The walls began to breathe in time with my lungs. Ripples flowed across the threadbare carpet, the pizza boxes and beer cans shuddering as it moved beneath. It all started to make sense: Seraphim — a dark, thick liquid; the smell of mushrooms and citrus; the stony, drunk feeling coupled with mild hallucinations. I had been drinking nothing mystical or enlightening, though it was indeed magical: citrus-flavoured magic mushroom extract. Bortho had had me sucked in big time.

Watching his legs twitching in the doorway, I realised he was so caught up in his imaginary world of conspiracy, lying there in a self-induced fit (Ha! Inducing!), he really had no idea what was going on. Sick of his twitching, I decided to let him in on the secret of Seraphim. With the walls still expanding and contracting with my lungs, and me still laughing, I took a step towards the kitchen doorway, bringing his entire body into view.

A bipedal creature crouched over Bortho, its skin a fibrous black mottled with orange and green. Long tendril-like fingers curled around Bortho's head.

One of the fingers slid into his ear. Bortho twitched

violently and vomited a mouthful of teal onto his chest. The creature pressed its face to the vomit and sucked it up, a shiver shaking its haunches as it did so.

"This shit is amazing," I said. "Not even on acid did I get this."

The creature jerked away from Bortho the way a small child does when caught reading dirty magazines. The buzzing in my ears intensified. The creature stood slowly, staring at me all the while with diamond-faceted eyes, unfolding its limbs until it reached five feet high. It held its slender arms out, as if trying to placate an upset pet. The fibrous glands around its throat puffed and the cloying scent of fungal mandarins filled the kitchen. The buzzing noise suddenly popped in my head like the stopper on a cheap flagon of port...

...and my head filled with silky modulations and valium vibrations that slowly resolved into:

"Welcome to the world that lies beneath. You've done bloody well to get here so fast, Luke. I'm sure you have many questions."

The glands puffed again and it took a tentative step closer. Bortho stirred on the kitchen floor. He tried to sit up. The skin beneath his eyes looked dark and mottled.

"Hey, Bortho, you're not going to believe what trip I'm on." I laughed. "I'm talking to a giant mushroom man who has little fruits growing on his skin."

"Wow," said Bortho. He held out an arm and the creature pulled him up with one of its slender arms. "I see you've already met my sponsor. Her name is Shemeshiel. You can call her Shelley — she doesn't mind."

"What?" The world teetered at that moment. If I

hadn't been high on Seraphim, I might have lost it. "You can see it, too?"

Bortho and Shelley looked at each other. They were smiling.

"See," said Shelley. "Standard reaction. You were like that, too."

I backed into the lounge, suddenly, desperately needing a drink. "What the Hell is going on, Bortho?"

They took another step closer. Bortho's eyes bulged. "Take it easy, Luke. There's nothing to be worried about. You've reached another phase of being. The Seraphim is a conduit and a relaxant. You've done the hard part, proven you're worthy. Now there's an easy way to do this or there's a hard way."

Shelley's spindly fingers reached out, hovering in front of my face. "This won't take long. It's much faster than asking and answering questions."

"You're not fucking touching me!"

"Calm down, Luke. This is your first Third Encounter. It won't hurt," said Bortho. "In fact, it's kind of nice."

The fingers hovered closer, spindly, black and fibrous. The smell of mushrooms and citrus was overpowering.

"I've seen how it doesn't fucking hurt, mate!" I backed into the coffee table. "It had its fingers in your fucking ear just before! You were twitching like a mad bastard and throwing blue shit up all over the place."

"Eh?" Bortho glared at Shelley. "You've been treating yourself to my essence without consent?"

"He's lying."

"How can he be lying? How would he know unless

154

he'd seen you doing it?"

The fingers in front of my face dropped and Shelley turned towards Bortho. "Listen to me. Do you want that ISD or not? He. Is. Lying."

"You think I'm stupid, don't you?" Bortho said. "You think as a species we're all stupid. I fucking knew it! It was bugging me why after so many years you were *still* stuck here on Earth. You're not advancing too fast are you, Shelley? You're addicted to us!"

"No, not—not addicted. It was just a little taste, you know. Look, I'm cutting back, it won't happen again. Just forget about it."

"Forget about it? Ha! I *know* that I *can* report you for breach of contract, Shelley. Maybe I'll report you to Ariel."

"Ariel? You've been talking with Ariel?"

I edged around the coffee table towards the hallway. There stood the front door and an escape to the outside world.

"I want my own Independent Seraphim Distributorship," said Bortho. "Otherwise..."

"Fine," said Shelley. "You'll have your ISD, but if you breathe a word of this to the others..."

I bolted for the front door and tripped over the phone books lying in the hallway. I hit the floor, crashing into the telephone stand. An empty flagon flew from the stand and shattered against the wall. The glass — or whatever the Hell it was — dissolved and began to flow across the floorboards towards me.

Shadows loomed.

"Fuck," said Shelley.

"What?" said Bortho.

"He's not in a position to absorb that yet without indoctrination. It may replace his humanity sooner than intended. We don't have much time."

"Whaaaaat?" said Bortho. He said it *very* slowly. He inadvertently took a step away from her. "Replace his *humanity*?"

If mushrooms could wince, I'd swear that was what Shelley did right then as she crouched over me. A sour puff of rotting fruit and fungus hit my face. The Seraphim on the floor hit my fingertips; a feeling of metal liquid and cold fire. Everything in the room increased in intensity: the silver lined cobwebs across the ceiling and its pulsing, poisonous owner's million glittering eyes; Bortho's skin in close up with each pore releasing orange oil, the black mottling under his eyes not dissimilar from the fungal flesh hovering over me, all mushroom-gilled and fibrous.

Shelley thrust her finger into my ear.

They say being born is one of the most traumatic experiences of your life and you don't remember it. I prayed to whatever God there was I wouldn't remember this. But somehow I knew I would, because she was *making* me remember, implanting the memories of her species into my memory. My brain reeled in rejection, and still it was forced in; of hundreds upon thousands of networked stars and galaxies; of species assimilation; of pyramid upon pyramid upon pyramid; of power and distribution and recognition; a massive scheme spider-webbing across the universe, connected and functioning as one, driving from the bottom upwards, spiralling up through the chain, past Ariel, past Azariel, past Emmanuelle and Ezekiel, past Uriel and Lucifer and Gabriel and on and up until…

I lay there shuddering on the floorboards, my vision filled with stars, fragments of a broken argument sliding between the white noise in my head.

"…but you said 'replace' his…"

"…no no…retain essential knowledge and identity… simply enhanced with our organic…"

"…body-snatching bastards! You won't…I'll stop…"

"…it's not like that; you've already begun the process…"

Then silence.

And the sweetness of sleep.

The bedroom appeared under my eyelids. And Bortho on the bed eating an apple.

"Welcome back, man."

I sat up and gripped his arm. "I know what's going on!"

Bortho offered the apple. "You want one?"

"It's one gigantic fucking pyramid scheme! Some horrendous fucking Amway type thing, leading… leading…I don't know! All the way back to…to…"

Bortho took a bite of the apple. "What?" he said with his mouth full of juice and flesh.

"To God!"

Bortho choked on the apple, coughing it up onto my

bed. "Don't be ridiculous! It's a commercial enterprise run by business-minded extraterrestrials. And it's not like Amway. It's different."

I threw my hands up. "It's just like Amway! We're on the bottom rung!"

"No we're not."

"Yes we are! How old did you say that spaceship was? At least fifty years?"

"See. You said 'spaceship'. Correct me if I'm wrong, but I don't think God had spaceships." Bortho tossed the apple core at my bin and missed. "We may be at the bottom of the ladder on Earth, but we're in the first picked to be the top of the ladder in galaxies where the human life form is pitched at a different frequency to the prospect cultures. Remember all those purple sections of sky? Up for grabs, man. We'll be like Shelley is here, unseeable, unknowable, moving amongst the masses. We'll introduce Seraphim into those cultures, gradually building our base and if they think it's a religious experience, well, I don't mind being the new messiah. Imagine how much pussy we'll pull."

"You're missing the point, Bortho! They'll be alien life forms. You won't want to pull them!"

"That's my boy." Bortho smiled smugly. "Alien life forms. You got it right there. None of that religious bullshit. Nobody buys that crap these days."

He whipped the sheets off me and flicked my penis with his finger.

Hard.

"Anyway, it's time you got up. Ariel — he's the head honcho here on Earth — is giving a motivational speech here in Melbourne this afternoon. You'll love it and it's a great opportunity to meet some of the others."

I realised then and there that Bortho was not only crazy, but he was stupid too. We *were* on the bottom rung. He pointed to the end of my bed. The thin plastic book I had found in his room sat shining, vibrant and urgent. "This is your copy. Protocol and procedure. Looks like a bastard to read, but it's a piece of piss."

"This is all bullshit, Bortho!"

He grinned, all cork-screw hair and blurry eyes. "It only *looks* like a book. All you have to do is touch it."

After he left the room, I lay there staring at the book. Shelley and her finger. The vision granted.

What if Bortho was right?

Eventually, I reached out to touch that vibrant sheaf of an alien sales guide. The swirl of Arabic-like characters crawled over my fingers and soaked into my skin. A deep resonant hum bubbled up from the back of my skull as the words took form.

I knew this book. I'd read it before. When I had not understood the true meaning of the word within.

When mine eyes had been closed.

In the beginning...

Lifelike and Josephine

Bernard arrived home late from work to find Denise sipping Bolli at the mirrored dining table. She wore the long red dress that split down the front, emphasising the cut of her breasts.

"What do you think, darling?" she said, a manicured hand adjusting the thick black curls that fell around her shoulders.

Go with it, Bernard told himself. Whatever it is has made possible a whole new troop of fusiliers.

He placed his briefcase on the floor next to the stand, and carefully removed his coat. Denise's hair looked the same, he thought, though she may have had it cut again. Surely she wouldn't bother asking him about something trivial like that.

"Very nice," Bernard said, unsure whether he had used the right amount of conviction. He hung his coat on the hook and loosened his tie.

Denise leaned forward in her chair, turning her head. Her chest rose, presenting a perspective of deeper proportions. "Well?" Her chin angled up towards the light.

Had she had her breasts done again? Bernard couldn't be sure. "They look great."

"No, no, no." Denise moved her head slowly from side to side.

If she opened her mouth, Bernard thought, she'd look like a side-show clown waiting for the ball to be popped in. Her finger circled her face in impatience. He'd doubted he'd be lucky enough to win a prize.

Bernard took the brandy decanter and a glass from the sideboard. He eased his paunch down on the other side of the table and poured himself a little stress relief from the half-empty decanter. The brandy spread through his belly, releasing a slow, reassuring heat through his knotted, middle-aged muscles. His head throbbed. He studied Denise again, unsure what he was supposed to be looking for. Surely she hadn't had a facelift. Maybe her chin had been re-sculpted.

"Oh, for God's sake, Bernard." She pounced out of her chair and stalked around the table to tower over him. She thrust her face up close to his. "Are you going blind in your old age? Open your bloody eyes!"

Bernard winced and leant away, trying desperately to adjust his glasses. He scanned her face, looking for something, anything. Her skin, pearl-white and smooth, pulled tight like a canvas over her cheekbones. Flawless, unblemished.

Ah-ha! He puffed himself and spoke with swagger, "Marvellous job, Denise. Your face looks absolutely beautiful. Not a day past twenty-five."

She allowed a curl at the edge of her lips. "Yes, it is good, isn't it? Audrey and Madeline and the rest of the gang will be awfully jealous. Latest formula. Won't need new injections for at least ten years." She touched up her lipstick in the reflection on the table before straightening to her full six-feet.

Bernard had convinced himself that her being taller

than him now wasn't intimidating.

"I thought perhaps you should take me out to dinner to celebrate."

Denise refilled her glass.

"I've had an eventful—" Bernard began.

"Mancini's. Nine sharp. I've made the booking already, so don't give me that face. You can wear the suit I've put on your bed." She took a sip and admired the fine line of the bridge of her nose. "Besides, Ila told me celebs will be there tonight. Oh, and I'll need some cash for the gardener. He'll be coming tomorrow afternoon."

"Yes, dear." Bernard swallowed his drink easily. He couldn't swallow his headache.

Bernard arrived at the hospital half an hour late from work.

"What time do you call this?" Denise snapped her compact shut and placed it into her handbag. She sat in a wheelchair, her legs apart, wearing an outpatient's robe. "It's a bloody Sunday. You should have been here for me when I called."

"Sorry, dear." He had learned to appreciate her last operation — she no longer scowled. He could appreciate this one, too.

A nurse pressed a packet of pills into Bernard's hand. "Make sure your lovely wife takes one of these after every meal. And no sex for two weeks."

Denise snapped her fingers. "Hurry up! I can't bear to spend another minute in here. Take me home!"

Bernard shuffled into position and pushed the wheelchair down the hallway to the elevators.

"Has Audrey called yet?" she asked.

"Yes, dear. She said she can't wait to see the results." For the life of him, Bernard couldn't remember what Denise had just had done. He hadn't checked his notepad on the way here. The pressures at the office were consuming him. He didn't think she'd had liposuction, but he wasn't sure.

Hadn't they had to wait a month last time?

As they drove home, Denise chattered incessantly about rejuvenation and gratification. Bernard answered in all the right pauses, but his mind was already strategising over the battlefield in his study. How much artillery should he use against Somerset's heavy cavalry? Or perhaps he should counter attack with a cuirassier brigade first, backed with lancers, thereby negating Picton's reserve? To achieve victory, his next move required delicate timing indeed.

Bernard surprised himself with a nervous flutter deep in his stomach. They had refrained from sexual activity for the last two weeks and, though it had been difficult, Denise promised him it would be worth the wait. He suspected she had tightened herself and hoped he'd be able to get used to the change.

He stepped out of the shower, dried himself off, and applied Denise's favourite body lotion to his chest and thighs. He dabbed on the aftershave she had made him buy, though not too much. She hated it when he overdid it.

"You have a retarded sense of smell," she would chide before making him wash it off to reapply the correct amount.

He slipped into her preferred bathrobe — a blue silk kimono — and adjusted his thinning grey hair in the mirror. It would annoy her if his pate reflected too much when they watched the recording later and he didn't want that.

"You ready, darling?" Denise called from the bedroom.

"Yes, dear."

Candles lined the dresser and the bedside tables, flickering shadows across the walls. Denise lay on her back on the four-poster bed, one hand under her head. Her legs were pressed together and turned to the side. The black satin lace chemise she wore ended halfway down her thighs. She raised a leg and the chemise slid down an inch, revealing dimple-free skin.

Bernard lay beside her, careful not to block the view of the camera tucked up in the corner of the room. Denise couldn't smile, but her eyes were kind as her hand nestled on the back of his neck.

"Hello," she said. She pulled his head close to hers, and they kissed, a soft tentative touching of lips. Bernard, almost used to the collagen, pressed his mouth more firmly to hers. She thrust her tongue in and pulled the robe from his shoulders.

He slid his hand over the chemise, tracing his fingers over the saline and briefly teased the permanently elongated nipples. Bernard suspected they didn't harden anymore, but it had been so long since she'd had them done, he wasn't sure. He needed to concentrate on his performance so he dismissed the thought.

His hand moved down again, her belly firm, making sure he avoided her navel. She hated having it touched. He encountered the thin strip of coarse hair dividing the electrolysised skin and wondered what he would feel next. He slid over the *mons pubis*. His finger encountered something fleshy and hard. Denise inhaled sharply. Something's wrong, Bernard thought. It feels too big.

"Check it out." Denise pushed his head down and, at first, he made the mistake of resisting. She shoved his head again and the stress-sore muscles in his neck twinged.

"Bernard! Don't you ruin the movie again!" She pushed his head between her parting thighs.

Bernard gasped.

"What do you think, darling?" Denise asked.

It wasn't just the size that had caught him off guard, but the colour of her sculpted *labia minora*. He struggled to form words, his tongue deadweight and temporarily paralysed.

"It's the new black, darling," said Denise. "Modelled after Naomi. They say she has the best in the business." She wriggled into view for the camera.

"And though it looks bigger, the vault's actually smaller."

Bernard stared transfixed at the chocolate lips bulging over her white *labia majora*, his thoughts of performance fading fast. It looked like someone else's mouth.

"Well?" When he didn't answer, she stopped recording and backhanded him around the head. "You're pathetic! I did it for you."

"I'm sorry, dear. It looks very nice."

She threw his kimono at his face and pushed him off the bed.

He sat in the dark in his recliner watching the television with the sound turned down while patterns of interference swept over the screen. She'd be finished soon. Bernard preferred the interference over the gardener.

After a while, the interference stopped.

Bernard added a flourish of red to the Cuirassiers' bayonet before placing the toy soldier back on the battlefield. This regiment hadn't been as accurate as promised. The heads were oversized.

This weekend he planned to re-enact the entire Battle of Waterloo again. And there would be no delay in the opening of *his* attack. He made shooting sounds and stormed the crest of the ridge, where Picton's 5th division were positioned. He would destroy the English like he had the King's German Legion holding the farmhouse La Haye Sainte. He made a mental note to whitewash the farmhouse walls — the unauthenticity of the exposed brickwork detracted measurably from his enjoyment.

"Have you noticed this?" Denise stood in the doorway of the study holding her right arm out parallel to the ground. She wore only her lace negligee.

He placed the soldier onto the table with a smidgeon too much force. His first weekend off in months. Bernard bit his lip and counted down from ten. Today was supposed to be *his* day. "What is it, dear?"

Denise tapped a finger on the skin beneath her outstretched triceps. It wobbled. Slightly. "See? When did I get the arms of an old woman?"

"You *are* forty-three," Bernard replied.

"Not this woman! Follow me."

"Denise, you promised—"

"Now!"

He trailed her into the kitchen where several brochures were displayed.

Denise specified one with glossy pictures of muscle schematics overlaid with electronic grids.

"Madeline is having this right now. Audrey's booked in next month. What do you think?"

"I don't know." Bernard studied the brochure. "Neuro-sub-muscular atomic repression. I've never heard of this."

"It's been in the States for months, darling. If I don't book an appointment now, who knows when I'll be able to get in."

"Wouldn't lipo—"

"Can't you read?" Denise thumped a long finger on the brochure.

"This is permanent. The entire body, every surface muscle. Nothing will sag again."

"But, Denise." Bernard scanned the fine print. "This says there is partial paralysis of the muscles. I don't think it's a good idea."

"Oh, come on, Bernard. When did you last see a

cripple with fat arms or legs?" She nodded slowly, up and down, up and down, the rhythm of victory. "Makes sense, doesn't it?"

He sighed, thinking of how many extra hours he'd have to put in at work. "This looks expensive."

Denise almost grinned. "Ah ha! You'll love this! You won't — and I promise you this — need to purchase any additional enhancements for the next five years."

Bernard looked at her dubiously. He had heard this before.

"We're going to save a lot of money doing it this way." She slid a second brochure in front of him. "Audrey and Madeline don't know about this one. See this procedure? It provides a soft yet resilient surface encasing the entire epidermis. It also applies pressure to the muscles beneath, keeping them firm, doubling the benefits of the sub-muscular procedure. It gains nourishment from metabolising and reabsorbing the dying epidermal layers. I'll never perspire in public again!"

"I'm sorry, dear. I have no idea what you're talking about."

Denise guided his hand to an inch-sized sample on the brochure. It felt soft and warm and looked sun-tanned.

"Skin?" Bernard recoiled and tried to rub the feeling off on his trousers.

"And this is the best bit." Denise adjusted a dial in the top corner of the brochure. "See! Any colour tan whenever you want. We can convert the sun-room. If only this had been around before my electrolysis."

She gave him a sympathetic look, though it wasn't

meant for him.

Bernard nodded. He might even be able to expand his library with the extra space. Denise squeezed his hand and passed the last brochure. A woman bent one leg over the back of her neck while she balanced on the other. Another women stood with her head beneath her legs, looking up at her bottom. Its title read: *Boning Up*.

"The clinic has a buy two get one free offer," she said. "And although beauty is noble, one mustn't neglect one's health. Osteoporosis is *the* silent killer, Bernard. You wouldn't want me at risk, would you?"

"No, dear." Bernard read how they injected a keratinase-based serum into the marrow of the bone providing a suppleness, much like that of a new-born baby. They claimed it rendered bone density technology obsolete.

"I'm still not sure about this, Denise. Are there any side-effects? Is it proven? How long bef—"

"For God's sake, it wouldn't be available if it didn't work! We're living in the twenty-first century, not the bloody nineteenth. You and all your bloody Nappyonic battles!"

She'd booked herself in before Bernard made it back to his study.

Bernard adjusted the saline drip in the crook of Denise's arm.

"Don't you dare!" she said. "I can still eat. My teeth aren't too soft. You just need to blend everything and then hand feed me."

He had dressed her in a red high-waisted French evening dress, circa 1815, made of silk, net and embroidered in chenille. Bernard parted her legs slightly, relishing the touch of her cyberskin. He'd come to like it much sooner than he would have thought. So warm and lifelike, yet so guiltily artificial. Like the accessories he had enjoyed in his youth. He untied several of the silk strings around the neck of the dress, revealing a generous curve of saline breast.

"Bernard, please." She sat straight-backed against the leather settee, unable to move. Her arms hung at her side, bent at the elbows. "If you're going to do this, don't make me watch."

He stood back, admiring her position, and scratched the stubble on his chin. *She might not be able to see the entire battlefield from here*, he thought. *I need something to prop her up with.*

The phone rang in the kitchen.

Bernard answered on the sixth ring, hoping it wasn't that damned gardener again. He'd be firmer this time and tell him in no uncertain terms his services were no longer required.

"Hello?" Bernard's eyes lit up. "Yes it is, Doctor McKenna. That's right. A soft, French timbre preferably early nineteenth century. Over one hundred phrases right? Great. You're positive there are no side-effects from the electronic voice box? Good. The larynx won't regress, will it? Excellent, see you tomorrow morning."

He cast his eye over the battlefield, mentally checking off regiment positions, calculating distances, and the camera in the corner.

"Bernard, please!"

He smiled at his beautiful wife, secure in his impending conquest.

"Soon, my sweet Josephine, soon."

Yum Cha

They say it comes in threes.

The first is my marriage — "You don't listen to me, you don't understand me, you don't love me" — and that's not true. I love my wife so bad I'd do anything for her. Maybe I don't understand her. I thought that would be the worst. It's not.

I've given up smoking. Haven't had one for six weeks and still counting. It's making me irritable and miserable to be around. I now have to pop a pill the size of a football with every meal; this one's supposed to be side-effect free.

And I'm doing it for her!

The third is the worst; I thought I was going mad, but I'm not. I'm just hearing voices.

Mr. Wong ushers me to a table in a tiny, crowded room hidden at the back of his restaurant. *Back again so soon?* He leans forward and asks discreetly "The same as Wednesday, sir?"

"No. It must be a woman this time."

"Certainly, sir." Mr. Wong bows as he accepts the money I slip him.

I ignore the gluttonous thoughts of the men and the hungry faces of the women around me as I wait for him to return. I place the pill carefully next to my cutlery and begin to read *Men Are From Mars, Women Are From*

Venus. I'm here for different reasons. Men and women *are* different species, after all.

🐱

This all started when the stray cat that adopted our house alerted me to the voices about three weeks ago. The wife and I were retreating to another cold bed so I asked him if he wanted to join us. You know, stupid cat talk. He shot me a yellow-eyed glare and flicked his tail once.

Not fucking likely, pal. As soon as you leave, I'm on the bench for those leftovers.

"What?" I stared at the cat and then at the bench scattered with Chinese takeaway and then back at the cat.

He just sat there, scowling and swishing his tail. I put the takeaway into the fridge.

You fucking bastard.

I heard the cat-flap bang shut before I reached the bedroom.

The following morning I heard voices from every cat in the neighbourhood. Not dogs, not birds, just cats. They didn't like me much and I didn't say anything about it to anyone. I put it down to stress; the strife with the wife and the nicotine withdrawal.

I spent most of that night shitting out the Vietnamese the wife brought home for tea. She was pissed off I'd kept her awake — "It's not the food, I ate the same as you" — and stormed off to work in the morning. I called in sick, got up late, had breakfast and went outside to throw out the leftovers.

174

The Doberman next door leapt up onto the fence, all slavering tongue and dripping froth.

You didn't eat that, did you?

I locked the door and stayed inside. Over the next two days, I edged towards madness. I locked the cat-flap and shut the curtains. I could hear the cat outside, incessant, whining, angry.

Fucking let me in, ya cunt!

With things so strained at home, I decided to go visit the folks on the farm in Werribee. I could talk to Mum. I didn't think she'd understand, but I needed to tell someone I was losing it. As I drove down the driveway with the window down, soaking up that clean, country air, I passed the new yearling grazing in the paddock. It looked up at me with those brown, docile eyes as it chewed lazily on its cud.

I haven't seen you before.

It released a steaming stream of urine and wandered off to annoy a couple of sheep that had arrived to investigate proceedings. The scragglier of the two shook its head and spoke in a slow monotone.

Hey. Can you fix this?

A strand of barbed-wire had wound around its leg, cutting into the flesh.

Well, can you?

I turned slowly back to gaze out the windscreen as my car lurched onto the flowerbeds lining the driveway. Something fluttered in front of the car and I slammed on the brakes. Two chickens scarpered up and over the fence and off into the paddock.

The crazy bastard almost hit me! Who the Hell does he think he is?

It's the son.

Oh.

They glared back accusingly and stormed off to the barn.

Mum's horse Casper wandered over to the fence to survey the damage.

"Hey Casper, do you know what is happening to me?"

Casper whinnied and turned away.

As I pulled up to the house I realised I hadn't heard Casper's thoughts.

But the cow and the sheep and the chickens...

That night I drove home confident and calm. I would've picked the pattern sooner if I'd lived in the country. There were no bloody farmyard animals in the city. Thank God for dodgy Asian food.

🐈

Mr. Wong presents a steaming platter of pale meat on a bed of Asian greens accompanied with several dipping sauces.

"Enjoy, sir," he says smiling. *May her herpes infect your tongue.*

"I think cooking her should've fixed that," I reply, popping one of the anti-smoking pills from its foil.

"Of course." Mr. Wong nervously backs away. *I didn't say that aloud, did I?*

I swallow the pill with a forkful of the delicate flesh and shake my head.

"No, Mr. Wong, you didn't."

By tonight, I'll be able to understand my wife's

thoughts perfectly. My marriage problems will be over.

A Tale of the Interferers: Necromancing the Bones

The heat hung over the wheat fields like a festering sore. Scwythe wiped the sweat from his forehead as he crested the hill overlooking the village. He squinted at the sign on the side of the path with his good eye. The other eye bulged uselessly.

"Vileville, good knight." Thorndyke slapped Scwythe on the shoulder. "Population: two hundred. One evil necromancer. One dark tower. And we are the Interferers! Piece of piss."

Thorndyke posed heroically. He held his staff aloft as if to strike the ground as he scanned the village below. "Think anyone can see me?"

Scwythe took the opportunity to wipe his face on Thorndyke's robe. It left a dark stain on the pale blue cloth. *Goddamn hangover sweats.*

"I knowed what it say, dat sign. Just a little blurry is all," said Scwythe.

Thorndyke raised an eyebrow. The wrinkles creased

his papyrus-like skin. He ran a yellowed finger through his greasy beard. "Do I detect an admission of failure, *Old* Man?"

"Be sweat in me eye, mage, nothing more." Scwythe adjusted the rucksack on his back by jiggling his knees. "Let's just get this bloody job done."

"I don't see much evidence of animal husbandry," said Thorndyke, as they strode down the mud track towards Vileville. "There better bloody be some! I'm not doing this just for the coin."

"How well you know this bastard? We're out o' coin, mage, and we be not eating for more'n two days. I don't like ta be cheated."

Thorndyke cackled, his throat rattling like a reed in a drought-stricken swamp. "And that bothers you? How ironic, good knight. The cheater and the cheated."

Scwythe scowled and strode ahead. The mud sucked greedily at his boots. *I'll have you while you sleep, mage.* "Not many people out about."

"The spell, poor fools."

"What's the one here? Festering Pestilence II?"

"You're learning. The residual suggests an airborne spell, probably Oral Herpes III. Now, which of these shacks do you presume is the town hall?"

Thorndyke sat at the table with the mayor and village council. Most were dressed in homespun tunics, though the mayor wore a wheat chain of office around his neck. A host of scabs distorted the shape of his lips. When he spoke it sounded like his tongue was swollen too tight for his mouth.

"Not until the evil necromancer McNabb be driven from his tower and our graveyards be left in peace. Nae silver till then."

Scwythe puffed up his chest and squeezed the hilt of his sword, making sure the mayor could see the scars ribboning his knuckles. Thorndyke doffed his hat and pretended to stand, while casting a subtle spell of Mild Persuasive Fear II, a teal nimbus on his hand. It was all the wizard could do with little preparation. Or, as Scwythe suspected, as much as he could be bothered.

"Then I fear our business has concluded, gentlemen," said Thorndyke.

His voice sounded like a slick of fertile eels as the spell took hold. "Perhaps news of this petty encounter won't deter others and your predicament will solve itself."

Concerned mumbles spread among the council, as hare-lipped sons and close-eyed fathers passed the word. The mayor appeared startled, confused, trying not to grimace as the scabs on his lips split. The council glared.

"Wait," the mayor said. "Praps we can make some arrangement." His words wheezed and gasped like tired old women.

Scwythe ceased his pose as Thorndyke resumed his seat at the table.

Stupid bastards. We're getting good at this. Soon, we can take on the bigger towns.

"A third of the bounty now, and the remainder with the necromancer dead," said Thorndyke. "We'll also need provisions for at least two days."

"Two days?" said the mayor. "But the tower be only an hour's march from here."

Thorndyke leaned forward. His beard dredged through the slops on the table. "That tower may appear thin and penile, good fellow, but its shaft is thick and runs deeper than you may think. Four days worth would I ask for, could I carry such."

"Can't you use one of them tally-portation spells to get there quicker 'n that? All the good wizards have them."

"You mean Lesser Teleportation IV from the *Deus Ex Machina* spell set?" Thorndyke laughed haughtily. "The energy required to cast such a spell, even a level one version let alone the level five that I'd need to teleport two people, is phenomenal. Phenomenal. Do you know what that word means? No? I'd need to harness the power of the heavens to cast that spell and *still* have enough fight left to fight the good fight."

"And dat's a lot a fighting," said Scwythe.

"Never having seen the tower, where, just where, would I fix my destination? It's the long way first, dear mayor, always."

The mayor glanced at the council, his eyes brimming as if contemplating the necessity of child labour. The council nodded as one. "A third of the silver, and two days' provisions then. You Interferers strike a hard bargain." The mayor pushed a purse across the table. "The rest when you bring his head."

"Done."

Thorndyke drew the drawstring and peered inside the purse. He licked his finger, pushed it down the side of the coins, and then nodded. The purse disappeared into the folds of his robe.

"But first," said Thorndyke. "It is late in the afternoon and we are weary. Perhaps a hot meal and a couple of strong ales to ease the mind."

Scwythe assumed Threatening Pose IV, rattling his scabbard and creaking his leather jerkin. "On the house, mind."

"I s'pose." The mayor picked at a splinter jutting from the table's edge.

Thorndyke grinned — a crooked leer of yellow teeth. "Excellent, my good man. By the way, does anybody have any..." he paused to rake his cracked tongue across his lips, "...pets?"

Scwythe woke from a nightmare. He had been caught running naked in circles through the court. The King had been standing on his throne beating a drum with a thighbone. The court attendants clapped in time with his every footfall. Thorndyke pinched Scwythe's arse whenever he passed.

He hated that dream. Now his head throbbed and his mouth tasted like someone had washed their cock in it.

Weak shafts of morning sunlight oozed into the room. Thorndyke stood naked in front of the window, his skeletal hands exploring his haunches. He yawned and loosed a gentle wind.

"Think we can screw them to break fast as well?" said Thorndyke. "I could do with some fried pig. Maybe some eggs."

Scwythe grunted. Someone had shit on his side of the

bed. He tried to pull his bulk upright, struggling until he sat on the edge of the bed with his feet firmly on the rotting floorboards. His lurching stomach hung heavy between his thighs. "Aye, why not."

"Good night, last night." Thorndyke struggled into his pale-blue robe, careful not to snare his freshly stitched penis in the folds. "We should have this endeavour over by tomorrow morning and be a tad richer."

"You be trusting this necromancer?" Scwythe strapped the daggers to his shins and pulled on his leathers. "He won't be ripping us off, will he? We be needing the coin if we're to buy passage to the continent. We will be paid?"

"McNabb's old school." Thorndyke grasped his staff, spat on his sleeve and polished the knobbed head. "This'll be like taking milk from a babe."

After the townsfolk had packed Scwythe's bags with carrots, a leg of mutton, a pot of honey and a flagon of mead, the Interferers trudged up the mud path towards the dark tower. Gilby, a teenager with a bulbous pocked nose, had been assigned escort.

"He be real evil, like. Killed my uncle when he was dead and dug him up'n that." Gilby's voice sounded like a donkey braying. He pointed to the sores weeping in the cracked corners of his mouth. "He be poisoning our water, so they say."

"Fascinating. Carry this, will you?" Thorndyke passed his staff to Gilby, then hitched his robe, which had been riding through the mud. "Evil, you say?"

"Oh argh," said Gilby. "Turned ol' Widow Gladstone's dog into a cow! Now she got no one to feed all that dog food to!" Gilby grinned, all swollen gum and broken teeth. "Heh heh. Big fat teats, that cow."

"Really?" Thorndyke moved closer to Gilby as they walked. "Where is this Widow Gladstone?"

Scwythe scowled. "No, mage. This one job and we be out o' here."

"Heh heh heh. Big fat teats." Gilby brayed again. "Got a rough tongue, that big fat cow. Heh. Big fat teats."

The more the boy talked, the more Scwythe wanted to crack the flat of his blade over the idiot's head. They could afford no distractions with Sir Henry Charles so close on their trail — goddamn fucking paladin! Sir Henry left little to chance and Scwythe's hangover left no room for a fool's conversation.

"Shut up, boy, or I'll chop your cock off."

"Huh?" said Gilby. He stopped and turned, his dopey mouth hanging open.

Scwythe jabbed his elbow into the boy's jaw as he walked past. Gilby's head rocked and he wailed.

"Tut tut tut," said Thorndyke. "Scwythe Winchcliffe, you shitty bastard. I wouldn't have pursued her. It's just nice to know she's there."

Scwythe grunted, then lengthened his pace, increasing his distance from the other two men.

"Why he do that?" Gilby asked Thorndyke. Tears brimmed in his eyes as he nursed his swelling jaw.

"Scwythe's just a little tense. After all, we're off to kill the necromancer and free your fine town. It's not going to be easy." Thorndyke fondled Gilby's shoulder as they walked. "A cow that was a dog, you say? I've not had one of those before. Have you?"

"This be far as I go," said Gilby. "Follow the path up into the poisoned grounds. It leads to the dark tower."

The tower thrust up from the top of the barrow ahead of them, stretching into the sky, a monument of crooked pain. Sunlight died on the tower's rutted ebony walls, and balconies jutted from the main shaft. Windows had been slitted into the exterior, and a huge wooden door studded with iron stood waiting to be opened. The grass had withered along the path, the blades curled in crisp brown. Fresh weeds had taken root, sprouting in clusters amongst the poisoned ground.

Scwythe shook his head. *Poor maintenance. Not good for the image at all. And Thorndyke says this necromancer be old school?*

As they approached, clouds spiked with lightning rumbled across the sky. Thorndyke tried to turn the squat skull doorknob, but it wouldn't budge.

"Shit."

"Be it locked?" asked Scwythe. "I thought you said..."

"I know what I bloody well said!" Thorndyke rapped his staff against the door and looked up at the approaching storm. Chubby drops spilled slowly from the clouds. "Must have tripped the alarm."

"You're knocking? Be he letting us in just like dat?"

Lightning struck the spire of the dark tower. Thunder roared. The earth trembled beneath their boots. The rain pelted, a cold angry barrage that seeped through the cracks in Scwythe's leather.

Thorndyke hit the door with more force. The pitiful sound of the staff was drowned in the storm.

"Well, what would you suggest?" Thorndyke wiped lank hair from his face.

Scwythe fumed, letting his anger swell inside, until rage swept through his body. He screamed and charged. His massive bulk smashed into the door.

The wooden frame creaked.

Slightly.

Thorndyke, smirking, pointed out the hinges in the corner of the doorframe. "The door opens *outwards!*"

Scwythe swung his fist into the mage's stomach, and brought his knee up into the descending jaw. Thorndyke sprawled backwards into the mud.

"I knew I shouldn't be letting you plan this..." Scwythe removed a thin, round handspan-length of steel from his belt. He punched the steel up and popped the hinges. The door sagged in its frame. Using the steel, he levered the door out, allowing them to slip inside the tower.

They stood at the midpoint of a wide staircase that curled up in one direction and wound down into darkness the other. Torchlight flickered on the stone walls and the warm air smelt of rodent spoor.

"Up or down?" asked Scwythe.

A vile stench wafted up from below, drawn to the promise of escape through the gap in the door.

Thorndyke shrugged.

"Damn you, mage! You be learning nothing of this tower beforehand?"

"I don't deal in details, good knight. Big picture, that's me."

"Details? You're a bloody wizard! It be all about details! No wonder your spells don't work!"

"There's no need to shout! Calm yourself, man. We're in now. Down's easier on the legs. Obviously."

"You sure? I no want be coming all the way back up if you be wrong."

"I lived in the Wizard's Tower at the Royal Court, didn't I?" Thorndyke pushed Scwythe down the steps. "The bedroom at the top, the laboratory at the bottom. Lots of stairs in between. Now go!"

Scwythe grumbled, adjusted the weight on his back, and descended slowly. His wet boots slipped on the stone steps. They hadn't gone far when the fetid smell of rot became overpowering. Scwythe paused and held his hand up for Thorndyke to stop.

"Listen," he whispered.

Low moans issued from the darkness below. And beneath the moans, a wet slapping on the stairs nearby. If they were to turn the corner of the staircase...

"I don't be knowing 'bout this." Scwythe drew his sword and tried to back up the stairs. He bumped into Thorndyke.

"What do you think you're doing?"

"Something be down there."

"Of course there bloody is! McNabb's supposedly a necromancer and down there is supposedly his laboratory. Is the smell of a decaying corpse too much for you, big man?"

"I just don't see why we be doing this down the lab."

Thorndyke sighed. "Because he's most likely working. Now move it!" He pushed Scwythe in the back, but Scwythe didn't budge.

Scwythe turned around to face the wizard. "This was supposed to be easy. The door was locked and I be soaking wet. You be fucked this up! You go first."

"You're a pathetic man." Thorndyke summoned a sickly ball of light and set it hovering a few yards behind Scwythe's head. "Look, you can follow Sallow Wisp II." His mouth dropped open. "Oh fuck, look behind you. I didn't think McNabb was this proficient..."

Thorndyke hitched his robe, turned and scrambled up the stairs.

There was a loud slap on the step below and behind Scwythe. Something moaned in his ear. The smell of damp rotting meat assailed the staircase.

Scwythe thrust his elbow back into a mass all soft and sticky. He leapt one step higher, swivelled and swung his sword in what should have been a decapitating chop. Instead, he struck the wall. The clang ricocheted through his bones and rattled his skull.

"Up. I meant up." Thorndyke's voice faded with every word.

The shambling mound of flesh moaned again. Its arms grasped at Scywthe's woollen braes. Two more undead creatures staggered up the stairs, the remains of their skin a shiny mottled purple under the wan light of Thorndyke's spell.

Scwythe kicked out at the chest of the closest. His boot sank into weeping flesh and the creature flew backwards, crashing into the followers.

"Up up," Thorndyke called faintly from above.

Scwythe tried to leap up the stairs, two at a time. He slipped and cracked his head on the wall as he fell. As he sprawled in dust and muck, the rage grew. It trembled first deep in his swollen gut. Rage rapidly shuddered out and up, through the dense muscles gilded in fat, until his brain screamed blood.

The undead, all low moans and stinking flesh, had regrouped and marched towards him. One of them with an oozing foot imprint in its chest.

"Fuck you, ya dead bastards!" screamed Scwythe.

He charged into their midst, battering the head of one against the wall. Its skull splintered but it kept moving, as the flesh sloughed from the broken bone. Scwythe thrust his sword into another's gut, twisted the blade and yanked. A swelter of pus sprayed from the wound and the reek of decay thickened the air. The creature faltered, moaned again, and reached for Scwythe's face. He pushed it away and hacked off the leg of another undead, the blade slicing through soft bone and moist tissue. Unbalanced, it toppled and rolled down the stairs. Scwythe whirled his blade, slashing and chopping, as the rage consumed him, until he stood amongst a pile of butchered meat quivering on the floor. The rage had passed.

More moans drifted up from the darkness.

Scwythe ran up the stairs towards Thorndyke's distant chanting. Too bloody late for spells now, mage. One flight up, Scwythe rounded the corner to find Thorndyke weaving a pale teal nimbus across the corridor.

"Quick," said Thorndyke, "come through. It can't harm you yet."

Scywthe stepped through the woven shards of light, shuddering as the spell sought to unknit his flesh.

With a flourish of his wrist that zinged the air, Thorndyke completed the spell. "Ah, the Consecrated Wall II! That should stop them, good knight." Thorndyke grinned. "And look at that! What a mighty bump you have on your head."

Scwythe growled and sheathed his sword. "You said this be easy. It looks like McNabb really be raising the dead. We could have been killed!"

"Yes, yes, yes, Winchcliffe," Thorndyke muttered. "Whatever. Come, let us make haste."

Scywthe grabbed Thorndyke by the throat and pushed him hard up against the wall. "Don't be giving me none of dat heroic speech. Save dat shit for your commoners. There be fucken undead down there, mage!"

Thorndyke spluttered and coughed as his scrawny fingers tried to pry Scwythe's hand away. Scwythe knocked the mage's head against the stone.

"Ow! I know, I know. None of the reports indicated McNabb was doing anything besides scaring the townsfolk with his syphillic spells. Sending the occasional monster down to poop in the fields, infect the barley, that sort of thing. Christ, I thought he was just idling away his time in that bloody tower of his! You read the reports."

Scwythe released his grip. Thorndyke slunk against the wall, massaging the loose folds of skin around his throat. *Bastard knows I can't read proper.*

"You're right, Thorndyke. Let's be finding this bloody McNabb."

After a few seconds of running upwards they came to an ornate door at the top of the stairs. A soft glow leaked from the crack.

"It's not a very big tower, be it?" asked Scwythe.

"Of course not, good knight. It's much cheaper to maintain an illusion than to build a real tower. God, can you imagine how much that would cost? And the time?"

"You be opening the door?"

"No, it might be trapped. You open it."

Scwythe growled. Rage trembled in his bowels, threatening to burst into his pants. He counted to three, then counted to three again. "Use one of your bloody divining spells. Find out and then be unlocking the fucken thing!"

"Watch your tone with me, boy!" Thorndyke waggled his staff in front of Scwythe's face. "Didn't you see that impressive spell I created back there in the staircase? Takes a lot of energy, you know. Magic's not just something you churn out." Thorndyke's eyes shone and he thrust his staff into the air.

"It's Art!"

Scwythe shook his head then spat on the floor. "Fuck it, then. If be I getting it, you be getting it." He grabbed the mage's robe in one hand and grabbed the door handle with the other. Nothing happened. No sharp buzz of sparks shocked his groin. No puff of poison gas left him retching on his knees. No slime, no fire. Nothing.

And the door was unlocked.

Scwythe glared and gripped the hilt of his sword. "Will I be needing this?"

"Shouldn't think so," said Thorndyke. "Chop chop."

They threw the door wide and strode into the room.

A short, skinny man glistening with sweat stood naked with his back to them. He squealed and pulled a sheet off the massive four-poster bed, quickly wrapping it around his shoulders. Something large and fleshy moved beneath the remaining sheets on the bed.

"What in the nine hells?" The man had a voice like a young lass, though too high-pitched for comfort.

Thorndyke laughed. "McNabb!"

McNabb squinted. "Thorndyke? Is that you?" He scratched at the small tufts of red hair that sprouted behind his ears. "What are you doing here so soon?"

Thorndyke spread his arms and walked over to embrace the necromancer.

"Business, my good man!"

The thing beneath the sheets writhed. Scwythe caught a glimpse of mottled flesh and a waft of perfume. Candles lit the room, and incense burned in tapers in an attempt to mask another smell. Dried petals were scattered around the bed.

The two wizards hugged each other, laughing.

"You bloody fool, Thorndyke. Look at you. You're all wet," said

McNabb. "You're not supposed to be here until next week."

"Eh?" Scwythe scowled at Thorndyke.

"Next week?" Thorndyke asked. "Oh..."

McNabb giggled as he wriggled into a soiled robe that had been lying on the floor. "I would have turned off the alarm system and unlocked the door. With all that thunder I didn't hear you come in. Heh heh, I myself had thought that perhaps the earth had indeed moved during my last marathon."

Thorndyke coughed and pretended to browse the bookshelf near the dresser. "You've, ah, had some success in the black arts I see, McNabb."

"Next bloody week, Thorndyke!" Scwythe scowled and started counting to three. "I almost be killed down there!"

"What?" McNabb's little pink face screwed up and his eyes widened.

"You didn't hurt my little boys, did you?"

"No, no, no." Thorndyke wandered over to the bed where the mound wriggled beneath the sheets. He wrinkled his nose. "Ew, that perfume's horrible, McNabb. Smells like a woman. Have you been up to your old necrosexual tricks again?"

McNabb giggled and rubbed the palms of his hand together. "Is it really necro if they're still warm?"

Scwythe set the rucksack on the floor next to the door. "What's still warm?"

McNabb whipped the remaining sheets off the bed.

A mass of heaving flesh squirmed on a battered mattress, large patches of tissue sewn haphazardly together, a warp of decaying breasts and gaping orifices. Patches of hair bristled from a bulbous stalk skewed off from the bulk of the flesh. A wet, toothy slit mewled in the middle of the bulb. A rainbow of eyes circled the slit. A gaggle of stitched limbs writhed, their extremities a sea of clutching fingers and toes.

"Oooh," said Thorndyke. "Very clever."

Scwythe, already at the side of the bed, reached out to touch the quivering flesh. "You really be a necromancer. I thought it be all bullshit to scare folks away."

McNabb slapped his hand away. "Elizabeth's mine." He pulled the sheet back over the creature, patting it tenderly. "I can make you your own if you want."

"Scwythe has other tastes," said Thorndyke. He wandered over to the table next to the window and pulled up a chair.

"Yes, your infamy travels fast. I hear the King has entrusted Sir Henry Charles to your capture. What a wedding feast you must have disrupted, Thorndyke! Such shame you have brought to the Royal Court." McNabb giggled again. "So this is the fallen knight? I heard you fell far, Sir. With the Princess' favourite gelding, no less?"

Scwythe growled, trying not to blush.

"Come, McNabb. Some wine. Have you forgotten how to host?"

Thorndyke removed the purse from the folds of his robe. "We have another dark tower to reach by the next moon."

"Of course, gentlemen. Please, Sir, take a seat." He scurried over to the dusty wine rack. "I believe a toast is in order."

Coins showered across the table as Thorndyke upended the purse. "And I believe this is yours, McNabb. We'll collect the rest when you're dead!"

They laughed a good throaty laugh that hinted of petty evil. Except for McNabb, who giggled.

Later, much later, when Scwythe staggered from the

table and collapsed on the floor, his head reeling, he thought he heard Thorndyke's slick of eels suggest a threesome.

In Scwythe's dream he was back in the Royal Stables on the night of Princess Beatrice's wedding, but this time it wasn't the gelding, but the gelding's owner, the Princess, that he lay naked next to. His nose was no longer split, and his bung eye had unbunged. His family of scars, as in all his dreams, had never been.

The Princess sighed and ran her fingers through her long golden locks. She rolled over to face him, her cleavage pushed tight by the corset under her wedding gown.

"I wish it were you I was to marry, Sir Winchcliffe," she said. "Perhaps if you were to fuck me, my father might call the whole thing off?"

Scwythe grinned as his great cock stirred in its scabs. "I think you be right there, lassy." *This be going great,* his subconscious whispered to him. *I'll make her take her clothes off. Fast like, no thumbs needed.*

The Princess stood and hitched her gown up above her waist. Scwythe followed the length of her legs up into the forbidden triangle. She wore no undergarments and her auburn bush beckoned him. He smelt her scent, strong and pungent, drawing his face closer to her mound.

Somewhere in the back of the barn, the gelding neighed. "Go on, do it."

Scwythe glanced over his shoulder, irritated. The

gelding stood nearby in the shadows, though its once muscular frame appeared emaciated, the bones jutting out beneath worn hide. A wisp of grey clung to its chin.

Get rid o' the fucken horse, Scwythe ordered his subconscious. *Sure, it replied, you're the boss.*

The Princess ground her vulva into Scwythe's face. Something wet smeared his chin. Scwythe grinned and opened his mouth to feed. This close up, her pubic hair suggested traces of gingery red.

"You sure?" asked the Princess. Her voice sounded strange. A little too high-pitched. "The spell will hold?"

"Of course," said the gelding. "I do it all the time. Think of it as a mouth wash."

The Princess giggled. A leathery cock smeared in pus sprouted from her vaginal lips, thrusting itself into Scwythe's mouth.

He gagged. "No, fucken no...wake...ugh...up!"

Scwythe woke retching on the floor. He managed to swallow the bile in his mouth and took several deep breaths. His head throbbed again. He had to cut down on the booze — it must be killing him, if he felt like this every morning.

In the far corner of the room, near the bed, Thorndyke and McNabb stood watching. McNabb, naked, looked nervous and clutched his robe to his chest. Thorndyke simply leered, his mouth full of big yellow teeth.

Scwythe vomited on to the floor, splattering his arms and chest with bright yellow. "Must be something I ate," he muttered, trying to stand.

"Looks like everything you ate," said Thorndyke.

"You said the spell would hold—" McNabb

whispered before Thorndyke clouted him around the ears.

"Hurry up, Scwythe. Get yourself together. We've a big day ahead and a sizeable bounty to collect," said Thorndyke. "Now, McNabb, you have the head?"

McNabb scurried over to the wall and placed his hands on two of the stones. They ground open and a secret receptacle revealed a large stone urn. McNabb plucked a head from within the urn and tossed it to Thorndyke.

"Very nice." Thorndyke turned the head slowly in his hands, admiring the craftsmanship. "It even looks like you. Real flesh too?"

"Of course." McNabb giggled. "From the village graveyard, but I've used a modified Mirror Image IV on it. Lasts for months because it doesn't have to duplicate my actions. There's still a few bugs to iron out, but I've applied for a patent anyway — Mirror Visage, I think I'll call it. A user-pays system with different royalties, payable for each level cast. What do you think?"

Thorndyke arched an eyebrow "You don't have any easy-to-learn, simple-to-master Summon Animal spells, do you?"

"I'm a necromancer, Thorndyke, not a druid. You're into nature, perhaps you should join a Ring?"

"There are certain...restrictions, shall we say. I do *love* nature, McNabb, but not in quite the same way as the druids." Thorndyke thrust his finger into the head's mouth. "Still moist. Hmm...you don't have a spare, do you?"

"You said a few bugs," asked Scwythe, strapping his weapons to his waist. "What sort of bugs?"

The two wizards looked at each other and McNabb giggled. "Don't you worry that tough little warrior brain of yours about such matters." They looked at each other again, sly smiles smeared over their faces.

Scwythe scowled. "I ain't just muscle, McNabb. I be a strategist."

McNabb raised his eyebrows and pursed his lips.

"Come, Scwythe, let's leave the man in peace," Thorndyke leered. He tossed the head to Scwythe, who caught it by the nostrils. "You can be the hero this time."

As the two Interferers readied themselves, McNabb wandered over to his bed and the bride hidden beneath the sheets.

"Hey," said McNabb. "What's this?"

Thorndyke strode towards the door, tugging at Scwythe's sleeve to follow.

McNabb dipped his finger into one of the multitude of oozing orifices and then took a delicate sniff. "This isn't mine!"

"Hurry," hissed Thorndyke.

He threw open the bedroom door and rushed into the stairwell. Scwythe trotted after him, casting a backwards glance at the necromancer. McNabb whirled around, flicking the scum from his finger. Blood flushed the little man's cheeks and the shadows in the room deepened.

"Thorndyke! You promised you wouldn't touch her!" Spittle flew from McNabb's lips. The red tufts of hair danced around his ears, weaving like flames in the wind.

Scwythe slammed the door shut. Something huge

and heavy smashed into the other side of the door. The wood sizzled and black decay spat through the keyhole. The stench of death assailed Scwythe, before he regained his senses and sprinted downwards after the fleeing robe of Thorndyke the Mage.

The mage chuckled as they walked down to the village. In the distance, McNabb's voice could be heard piping from the upper windows of the dark tower, though the Interferers were too far away to distinguish any words.

"You couldn't help yourself, could you?" said Scwythe.

"You saw how he was, all gloating and proud of his Elizabeth. Smug little bastard. Just like he was back at school. Always trying to one up me."

"Which spell you be using on him? Mild Persuasion II?"

"No, very similar. Brotherly Love III. He was always a sucker for that one." Thorndyke cackled. "He'd always share anything when I cast that one."

"You coulda woke me for a bit o' the fun." Scwythe tossed the head up and down in his hands, studying the tufts of red hair and rosy cheeks. "I didn't much like the man and I would o' enjoyed rooting his missus."

For a second, Scwythe thought he saw the eyes in the head move to focus on him. The blue orbs were congealed in a thick film that had crusted around the eye socket. The eyes didn't move. They couldn't move. The head was dead.

"Yes," said Thorndyke, "she was a good root, too.

Not had anything like that before. Speaking of which..."

Gilby sat at the base of an old oak, studying what was once the contents of his bulbous nose now smeared over thick fingers. "Heh heh, you're still alive!" Gilby clambered to his feet, cleaning his fingers with his tongue as he did so. "You must o' killed that bad man good."

"Thorndyke, you promised you wouldn't pursue this," Scwythe growled. "Let's just be getting this job over with."

Thorndyke grinned, his mouth of yellow teeth. "Now, now, good knight, it would be foolish to waste an opportunity such as this. Think of it, man! A cow that was once a dog!"

"I dunno, I reckon we get out of here before McNabb be coming after—"

"McNabb? But ain't you s'posed to have killed—"

"Gilby!" Thorndyke slapped the boy on the shoulder, glaring at Scwythe to shut his mouth. "The Widow Gladstone. How far from here?" He motioned furiously for the head. "Show it to the boy."

Scwythe thrust the head forward.

"That don't much look like him," said Gilby.

"Death is a funny mistress, boy," said Thorndyke. "Necromancy held its sway with youth and desire. It's McNabb alright. See?" He pointed to the greying tufts of red hair.

"I spose," said Gilby. "Well, okay then, let's go see the Widow Gladstone. Heh, heh, those big old teats! You can hardly get two of them in your mouth."

The three of them strolled down the muddy path towards the Widow Gladstone's, the mage with his long scrawny arm draped over the shoulder of the enthusiastic Gilby.

Scwythe turned the head over in his hands, studying the balding scalp. *I don't remember the red hair going grey.* The skin appeared blurry and refused to focus underneath Scwythe's gaze. Sometimes it looked bald, but every now and then, a thick, coarse mat of grey hair would seem to sprout then disappear. *And the bloody eyes have moved!*

"Thorndyke, I don't be knowing about this head—" Scwythe said.

Gilby threw his arms wide. "Here we are!"

A fat cow stood tethered to an old fence, near a thatched cottage. The cow snarled and pawed at the mud.

"Heh, heh, she don't like me much anymore," said Gilby.

"I wonder why ever not."

Thorndyke moved warily to the fence. A hot stream of urine jettisoned from the cow as it tried to cock a leg. It staggered and the rope around its neck pulled tight. Thorndyke glanced back at Scwythe, a grin spread over his face.

"You can smell it's true! Cow and dog!" Thorndyke loosened his robes and clambered over the fence. "You'd better check on the widow, Scwythe, make sure she doesn't see anything untoward. I'll check the rear."

"I don't think so, wizard. I be going first this time." Scwythe tossed the head to Gilby, then unbuckled his belt and draped it, clinking and jangling, over the nearest post.

The cow snarled again.

"This was my idea, Scwythe. Check on the widow."

Scwythe heaved himself over the fence. "You touch that beast before I do and you won't get the chance to come. I'll beat you off so bad." He dropped his woollen braes.

And then everything happened at once.

The cow began to bark.

An enormous bulk of swaddled breast and chin waddled from the cottage, waving a broomstick and shrieking. Apart from the bed sheet clinging to the rolls of fat, the Widow Gladstone was quite naked. "Gilby? Is that you? Worrying my Doreen again? I told you to stay away!"

Gilby screamed and dropped the head. "It's my uncle!"

And the head screamed, too. In the high-pitched whine of McNabb the Necromancer. "Thorndyke, you bastard! Where are you? You won't get away with this. I'm coming for you!"

It rolled through the mud, somehow dragging itself towards the Interferers. It cursed and spat out sludge as it slid beneath the fence. The scalp was no longer bald with red tufts of hair, its cheeks no longer rosy red like McNabb's.

"*That* orifice was virginal. For my wedding night! You bloody knew that!" the head squealed.

Gilby screamed again and sprinted down the path towards the village. "That's my uncle's head! The necromancer's coming."

The cow reared, the rope snapping under the weight. It barked again and its mouth housed no teeth belonging to an herbivore; instead sharp fangs ran ragged with saliva. *And Gilby knows what its tongue feels like!* Scwythe stumbled backwards, tripping over his braes and falling into the mud. He crawled on his knees towards the cottage.

"Bloody hell." Thorndyke struggled to clamber back over the fence, but his robe caught on something. "McNabb's Mirror Image spell has worn off. He lied to us!"

"You deflowered my Elizabeth!"

The hooves crashed down, and the high-pitched whine ended in a soft explosion of skull and brain.

"Gilby? You're not Gilby!" shrieked Widow Gladstone. Her enormous breasts shuddered as she swung the broomstick into the side of Scywthe's head. Her thighs shook and wobbled with the impact of wood on bone.

A man emerged from the cottage with a sheep's intestine wrapped over the end of his cock. "What the Hell is going on here?"

Scwythe recognised the man to be the mayor. And the mayor was reaching for a pitchfork. Scwythe managed to say fuck before the broom mashed his lips.

Thorndyke began to scream. He had managed to free his robe, but his stitched penis had snagged on a jagged splinter. He worked frantically beneath his reddening pale-blue robe.

"You dirty bastards," shrieked the Widow, bouldering her bulk and broom towards the wizard.

"Come on, lads!" The mayor ran towards Scwythe with the pitchfork held forth like a lance.

Lads? Scwythe thought, trying to pull his woollen braes from the snarling, tearing mouth of the cow. *What lads?*

Three naked men charged from the Widow's cottage with their weapons in hand.

"Cast a bloody spell!" Scwythe twisted in the mud as the pitchfork speared the earth where his head had been. He punched upwards into the heavily-veined scrotum dangling above his face. The mayor went down.

"I'm stuck," the wizard wailed, his face whiter than the inside of the widow's flabbulant thighs.

The cow reared again, the woollen braes snared between its teeth, and charged through the fence, knocking the Widow sideways. She hit the ground with a fat-shattering thud, the air in her lungs expelling in a spermy garlic gust that hit Scwythe full in the face. He gagged and rolled over. *Lucky I've already been sick this morning*, he thought. He forced himself up from the mud as the other men gagged helplessly on their knees, awash in each other's sputum.

Thorndyke lay squirming on the ground, blood oozing between his thighs. His mouth worked speechlessly and sweat coated his face. On what was left of the fence, hung a loose shred of bloody skin.

Scwythe grabbed his belt and buckled it around his naked groin. "Get up, Thorndyke! For the love of Princess Beatrice, get up!"

Thorndyke's mouth popped open and closed like a dying fish.

"You bastard Interferers!" The mayor plucked the pitchfork from the suckling mud. "This'll be the last time you try to diddle good folk like us!"

"Come on, Thorndyke!" Scwythe grabbed a fistful of

the wizard's beard and yanked him upwards and sideways.

The mayor roared as he charged, bearing the pitchfork towards Scywthe's barrel chest. Scwythe turned in one impossibly fluid movement for a man gone to seed, his blade flying from its sheath, slipping underneath the pitchfork prongs and sliding down the shaft. Scwythe pushed upwards, deflecting the course of the pitchfork. With his other hand, Scwythe unwound the mayor's intestines with the blade he had had strapped to his shin seconds before. Blood spattered over Scwythe's groin. The mayor gave him a look like a man caught eating his own ejaculate and toppled to the ground.

"Who wants some?" Scwythe waved his bloodied weapons as the other naked men drew closer. "I can kill you all!"

The men drew closer still. "Go on then," one of them said.

Shit, Scwythe thought. Gilby could still be heard screaming amongst the villagers. Voices were raised, too many voices. The thud of the mob would soon be upon the Interferers. From the direction of the dark tower, a foul wind began to blow, gathering strength as it tore through the leaves. McNabb's face formed in the clouds as the sky crackled and spat. From his eyes, he began to weep dark acid.

"Thorndyke!" Scwythe yelled, as the first droplets seared his skin. "Cast some bloody spells!"

"My penis. I'm ruined."

The clouds roared with McNabb's pestilent mouth. Lightening hit the cottage and the thatch burst into flames. The widow wheezed in anger. The widow's other lovers dropped their weapons and fled towards the thick of the forest. Up the path towards the tower, could be heard the slow shuffle of the undead, their stench carried on the plague winds.

"Spells! Cast some spells!"

"I'm trying! Step close to me." Thorndyke's body was encased in a teal nimbus. "I don't know if this will work — that rain really hurts. Even more than my penis."

From below, the village mob marched towards them with pitchforks, clubs and flaming torches. The cow raced ahead of the mob, barking madly.

"Oh, shit." Scwythe hung his head. "How many times have I seen this happen?"

"Not this time!" Thorndyke struck his staff to the ground, channelling McNabb's lightening spits. Electricity arced around them, sizzling out the air, and then—

Poof!

They were gone.

McNabb watched with duty from his tower, as the zombie army engaged the villagers. He watched with amusement at the hacking of limbs and the torching of flesh. He watched with dismay as the villagers, what little was left of them, triumphed over his boys, an armour-clad paladin riding amongst them smiting any undead — Sir Henry Charles, no doubt, hot on the stinking trail of the Interferers. He remembered watching in anger as Thorndyke had channelled

McNabb's own energy to cast — and who would have ever believed that weak bestial practitioner could ever cast such a high level spell? — Lesser Teleportation VI, no less from the *Deus Ex Machina* spell set. As far as McNabb was aware, Thorndyke had never managed more than a level three spell in the past. It was terribly unfair.

He'd already sent warnings to the other dark towers. This time, Thorndyke had pushed the boundaries of decency and friendship too far. McNabb had made sure people knew what to look for — a wizard in a pale-blue bloodstained robe, and a swarthy knight naked from the waist down. He'd give Sir Henry a helping hand when the paladin came poking his head into McNabb's tower passage.

The sound of flesh and bed sheet rustled from the far corner of the room.

"Yes, Elizabeth," said McNabb. "I won't be long."

They were out there, McNabb knew. Probably not far from the village, perhaps lurking in the woods. Without his army, McNabb would be weak for a while, but soon, oh so soon, after he had raised the dead from today's battle, he would hunt them down and kill them. Or perhaps tell the ugly knight what Thorndyke had been doing to him in his sleep. McNabb smiled.

Let them kill each other.

The rustle of bed sheet again, this time more insistent, urgent. A musky perfume filled the room.

"Yes, dear." McNabb bit his lip, trying not to raise his voice. "I said I won't be long."

She wasn't the same anymore. Not since Thorndyke had...put...McNabb shuddered, unable to bear the thought.

The bed sheet rustled again, demanding.

McNabb whirled towards the bed, his cheeks flushed, clenching his tiny fists. "For God's sake, woman, can a man not have some peace! I'm coming already!"

Shot in Loralai

The news preaches terror and the world is closing its borders. Hatred and mistrust printed across dark skin and long beards, tattooed in blonde hair and blue eyes. For me it was a Western ignorance buried deep in the fear of a different skin, a foreign culture. For them? I can only guess. I thought envy, I thought fear, I thought awe. If you look back further than my life, that misnamed thing masqueraded as a battle fought with religious steel. And if you open your eyes and ears, we're told it does once again. When wars are best viewed on digital wide-screen, it's hard to believe Hollywood does not have a guiding hand.

The photos I'm holding show a version of the truth from the spring of 1998, after the thaws, before the heat cooked the earth again. See this one? With the woman dressed in *purdah* pointing an automatic handgun at the tall, white man with the short brown hair. See the liquid eyes of the dark man with the moustache, muscled and sweating in the background? See how they shine? He wants to kill the white man whose name is Simon. I travelled with Simon for a while.

And this photo here? You can still see the handgun in the corner pointed at Simon's head. He's half-sprawled on a stretcher, trying to prise the dark man's hand from his throat while his other arm pushes up against the wrist bearing down on him with a thick steel blade. Why doesn't the woman just shoot him?

And what am I doing while this is happening? I'm standing watching.

Someone else took this photo. Could I have helped? Perhaps, but I wasn't big enough and the dark man was a Pakistani policeman.

Yes, there is truth here, in these photographs, but what is that truth when you are shown what people want you to see? Here is part of that truth.

Dusk settled upon the desert as our truck pulled into Loralai — a seedy, frontier village choked with dirt and grimy used-car parts that littered the roadside through Pakistan. The narrow street flooded with dark shapes and white, peering eyes.

The *shalwar qamiz*-clad crowd surged towards us — our welcoming committee. Few white men stopped overnight here, even fewer white women. They liked white women, we knew, and our truck carried fourteen of them. One of the younger girls, Steph, shuddered as she peered out the window. She'd been molested in her hotel room the night before when we had stopped over in Dera Ghazi Khan — a dirty, cluttered city banking the Indus River. The hotel we stayed in had been the most expensive in town, but in this part of the world, money doesn't mean safety, though sometimes it buys it for a while. There had been blood on the walls of my room, but the bed had been free of lice. I had slept well.

Tonight we had arranged to make camp in the police

compound near the outskirts of town. Apparently we would be safer there, but we all knew if anyone would fuck you over in these countries, it would be the police. The compound looked like cheap army barracks made from wonky, lilted prefabs. A few light bulbs strung up on poles cast a dim light, and we were directed to a large enough area to park the truck and pitch our tents.

"Okay, girls," Chris the driver said, bringing the truck to a stop. "Time to put on the robes. You know the drill. Just because we're with the cops doesn't mean we won't have a repeat of last night. The repercussions will be a lot harder on the offender if they try anything within the compound. You should be safe. Just follow the rules and obey the customs."

The women muttered and mumbled as they pulled on their *chadors*; tempers frayed with restrictions, continual groping hands and probing eyes. I watched with male amusement, immune to their complaints. They'd been bitching amongst themselves for the last two weeks about the conditions and it was only going to get worse. What did they expect from a tour of the Middle East? Greenie feminists, political correctness, beer and kebabs?

"One last thing, and I shouldn't need to say this." Chris leafed through his guidebook. "No booze or drugs tonight. It's too risky."

Bill slumped in his seat. A small, scrawny man who looked a little like Willie Nelson, he had left the mines in Western Australia, shouldering a 20-year-old alcohol addiction in search of greener pastures. "Ah, Christ," he moaned. "Not that it matters. That Paki whiskey is killing me."

Although a seasoned alcoholic, Bill's liver preferred a constant soaking of five percent alcohol. He'd stood silent as we gave away the Indian-brewed beer at the Indian/Pakistani border. Not that he could drink that either — it made you sick before the alcohol entered the bloodstream. Probably why he'd been silent. If it had been San Miguel, he would have attempted smuggling it across the border. The whiskey he'd purchased since in Peshawar, a smuggler's paradise of a city, *was* most likely killing him — if it didn't make him go blind first. We all knew he was struggling with his newfound sobriety.

As the women disembarked, police numbers swelled, emerging from the shadows. But unlike the villagers the night before, they kept a respectful distance. A sergeant moved amongst them, waving his arms and talking quickly in a tribal language. Most of them soon moved back to their huts, leaving us to pitch our tents in relative peace.

Being last off the truck left Steve and I with a rough, uneven patch of rock near the toilet block to stake our tent claim. The smell of shit and urine wafted over the dry, stale, evening air. After struggling in the dark to find a softish, somewhat level area to lay out the tent, Steve stood up quickly.

"Gotta take a dump," he said, and walked carefully and slowly to the darkened toilets. I heard him take a large breath of comparatively fresh air before he entered. No lights came on.

I struggled with hammering the tent pegs into the ground and fixed the poles upright inside the tent before Steve returned.

"Jesus fucking Christ," he gagged, "those are the worst so far!" His face shone with sweat in the dim light.

"You hungry?" I pointed toward the truck, where the group on cooking duty was unfolding the tables and attaching the gas bottles.

"Nah, but I gotta get away from this area. It stinks too bad."

The sergeant stood in discussion with Chris as we approached the truck.

"I don't know, mate. It's not up to me," Chris said.

"But you must," the sergeant implored. "Please. It would be great honour."

"What's going on?" I asked.

The sergeant turned to us and grinned, his teeth white beneath his black moustache. "You are come dinner at my house. All of you."

"Hold on." Chris rolled his eyes at us.

"Is ten minutes walk from here. Very close."

The sergeant was almost six foot — tall for a Pakistani — and his uniform appeared packed with muscle. I was pretty sure he could beat the shit out of any one of us, if he chose to. Or perhaps just open up with the Kalashnikov dangling from his shoulder. His eyes oiled over the two women pulling out the food baskets.

"Please. Is Muslim custom. I must offer you."

I watched Karen remove potatoes and cauliflower and put them on the table. Nothing else came out of the baskets. Alicia reluctantly began to chop. It looked like another minimalist effort.

"I'd be keen," said Steve. "Let's do it."

Chris scowled for a second and then called us all over and explained what was on offer. Nine accepted; five guys and four girls — less than half of the tour. Steph, wisely, had decided not to join us, and took over cooking duties from Karen and Alicia.

"Just remember. You'll be outside the compound. Be careful." Chris climbed back up into the cab of the truck and lit a cigarette.

"You're not coming?" I asked.

"Not fucking likely." He pushed The Chemical Brothers into the cassette deck. And then in hushed tones under the beats, "Watch yourself, eh? These guys are corrupt as Hell."

And so I found myself wandering up a road in the dark with a bunch of Kiwis, Aussies, Poms and a Yank, accompanied by several Pakistani policemen and students.

We had women. They had guns.

We introduced ourselves to two young, non-uniformed men, who had attached themselves to our group as we walked towards the house of our honourable host: Officer Mirza Khan.

"I am Rashid," one said, trying not to look too much at Alicia, who walked between Steve and I. He sprouted a thin moustache and looked to be in his late teens.

The wiry fellow next to him spoke up, his eyes skimming over Alicia before settling on me. "I am Omair." He too sprouted a thin moustache, and was of a similar age to Rashid. He glanced once more at Alicia, and then looked ahead.

I smiled at Alicia. Even though she wore her *chador* and dressed in *purdah*, there was no mistaking the mountains her breasts made. She nodded and gave me the what-can-I-do-about-it-look. She knew. Blonde with big tits.

Thank God she was sensible enough to follow custom. At nineteen, Alicia was the youngest on the tour, but she handled this part of the world a Hell of a lot better than the rest of the women.

"I am a student here," said Rashid. "I am study English, Drama and Political Science. I am wanting to be a romantic actor."

"I too study," said Omair. "The same things. However, I will be wanting to be an emotional actor."

"Right," I said. What the Hell were they studying in a Loralai police compound?

I'd already met a lot of young men who were studying English and Political Science, but not too many actors. How to act like a Hard Cop? A Hard, Romantic, Emotional Cop?

"Which actors do you like?"

"Leonardo Di Caprio." They beamed.

Steve laughed and Alicia elbowed him in the side.

"What about Pakistani actors?" she asked.

"You would not know the Pakistani actors." Rashid shook his head sadly.

"Pakistan does not make many movies. The government does not approve. We are thinking of going to India. They make many movies."

"Yes. Bollywood," grinned Omair.

At that moment, I'd swear the road lit up from the

sparkle in their eyes.

There are three questions you will be asked when travelling through Pakistan. The first question is, "Where you from?" And now, feeling a degree of comfort between us, they asked the second question.

"Have you got any alcohol?" Rashid said quietly.

"No," we lied in unison.

The sparkles died and we walked in relative silence until we arrived at Mirza Khan's abode.

As custom required, the girls were taken into the interior of the house to be with the women and children, and we were led into the Muslim equivalent of the entertaining room. Wall hangings draped the white, earthen walls, and tribal rugs and cushions adorned the floor. A big-screen television, with accompanying video recorder, sat displayed on a cheap shelving unit against the middle of one wall. A small cassette recorder sat meekly next to the television.

"Welcome," said Mirza, his mouth a wide grin. "Make comfortable." He indicated the cushions and then pointed at the television. "Home theatre." He glanced at the other tribesmen and then said to us, "Back soon."

We sat down on the cushions, five tourists, two policeman and two students, eyeing each other nervously. Steve began picking at the rug he sat on, lifting the corner, examining the tightness and number of knots.

"Very good," he said.

They nodded and grinned.

"This is the real thing, mate. No tourist shit here." Steve picked up a cushion, studying the weave and pattern. "How much?"

Rashid laughed. "We pay maybe five dollars US. Tourist, maybe ten, fifteen. Depends."

Brief silence.

"Well," said Bill. He lounged back, stroking his beard. "You guys got any hash?"

My stomach lurched. Steve dropped the cushion. Jeff, Simon and I stared at each other in horror. Passports confiscated. Money drained. Big, blunt cleavers, chopping off hands. Fucked up the arse by sweaty soldiers in the shit-reeking toilets of the Loralai compound.

Rashid glanced at the two remaining policemen. "Do you want some?"

"No," said Simon.

Bill looked at Simon disinterestedly. "Yeah," he said to Rashid. "If you've got some. I heard you guys got pretty good stuff."

"Is very good," said Rashid. He flicked his hand and a policeman stood and left the room. "Some of the best."

"Bill," Steve warned.

"Is okay," Omair said. "We are allowed not much, but this is...gift of Allah."

Bill laughed. "What about alcohol? You got any of that?"

"No," said Rashid.

"We hope you have some," said Omair. "Perhaps whiskey?"

"Nah," said Bill, making himself comfortable on the rug. "You got any beer?"

"Not much beer in Pakistan. Can get Indian beer maybe. You want I get?"

Bill shook his head and began to talk about the beer in India, the beer in Nepal, Australian beer, pubs, beer in pubs. And drugs. The Pakistanis crept closer, fascinated by this weathered, hairy little man, who spoke of things banned in their country.

"This could be bad," whispered Steve.

"No kidding," Simon replied, his six-foot-three frame coiled and ready to spring.

Jeff and I sat in stunned silence, listening to Bill's tales, waiting for God knew what to happen next.

Mirza came back into the room with the policeman who had left. Mirza had changed from his police uniform into a dark blue, *shalwar qamiz*. They both carried large serving trays that contained bowls of *dhal bhat* and unleavened breads. They placed them on the floor and we huddled around, dipping the bread into the thick, spicy soup. Mirza did not eat with us. He stood apart, smiling, resplendent in traditional dress, his eyes continually flicking between the door and his guests.

I couldn't tell if he was happy or nervous. At least the hashish request had been politely ignored. What the Hell was Bill thinking, asking the cops for drugs? I mopped up another mouthful of soup.

"Is good?" Mirza asked.

We nodded.

"Good!" Mirza's smile widened. "I bring mutton curry next. And hashish."

Simon spluttered into his bowl, and Bill yelled "Yeah!" through a mouthful of bread.

"How come Mirza doesn't eat with us?" Steve asked, oblivious to what had just been said. He wiped up his second serving of *dhal bhat* with a pita.

"He will not eat until guests finished," said Rashid.

"Oh," Steve said, his initial onslaught on the meal slowing guiltily. "I see."

He put the bread in his hand back on the tray. Omair tore a chunk off and dipped it into his bowl.

"There is more. He is Mirza Khan. Don't worry."

"Be 'appy." A policeman laughed, soup dripping from his chin.

Steve looked quizzically at me. I knew what he was thinking. I was asking it myself. Just who was Mirza Khan? And how high up the ranks was he?

Mirza returned with a tray, carrying a huge bowl of curry and a mound of steamed rice, and placed it on the floor in front of us. As we dug in, Mirza sat down and produced what appeared to be a large braid of liquorice from the folds of his *shalwar qamiz*. He sliced off a chunk and briefly held a lighter to it. Satisfied it was heated enough to crumble easily, Mirza mixed it with tobacco and rolled a fat spliff. He passed it to Bill and gave him the lighter.

"Thanks, mate." Bill pulled a bit of goat gristle from between his teeth. "Smells good."

The room fell quiet, and I noticed all eyes in dark skin were staring intently at Bill. So were the eyes in white skins. I could have walked over and left the room. No one would have noticed. Walked back to the compound.

Fucked off out of there.

And with a flick of the lighter, Bill pulled us across the threshold, whether we wanted to or not. He dragged deep and exhaled. Mirza grinned slyly, and Omair nodded to Rashid.

Bill dragged again, smoke curling from the end of the spliff. "It's fucking good gear." He passed it to Mirza, who declined. Rashid and Omair also refused. We started to get a very bad feeling. Even Bill's eternal optimism seemed to waver. "What? You...you don't want any?"

Mirza shook his head.

Bill tried to palm the joint off to Steve — easy, swayable Steve. He didn't want a bar of it. Bill tried Simon. I don't know why, I guess he was nervous. Simon hadn't smoked a joint on the whole trip. We suspected him of being a Christian, we'd even accused him, but he denied it. Naturally, he refused the spliff.

"What's wrong?" The smile leaked from Mirza's mouth. "Is good hash, yes? Is best."

"It's good, alright." Bill leaned back, somewhat pale. "Looks like nobody wants it."

"Why aren't you having some, Mirza? Rashid?" I asked.

"You my guests. I cannot. You must go first," said Mirza, visibly stressed.

"Like the food," Steve said, understanding dawning. "Here, giz a go, Bill."

Steve sucked greedily and passed it me. I took a tentative drag, worried the tobacco would rip my throat, but found it pleasantly smooth. I took a deeper toke, inhaling the spicy aroma and passed it on to Jeff.

He took a small hit and then the Pakistani boys devoured the rest of it. All except Mirza, who sat nodding and smiling and watching. Bill was right. It was good. Fucking good.

Too good.

My tongue felt thick and heavy inside my cheeks and the corners of my eyes, along with my temples, buzzed comfortably. I was a little too stoned to talk. Bill lay on his back grinning at the ceiling, his conversation rambled to a stop. Mirza left the room with the empty trays. Luckily, reliable Simon had taken up the reins and had thanked our hosts for the dinner, discussed physiotherapy and had begun edging around the fundamental differences between the Bible and the Koran.

"Safe topics for dining conversation, eh?" I whispered to Jeff, who had been silent and immovable since we arrived. He sat staring at the floor. I wondered if the metal plate in his head — he'd had his head caved in when boxing at university — combined with the strong hash, was fucking him up. I elbowed him. "Jeff?"

"Yeah, sports and sex," he drawled in his Mississippi accent. "Stick to sports and sex."

"What was that?" Rashid said, staring at me. He was frowning. "Who said that?"

"What? Sports and sex?" said Jeff.

"Ah!" Rashid declared, as if he'd caught his best friend sleeping with his mother.

In a flurry of knees and robes, Jeff and I were surrounded by the two students and the policemen. They almost sat on top of us.

"You!" said Omair, his face now dark with blood.

"Him!" Rashid glared at me, jabbing his finger at Jeff.

"What?" I asked nervously. "What's wrong?"

"He," Rashid's finger jabbed again. "He speaks like Bill Clinton."

"He has the same voice," accused Omair.

"What...what the...?" Jeff whispered to me.

Rashid glared at me once more, as if I were the one who led his best friend between his mother's thighs. He turned to Jeff and spoke in measured tones. The voice of a man who had waited years for the opportunity to interrogate the Infidels. The dreaded third question.

"What do you think of American Foreign Policy toward Pakistan?"

"Oh, shit," Jeff moaned. "Mississippi borders Arkansas. Same fucking Southern accent."

"What...do...you...think...of...American...Foreign...Poli cy...toward Pakistan?" Rashid's finger hovered in front of Jeff's face, stabbing every word.

Jeff retreated from the finger, his eyes red and pleading for help. "What?"

"We don't know anything about it," I cut in. "We don't see much about your country at all."

Their heads swivelled, a look of incredulity briefly rising over the anger.

"You don't know?" Rashid said. "You don't know what they have done?"

"About all we get is cricket, mate," I placated.

"He knows," spat Omair, his gaze directed back at Jeff. "He is American."

"Omair!" Mirza stood in the doorway glaring at the students. He barked something sharp in dialect and they backed away from us, eyes downcast.

Once more, the smile spread across his face and he waved a video-cassette in front of us. "Movie! You like to watch?"

And just like that, the mood lightened, the impending conflict — we hoped — forgotten.

We all nodded, relieved, keen to distance ourselves from foreign policies. I was also interested to see what was on offer at the local video shop out here on the edge of the Baluchistan desert. What was a Pakistani movie director allowed to film? Bollywood-style musicals, perhaps?

"This just started in movie theatre in Lahore." Mirza grinned. "And I have copy already!"

The tape started, grainy, lots of hiss. Suddenly the score wobbled distortedly out the speakers, and the opening credits flickered onto the screen.

Rashid and Omair both cooed and clapped their hands.

"I love this movie," said Rashid. "Have you saw it?"

"Yeah, I've seen it," I replied.

"Isn't he wonderful?" said Rashid. "I am wanting to be an actor like him."

"And me," said Omair. The sparkles were back. With brief attempts at political and religious discussions over, the sporting achievements in cricket acknowledged and the hints of sex with Western woman cleverly by-passed, we moved into the greatest unifier of our times — the television. Mirza rolled another huge joint, but did not partake. We laid back and watched the latest, pirated movie to hit the sub-continent: James Cameron's *Titanic*, starring everyone's favourite cunt: Leonardo Di Caprio.

I staggered out of the tent toward the toilet block, as the crew was packing up breakfast and loading the truck. The rich stench of shit assailed my senses and I decided I'd break my bladder on the first piss-stop of the morning's journey. I didn't want to face my imagination in those damp, dark toilets. Instead, I packed up the tent.

Karen gave me a dirty look as I passed up my tent to be stacked on top of the truck. She was still pissed with us guys for taking drugs the night before. They'd been offered, but had refused.

"You're supposed to be representatives of the tour! What sort of example are you setting for these people about us?"

I reckoned she was bitter because we'd gotten into it and they hadn't.

Mirza whipped past in his uniform, clapping hands, smiling. "*Salaam Aliehkum*. Good morning, good morning. See you soon." And then he was gone.

We climbed onto the truck and I took a seat next to Steve. As we pulled out of the compound, flanked by white-toothed smiles and waving, dark- skinned hands, I asked Steve if Chris knew what had happened last night.

"Yeah, the girls spilled their guts. He didn't care."

I nodded. "Cool."

"Yeah, that Mirza's one crazy bastard. He's invited us out to his mother's place for a Muslim breakfast."

"Eh?"

"Some place about five kilometres out of town. What

do you think?"

What did I think? He was a cop we'd accepted drugs from. "I dunno. There's nothing on the truck, is there?"

"Can't remember." Steve scratched the stubble that smothered his face.

"Do you think he's going to fuck us over?"

"What do you mean?" I tried not to think too much about the answers that came to mind. I realised we were following what passed for a police car here on the desert fringes.

Steve just stared at me. "Nothing," he said after a while.

I knew they'd beheaded tourists in Kashmir. People in the wrong place at the wrong time. Did they take hostages in Pakistan?

Mirza's mother's house was a low, flat complex the colour of the desert. I'd guess it was a farm but I couldn't tell what it was they grew or husbanded.

Camels probably.

More importantly, I noticed Mirza's mother had no neighbours. Steve made sure I knew this with a quick statement hinting of imminent betrayal, but then he'd been a paranoid bastard for weeks. His evening hash intake kept that fire fuelled. Once again we were split by sex, the women taken into the interior of the house and the men into the guest rooms. This one was barren compared to last night's. A thin rug spread over the floor and several camel-bags served as cushions. Simple weavings hung on the wall covering alcoves and recesses. A couple of elderly faces poked through the door leading to an interior courtyard, and shortly four other, younger faces peered in. They scattered when Mirza entered, carrying a tray of chai and hard-boiled eggs.

He placed it on the floor.

"Welcome, welcome. This is where I grew up," he said, before leaving the room again.

Simon poured the chai into cups and Steve passed the eggs around. They were still warm.

"Full-on breakfast, eh?"

"Continental breakfast, Muslim-style," I said.

Mirza returned and handed Bill a cheap, plastic, photo album. "Is of me," he said with a puffed chest. "I be back soon."

We huddled around Bill as he turned the first few pages. They were blank. He flicked the pages quickly and discovered that there were indeed some photos in the album. We, being the ignorant bastards we were, had forgotten that not all nations read from top to bottom, front to back.

"He wasn't kidding, was he?" I said. "It is of him. Just him."

The first photo showed Mirza taking a shower from the chest up. He gazed into the camera's lens as water poured down his face, spray cascading off his chest, flexing a bicep dramatically, his fingers running through the black hair sculpted to his skull.

There were five similar photos on the first two pages, one daring enough to show a full length shot, his back toward us, buttocks tensed.

"Maybe he doesn't want the women." Steve prodded

Jeff in the ribs.

"Maybe he wants a fine piece of American "ass". Some tight, Bill Clinton butt."

"Don't joke about it," Jeff said.

The next page showed Mirza in cowboy boots and denim jeans, bare-chested and gleaming in the sun, cresting a desert dune and staring through dark sunglasses. He had shaved his moustache in this series of photos. Another man stood next to him, similarly attired, striking an equally heroic pose.

Mirza in combat gear; Mirza swimming; Mirza disassembling Kalashnikovs, firing weapons; Mirza smiling and laughing; Mirza swirling long, mean blades overhead; Mirza, Mirza, Mirza.

"What the fuck is this?" I asked.

Chris had started laughing. "Does this guy love himself or what?" And, as if Chris' laughter was an infection, we all caught it.

"What's so funny?" Mirza said from the doorway. He had changed from uniform into blue jeans and a white singlet, but it was the automatic pistol he brandished in his hand that choked the laughter in our throats. A boiled egg and a cup of tea didn't seem like much of a last supper.

"Nothing," I said, perhaps too quickly. Mirza's forehead furrowed. I quickly spouted some shite from the movie we had watched last night.

"Ah," he said, unconvinced. The handgun jerked carelessly around the room. The room fell silent for what seemed an eternity, but was less than half a minute. Mirza swallowed. "I have other reason for bringing you here."

Silence. Thick and penetrating, when one can hear Adams-apples grinding up and down in dry throats and the trickle of bladders filling.

"What reason?" Chris asked, taking control. "The tour company knows we're here."

The edges of the room seemed to take on an unreal quality, slightly out of focus. Did he want money? Passports? The women? Our American?

He pointed the gun at Bill. "See the photos?" Mirza then pointed at Simon. "I want with him. He is the biggest."

Good old six-foot-three, country boy Simon. Tall, strong, Christian-like and clean.

"I dunno about this." Simon shook his head, sliding back on his haunches.

"Is for photo!" Mirza stared at our faces and laughed. "You no understand." He knelt down next to us, put the handgun down and flipped through the photos. I saw Steve eyeing up the gun. "See me here. And this? I want to be action star. Movie hero like Arnie or Stallone. This is my...what is the word...polio. Is for Bollywood, yes?"

"Your portfolio?" I could hear the breath exhaling from around the room.

"Yes!" he cried. "My portfolio. And with you here, I get great photos. Me against the West! Such advantage I will have! You no mind?"

We started laughing again, and this time he laughed with us.

"When you came in with the gun," Steve said, "and after last night..."

Mirza smiled and pushed the gun toward Steve. "You have been my guest, you have eaten in my house.

No harm would come to you, *Inshallah*. It is the way of Allah, my friend. Please photos, yes?"

"Jesus," Steve said, removing the clip from the chamber. "It's loaded."

"Is it?" said Mirza. "Forgive me; I am very excited of this."

We went out to the courtyard where the women were waiting. Mirza's family and friends clustered around the walls, cameras and smiles ready. Suddenly in his stride, Mirza assumed a Scorsese-like role, directing positions and cameras and barking orders.

Alicia accepted the handgun and struck poses, holding the gun against Simon. Mirza whirled in the morning light, blades flashed in the sun, guns were cocked, muscles flexed and strained. Sweat was applied from a small bowl to the skin of the warring combatants, and cameras clicked, whirred and popped.

Under a blue sky on the edge of the Baluchistan desert, I watched Mirza begin to realise the first of his dreams. An escape to a better life. A life most of us in the "civilised" West wanted to be a part of, where men and women altered their bodies, lessened their minds and soiled their spirit to achieve fame and fortune, Hollywood-style. Where truth is a world of plastic gossip and entertainment, where role models are shallow, selfish fucked-up puppets that we adore and worship. The new faces of the gods of the Western world presented in all their wide-screen glory in surround sound. Which version of the truth would you like today?

I'm meeting Simon in a café in St Kilda shortly. He's just passing through. I haven't seen him since the tour ended more than three years ago. I want to ask him how he's changed since his travels through what he's learned. I know I've changed. I want to ask him what he thinks of this war on terrorism, the shame of Islam and the scourge of capitalism.

So I take a tram down to meet him, noting the way people avoid each others' eyes, careful not to touch, strangers afraid to speak to strangers, God forbid if someone asks for help, lest they rob and rape and kill each other through an ill-conceived invitation.

But, as I said before, this is just a part of that truth.

Doof Doof Doof

"Please don't take this the wrong way," she murmured, pretending to pick a piece of fluff off his coat, "but I think I'm falling in love with you." She left her hand upon his arm after she finished speaking, stroking him with short, delicate movements.

"You have no idea how long I've waited to hear those words," he said, as blood soared throughout his veins. He swam deep into the green grass of her eyes. The scent of her body, her perfume strong and seductive, her lips soft, red and full, her hair gold and shining in this perfect summer afternoon.

She moved closer, pressing against him, her bosom firm but yielding against his chest. He fought to control and hide his instant reaction.

She smiled shyly, moving her mouth inches from his own and whispered "Would it be too much to ask for a kiss?"

An orchestra of a thousand fluting birds piped into his brain, almost dizzy, blood rushing behind his eyes. "Of course, my beloved Little Red Riding Hood," he replied, bending towards her, preparing finally to taste her tongue, to drink the sweet nectar from her lips.

"Oh, but wait," she said, stepping back from his arms. "Listen. Can you hear it?"

A low doof-doof-doof grew louder and louder, until

the sound surrounded them, overwhelmingly powerful and deafening. Little Red Riding Hood began to dance wildly, throwing her arms and legs around manically, pumping her body to the beat.

Doof-Doof-Doof!

"I love this song!" she said jerking her head up and down. "Sorry Wolfie, gotta dance, ciao!"

"Nnnooooo!!!!" screamed Wolf. "Wait, wait! I'm so close, she loves me, she finally loves—"

Wolf awoke to the ceiling fan above him shuddering to the doof-doof heavy bass of music thudding through the walls of his apartment, the ecstasy of his dream ripped quickly from his head.

His raging hard-on rapidly failed as he glanced despondently towards his alarm clock.

"It's three in the fuckin' mornin'," he growled, climbing out of bed and throwing on a beaten old yellow bathrobe he'd stolen from Papa Bear's place a few months ago. And in case he had to venture out, he whipped on his kippar, and had to adjust the skullcap slightly as it slid upon his bald patch.

He blundered his way towards the kitchen, flicked on the light, grabbed a broom and beat futilely on the ceiling against the bubblegum squeak, chanting soullessly to the thudding beats.

Ooh Baby, boogie baby, yeah yeah yeah,
Everybody, everyone, yeah yeah yeah.

"Turn that shit down!" he screamed, bashing the ceiling with the broom again, this time punching little round holes into the plaster.

Ooh baby, yeah baby, yeah yeah yeah.

Wolf shook his head in despair, eyeing the half-eaten chickens strewn around his lounge floor, the beard of mould that grew stubbornly and silently across his kitchen bench, and his grubby, dishevelled, barely rooted-on double-bed. This wasn't the best place in the world, Hell all it needed was some new wallpaper really and maybe a bit of a clean, but this was what he called home. His fucking home for Christ's sake! And worse, all he could afford if he wanted to live anywhere near Little Red Riding Hood, who had the Penthouse suite in the very same building.

"But I can't fuckin' stalk her if I can't get any fuckin' sleep!" he yelled, pounding the ceiling.

Doof doof doof.

Yeah baby yeah baby.

"Fuck you!" he howled, swinging the broom into the cordless phone set on the wall next to Miss December. It splintered into little black pieces of plastic scattering across the brown and orange chequered lino, as useless in pieces as it was in whole. He'd been disconnected last week for not paying his bill.

Not much satisfaction though.

Doof doof doof.

Not much at all.

He opened the cupboard beneath the sink. Shoving aside some old plates caked in grime, he found a fried egg sporting greenish veins over the yolk. Pleasantly surprised, he peeled it from the congealed fat in the roasting dish and popped it into his mouth and then pulled out his trusty crowbar from behind garbage bags he'd filled and discarded some weeks back.

He felt reassured with the cold weight in his hand. Made of tungsten, too. Heavy duty, twice the cost and worth every cent. He knew where that beat was coming from.

Wolf stormed out of his apartment, slamming the door behind him. He marched up the stairs to the third floor, nostrils flaring, a mistake he soon realised as the stairwell stunk of stale dwarf vomit and piss. Those little bastards must have snuck in through the fire escape door again.

He threw open the third floor entry door and stomped down the hallway towards the noise. People in this building would appreciate this. For sure, this time *he* would be the hero.

Doof doof doof.

This sort of carry-on was unacceptable, especially mid-week. Good God, this racket would even wake Little Red Riding Hood, asleep in her Penthouse suite. Maybe she'd thank him for this later, this heroic deed of his.

Yeah, maybe she would.

Christ, he'd almost kissed her. And then that bloody music had woken him up just as he — just as — it was just too much.

Wolf watched the walls vibrating as he stood outside the guilty apartment. On the wooden door a gold plaque proclaimed to the world "412". Big gold lock. Tiny silver peephole.

He thumped on the door.

Doof doof doof.

He thumped again, trying to thump his thumps

between the drumbeat, but the BPMs were too fast for him.

"Little Pig, Little Pig," Wolf yelled, cracking the crowbar against the door, "Let me come in!"

The music grew louder.

"Right then," he muttered under his breath, and swung the crowbar into the door. This baby would even rip through brick. Special designs for special purposes. He grinned, and swung again.

The door splintered and Wolf laughed, ripping away large strips of wood with the crowbar, his energy high, his blood boiling. And behind the wooden door stood another, a door of thick solid steel.

Cold, hard, unrelenting steel. Impenetrable.

Wolf stood there stunned, as defeat rose in his mind, eroding the anger infused in his limbs. He howled and beat upon the steel door with the last of his strength, steel on steel clanging, bouncing from wall to wall down the hallway, staccato with his sobbing.

Broken, Wolf ceased his hammering and faced the distant stairwell. It's what's always happened, he thought bitterly. To his father, to his grandfather, and to his father before him. An endless cycle of losers, eventually beaten down and whipped.

Suddenly the volume went down. He heard bolts being drawn from behind thick inches of steel. It opened silently, ominously and a high pitched voice squealed from behind it. "Hey guys, I think the pizzas are here."

A savage grin crept across Wolf's visage.

A pig wearing a bright blue shirt thrust his head out the door. His eyes were unfocused, the pupils dilated.

"Hey, you ain't the pizza guy!" said Stupid Pig.

Wolf saw flecks of white powder crystallizing in the snot dripping from Stupid Pig's nostrils. He remembered smashing down Stupid Pig's wire-mesh fly-screen door last year and beating the shit out of him for late night drug parties. Thought he'd fucked off since then.

"Nope, I'm not the pizza guy, but I got something for you anyway," Wolf growled, pushing Stupid Pig back through the doorway and clubbing him around the head with the crowbar.

Stupid Pig fell to the floor, already unconscious, and Wolf put in the boot until blood leaked from Stupid Pig's ears.

Feeling invincible, Wolf strode into the room and stopped speechless, his heart frozen, the scene in the room burned in his brain. His first instinct was to tear them limb from limb, but he knew he couldn't. It wasn't allowed, according to the scriptures.

Little Pig lay grinning, sprawled naked on the rotating king-size four-poster bed. He was handcuffed to the headposts. Little Red Riding Hood, clad only in her satin red cloak, kneeled over him, her head bobbing up and down over Little Pig's groin. Little Pig squealed in delight thrusting upwards, ever upwards.

Fat Pig grunted frantically, thrusting his fat little hips against Little Red Riding Hood's arse as he fucked her from behind. His body was slick with sweat, he looked like he had been at it for a long time.

Wolf could hear Little Red Riding Hood moaning

with every thrust, as Fat Pig porked her, and Wolf threw up over himself and began choking.

"What the fuck?" said Little Pig, noticing Wolf for the first time.

Fat Pig kept pumping.

"Oh sweet Jesus," wept Wolf as he attempted to wipe the spew matting his chest fur. This couldn't be happening, he must still be dreaming. The vomit burning in his nose assured him that he was in fact, wide and horribly awake.

"What you doon here?" slurred Little Pig. "You want some this?"

"Hey, no weird shit," said Little Red Riding Hood, unhinging her jaw from Little Pig's loins. "No inter-racial stuff. That costs extra. And turn that music back up, I love that song."

Wolf watched in horror as his own fingers turned the dial on the stereo back up.

Doof doof doof.

Fat Pig kept pumping, pumping, pumping...

Wolf wandered dejectedly back towards his room. His mind was closing down. Blotting out everything, everyone, his emotions, his feelings, his love, his hatred. There was no point, none at all. She had been his reason to live.

Fuck this. He'd save them the trouble. He'd go the same way as his old man.

Christ, if only pork was *kosher*!

He staggered into his bathroom and filled the

cauldron he'd pinched off the witch in the forest with cold water. He hadn't paid the bills. He found a match and lit the coals beneath the cauldron and climbed on in and waited for it to boil.

It was a stupid way to die he realised, watching the surface of the water ripple with every doof-doof beat.

Where is Brisbane, and How Many Times Do I Get There?

Monday — Buying Explosives and Propellants

I'd been having another bad week at the tax office when I received the phone call. "Hi, Paul, it's me," said a familiar voice. "You downloading porn under someone else's account?"

I killed the remote session to Gary's PC and glanced around the office, expecting to see someone peering over a partition. I maximised a couple of complicated-looking spreadsheets. "That's good. Funny. Who's this?"

"It's me. We don't have much time."

I still couldn't place the voice. "Right..." I stood up from the desk and looked around. People sat tapping at keyboards, yawning into telephone headsets. I still couldn't tell who it was.

"You need to get up to Brisbane. Fast."

"Scott? Is this you?" I sat back down. "You back from England?"

"I'm not your brother," said the voice. "I'm you."

I laughed. "Not bad, mate, not bad; you've got a little too much Aussie twang in the accent though. I'm a Kiwi. Who put you up to this?"

"Listen! We don't have much time! This is like that scene out of *The Matrix*, where you look up and see the boys in black moving towards you, ready to bust your arse."

I spun round in my chair, checking out the room. "No, there's not." And there wasn't. I prepared for the ding of arriving elevators.

"Is today Tuesday?"

"Nah, mate, it's Monday. Come on, who is this?"

"Shit. I've got the wrong time zone. Sorry."

The line went dead.

I hung up, puzzled, stole another glance around the room. There was no Hugo weaving towards me. I wondered if it was some fuckwit under investigation for tax fraud hassling me. Probably, but death threats were more interesting than prank calls. And then there was bribery...

I reconnected to Gary's PC and resumed diverting files. I only had about twenty minutes before he waddled back from lunch and this connection was S.L.O.W.

In the dead hours between lunch and knock-off, I decided to compile a new backdoor key on my computer; I didn't want to run the risk of crashing someone else's machine and encouraging the eye of the network geeks. I minimised the compiler and monitored available memory. If it started to go into a loop, the memory would be the first thing to be sucked up before the machine crashed.

Gary waddled over and propped his arms on the partition, and leant into my desk space. "Got yourself citizenship, yet?" The sweat from his armpits soaked into the fabric lining the partition.

"Nah. Why waste fifteen hundred bucks and become eligible to be fined for not voting?"

"The writing's on the wall, that's why. They picked up several Muslim extremists for violating the anti-sedition laws this morning. Once we've finished clearing out the towelheads," Gary said with a wink, "you Kiwi dole-bludgers will be next to get the boot."

"That'd be discrimination." The available memory on the PC dropped to half. "Shit." I flicked through the open applications, but the system still seemed stable.

"Not if there's evidence," said Gary.

"Yeah? What did they find?"

"Well, nothing...yet. But they will! They're terrorists. Simple facts, my friend, simple facts."

"Jesus, Gary, how fucking dumb are you? The government can plant whatever evidence they want to support whatever these sedition laws need. Those guys aren't terrorists."

Gary pursed his lips, raised his eyebrows and mimicked, "Ooh, those guys aren't terrorists." He leant closer, spittle shining on those fat lips. "Who gives a fuck as long as they're gone? Australia is for Australians!" He straightened and laughed. "Your brother got deported, didn't he?"

"He was framed!" I tried not to bite.

Gary laughed, his eyes lost in the folds of his cheeks. "Yeah, right! Remember, if you become a citizen it's harder to kick you out of the country. Only fifteen hundred bucks. Mind you, there's always a few legal loopholes left in place so we can always get rid of the foreign *citizens* we don't want."

I watched him waddle back to his desk. The stink of his deodorised sweat still clung to the partition. If Gary had been higher up the food chain, I'd think about planting a little evidence on him. Let him have a taste of the new sedition laws and see how much he'd want to stuff into that fat gut of his before he choked. I tried to tab back to my compiler, but the screen had frozen. While I had been soaking up Gary's vibes, the PC had hung, spiralling into a memory loop, eating up all the resources. Rebooting, I found the operating system had fragmented the files I had had open before taking a backup copy. And, of course, the copies were corrupt. I didn't care though, as they were work-related. I had larger fish to fry.

Melbourne is a big place, so after work I took a forty-minute tram ride to Northcote and got off at the northern end of High Street. I walked two blocks south to an internet café I'd heard about, and logged on using the hotmail account of a guy called Charlie I'd met in Wellington a few years ago. I didn't think Charlie used his account anymore, but just in case, I'd set up some spam filters to divert anything from one of my handles into his junk mail folder. I retrieved the files I'd downloaded from Gary's PC and burned them to disk. I then walked down to the station, caught a train to Flinders, changed onto the Williamstown line, got off at Seddon, then walked a distracting fifty minutes instead of the usual fifteen to my flat in Kingsville. Maybe I was being a little paranoid, but it was better to be safe. After all, Melbourne is not that big a place. And I'd never bothered to learn to drive.

My phone rang shortly after midnight, jarring me from dreams of pleasing softness. I lay in the darkness as my phone repeated, "Paul, answer the phone" until the message bank kicked in. People often think it's a family emergency and rush from their beds, but more often than not, it's only the slurred words of a drunk or the silent appraisal of a rogue computer. Or ASIO checking out its taps. I tried to close my mind and lose myself in the softness I'd been pulled from. But those downloaded files intruded on my dreams in all their uncensored, sedition-free glory and I woke in the morning realising I needed a huge pile of shit to cement the evidence.

Tuesday — Explosive Recipes

While waiting for the morning train to the city at Yarraville station, I noticed a man who had been in the internet café the night before. Short mousy hair, a little too tidy looking. I couldn't be sure though, but I'd caught him studying my reflection in the arrival and departure screen. I moved to the other end of the platform, and checked for messages on my phone, trying not to feel insecure or obvious. He took a few tentative steps closer, hoping to get within earshot. I turned my back to him, but soon realised this left me vulnerable. I faced him again, but he stared nonchalantly at the used condoms decorating the tracks.

The first message was from 12:06am. It sounded like me saying, "Just testing, but this should be Tuesday. Paul, you need to...up here...Brisbane, as fast as...fucking batt—"

The second message wasn't even there.

I looked for the mousy haired man, expecting him to be snaffling the airwaves around me, but the train pulled up in a gush of hot, dusty air and people swarmed into the packed carriages.

Was it possible to ring your own phone? And in your sleep? I squeezed between sweat and armpits, braced my legs so I wouldn't fall with the train's motion, tried not to lean into any breasts or groins, and phoned myself. I'd get my message bank, surely. And surely, I didn't.

"You at work yet?" my voice asked from the other end of the phone. "Today *is* Tuesday, right?"

I hung up.

If I'd been on medication, I'd have an explanation for this. The train braked sharply into Footscray and I lost my footing. A woman screamed. I apologised, mumbling something about how my fingers were clean; I'd washed my hands before I'd left home, and that it was I who ran the risk of infection. She still insisted she'd be pressing charges. She took a photo of my fake driver's license with her phone. The week was getting worse

Paul sat in his cell. Outside an electrical storm lashed at the detention centre in which he was imprisoned, but his focus was upon the phone in his hand and the memories, fragmented and fuzzy, slipping in and out of his mind. Only a second ago (had it been seconds, hours?) he had known what he needed to tell the version of himself back in the past, but the clock on the phone looped back faster through the days of the week than his mind could hold. When the clock had indicated Thursday, he had known where not to go, but that memory had become vague, insubstantial. Something about Mr. Browne, something bad. And when the phone had looped back through Wednesday he had known what he needed to buy to bring the seventh file into the world, but now...

Now the clock said Tuesday and he wasn't sure anymore. He made the call and the version of himself in the past answered the phone. "Are you at work yet?" Paul asked. "Today is Tuesday, right?"

The phone cut out, but not before the storm rushed through with a thousand yabbering voices screaming it was them, it was them, it was them.

I was early enough into work to install another rootkit onto a colleague's PC, an elderly woman called Marlene who always had problems with her email. I'd divert some stuff through her account when she logged on later that morning. Gary waddled in and gave me a nod, and I returned a sincere-morning smile. He'd be off for his half-hour morning dump in approximately forty-five minutes. I'd take over his PC and divert some files while he was losing weight. And that got me thinking about that huge pile of shit again.

More specifically, the ammonium nitrate present in that huge pile of shit. I knew a place down by the river in Yarraville that still manufactured fertiliser.

My contractor's pass would still be valid too. When the guard at the security gate asked me whom I was there to visit, I'd divert his call to myself. Perfect.

A call to myself? I laughed. Now that was weird.

Back at my desk, I leafed through a document I'd stored on Gary's home drive. *Almost any city or town of reasonable size has a gun store and a pharmacy.* Interesting stuff, and a useful introduction to buying explosives and propellants. I could seed this on the Commissioner's PC — he was high public profile enough to test the validity of the sedition laws — attach a worm, and then leak it to the media.

My phone rang. It was 10:45am. The number listed as the caller was my own.

"Hello?"

"Paul, it's me and it's Tuesday," said my voice. "We

don't have much time! This is like that scene out of *The Matrix*, where you look up and see the boys in black moving towards you, ready to bust your arse."

I shook my head, cheeks hot. "For fuck's sake! Who is this?"

The elevator bells chimed.

Four security guards marched from the doors and headed towards my section of the office.

"You've got to get out. Now!"

"Who is this?"

"The same guy who managed to suck his own cock for three weeks when he was sixteen! Now fucking move!"

A burst of panic tickled my bowels. Nobody knew about *that*. Nobody. Except me. Oh shit. This really was me.

"How?" I asked. "They'll see me. In fact, they can already see me."

"Just get up and leave. You'll be in temporal displacement for the next five minutes. Reality, for you and me in the space we currently co-inhabit, is in a high flux of distortion. No one in the building can see you. Move!"

That sounded like bullshit, but he knew about the cock-sucking thing. I pulled the power cord out from the back of the PC, then stumbled awkwardly towards the bathrooms at the opposite end of the office, away from the elevators. The guards, puffed chests and shuffling boots, were almost upon me. I strode away, eyes to the floor. I felt the office being sucked past me into a vacuum, a huge roaring sound that mashed my ears. As I went to push the bathroom door it swung in.

"Oh." Marlene adjusted her glasses as she shuffled out the door. "Sorry, Paul, almost didn't see you."

"Eh? You can see me?" Hold on, I thought. Hadn't I told myself I'd be in temporal displacement?

"I'm not so old that I'm blind yet! Ooh, look. I wonder what Gary's done." Marlene pointed a gnarled finger over my shoulder. "He's being marched from the premises."

I stared after the protesting Gary, then at my phone.

"He's probably been downloading pornography again," said Marlene.

"Are you still there?" I asked my phone.

"Not for much longer. I'm in Brisbane," my voice replied. "I've been arrested for writing a story about terrorism. I'll explain every...need to...quick...fucking batt—"

"Yes." Marlene stared at me with her ancient, faded blue eyes. "Loves his cum shots, does young Gary, the dirty, fat fuck."

I left the building and headed to Douglas Braid Park — a small patch of dead grass containing a couple of peeling, painted iron seats, nestled between a tram track and a four-lane intersection. Douglas Braid, whoever the man had been, would be proud.

I called my phone.

"Do you have a landline I can call you on?" I asked.

"No, if you rang on one I wouldn't be here. It's not part of the displacement."

"I don't understand. We can ring each other on the mobile—"

"If I were to give you a number to ring, you'd be calling me in your time zone — Tuesday. I'm actually in the Sunday coming. So is this mobile."

"Look, I'm not sure how you can be me, it doesn't make sense, but how could you know—"

"Because I am you! Listen, the battery is going to die again soon. Bloody loop I'm in keeps cycling through the power supply. I've been...*you've* been downloading a series of files through colleagues' computers that make up the *Terrorist Handbook*. You've got six files so far, but you haven't found the seventh."

"There's only six. Hey, how'd you know I was—?"

"Shut up and listen. I'm you, right? You can only find six on the net, but there is a seventh file. It talks about assembling cloaking devices, barrier shields, and temporal displacement fields, that sort of thing, using inexpensive commodities you can buy at the pharmacy. You need to get this file!"

A man sat down on the opposite park seat. He pretended not to look at me while he ate a sandwich. He had mousy hair and was tidy looking. Different coloured shirt, but any moron would think of that.

"I'm being followed. Is it ASIO?"

"You're just a little more paranoid than normal. You need to get the seventh file."

"I'm not paranoid."

"Yes, you are. I'm not sure exactly how this works, but because I'm up here in Brisbane...new centre of cultural...like when Melbourne stole Adelaide's Grand Prix...temporal split...fuck—"

The man teethed a smile full of sandwich. I pretended to return the smile and hurried back to the office, ducking through Book City and slipping in and out of a busy café so he couldn't follow me.

Marlene, loitering in the tearooms, called out as I walked towards my desk. "Oh, Paul, there you are." She adjusted her glasses and sipped at her steaming cup. "Gary. Kiddy fiddler photos."

I nodded, surprised. I hadn't put them there.

Back at my desk, I booted the PC, and logged on. Book City reminded me of something the other me had said. I called my phone.

"You took your time," my voice said. "When I start to cut out, call me back straight away."

"I'm not writing anything about terrorism."

"You are. Or you're about to."

"No, I'm not. I'm an activist. I'm doing something about these sedition laws. Framing the big guys with the same stuff they're framing anyone they want to shut up with."

"No, you're not, you're writing about it."

I felt my cheeks begin to slow burn. This guy was starting to piss me off. I restored a hidden worm and attached the first three sections of the *Terrorist Handbook*. I'd show him who was real about what they were doing.

"Listen to me! I'm an activist—"

"If you don't get that seventh file by the end of tomorrow, you're going to be executed for treason."

"This is Australia. That'd be un-Australian!"

"A new state law will be passed this Friday, applicable to Queensland, Western Australia, and the Northern Territory. The illegal immigrant borders."

"No one would agree to that."

The other me laughed. "Why would that stop the government? You need to secure the seventh file, build a temporal displacement field Mark III, and get to Brisbane before Sunday."

"Or what?"

"We die."

"I don't think so. If I don't go to Brisbane, I can't get arrested. If I don't get arrested, I can't get executed."

"I die; you die."

This time I laughed. "I don't think so." I inserted the worm into the network, modified the Commissioner's email rules and deleted my audit trail.

Now I just had to get the fertiliser sent to his home address and whammo!

One down, one government to go.

"I was arrested in Melbourne, idiot. You think I came to Brisbane on my own volition? This place is teeming with rednecks. A cultural bloody backwater! You haven't sent that worm yet, have you, Paul?"

"Uh, maybe...why?"

"That's what gets you arrested. Don't...they'll...batt—"

Somewhere alarm bells were ringing. I hoped they were just in my head.

Around the office, perched at desks in front of grimy keyboards and dusty monitors, several people with mousy hair pretended to be busy.

I left work early and took a taxi to the city, got off at Collins Street and took the tram loop to Spencer, then took another taxi home, peering out the rear window just in case. Things didn't add up. How could I have been arrested for writing about terrorism if I hadn't written anything yet? I was merely distributing information. Proving a point. The taxi driver ranted in the rear view mirror, punctuating everything with a "fuck".

"Just close the fucken borders, mate, or else." He turned to face me, one hand resting on the passenger seat, the other waving thick fingers in my face. "I'm European, mate, Mediterranean an I got fucken the blood. If something happens fuck I tell ya, mate. We don't mix, mate." He turned back to the road, swung the steering wheel to avoid a tram, then fixed me with another rear view mirror stare. "They come here with their fucken traditions an' that, mate. I tell you, fucken leave it at home if they want to come here! This country is for us, mate. For Aussies, mate!"

I nodded and called my phone.

"I haven't written anything — how can I be arrested for that?"

"This is the thing, see? The closer it gets in time to Sunday and in space to Brisbane, the more aligned we become. At the moment you think you're an activist, but by the time you get up here, you won't be!"

"What? I'll be a writer about to be executed for voicing his opinions?"

"Yes! Well, uh, no, no, we won't be executed, we'll be, um...freed! Have you got the seventh file yet?"

"What seventh file? What's it called? Can I Google it?"

"No, it's not on the internet. How much longer before it's Wednesday?"

"About another nine hours. What the Hell has that

got to do with anything?"

"Well, at the moment there's the good me stuck up here in Brisbane, and the paranoid you down there in Melbourne. Coincidentally, I think that also mirrors the psyche of each city, and that could be having an effect on us due to the temporal displacement. And in this space-time between us, there's another chunk of you and me still floating about looking for a brain to cement memories into."

"What's that got to do with Wednesday?"

"Exactly! On Wednesday we'll both know more. Batteries about—"

And I was gone again.

"If they have a European passport then let them in. If not, then fuck them off back to their own country!" said the driver. "You know what I mean? You know?"

"I'm a Kiwi. What about me?"

He thrust his hand into the air. "Ah, for fucken! That's European! New Zealand, Australian, Greek, France, England, Italy. We're all European." He glared at me in the rear view mirror again. "Look at the face! Look at the eyes!"

"People can forge passports, even European passports," I said.

He screwed up his face and shook his head, while making a sheeshing sound. "I don't think so, mate."

I needed to find that seventh file.

"Fucking idiot," the driver muttered, as I got out of the cab.

I spent the evening browsing the net, lurking in chat rooms, hacking into bulletin boards, even tuning into the Citizen Band frequencies, but there was nothing about a seventh file. I assembled the six existing files into a complete document. The contents page matched the contents. Numbers equalled numbers. Nothing missing. The other me was full of shit. The other me was paranoid. I went to bed shortly before midnight, knocking back a couple of glasses of cask red wine to help me sleep.

I woke shortly before 1:00am. I needed to buy a Blackberry. My phone rang. It was me.

"You need to buy a Blackberry. Get hold of as much cash as you can. Buy a ticket to Brisbane today. Don't use your credit cards."

But I already knew that much. Our memories were coalescing.

Wednesday had arrived.

Wednesday — Using Explosives

By midday I'd purchased and activated my Blackberry. There were too many buttons and the English section was missing from the manual.

I rang me, using the mobile not the Blackberry. "I've got a Blackberry. You know how to use it?"

"Not yet."

"I can't find the seventh file."

"You won't need to."

"But you said—"

"I know what I said. Time is rapidly cycling backwards up here. Things I remember get fragmented and sometimes when we speak the day changes and so does my memory. The file will find you. Have you bought a ticket yet?"

"Just about to."

I hung up and walked into the travel agent, where I was ushered into an uncomfortable chair to stare at posters of the Colosseum, the Parthenon, Big Ben, the Eiffel Tower and the Statue of Liberty. My travel representative wasn't the young, smiling, sexy thing they advertised on television, either. She was a slightly anorexic man in his early twenties. A shiny badge indicated I could call him Cameron.

"I'd like a ticket to Brisbane, for anytime today."

"Certainly, sir." Cameron smiled, tapped the keyboard, frowned, smiled and tapped again. "I'm sorry, sir, there are no available flights to Brisbane today."

"What about standby?"

"Sorry, sir, you misunderstood. There aren't any flights going to Brisbane today."

"What about tomorrow then?"

"Nope, nothing then either."

"How can that be? It's the capital of Queensland. There must be dozens of flights daily."

Cameron tapped, frowned, tapped. "Very strange, this. There are no flights until next Monday. Would you like me to book you onto one of those?"

"I have to be there before Sunday. What about to the Gold Coast? Ballina? Or maybe one to Sydney and then to Brisbane?"

Cameron tried not to roll his eyes. "I've already checked those options, sir. There are no flights whatsoever going to Brisbane, from any airline, from anywhere in Australia. If you'd like to wait, perhaps I can find out why."

"What about via Auckland? Or Wellington? Suva?"

Cameron smiled politely, tilted his head slightly, and batted his eyelashes. "That would be quite expensive, sir. You must be desperate. Would you like me to check?"

My Blackberry vibrated. "Please."

An email came through with a massive amount of text pasted into the body. The subject was entitled "The Seventh File". The sender: me.

"I'm sorry, sir," said Cameron. "There's a note here saying all flights into Queensland south of Cairns have been disrupted due to severe storm warnings. These are expected to pass by late Sunday evening."

I noticed, then, that Cameron had mousy hair. Cut short and tipped to disguise that fact no doubt, but mousy nonetheless.

Paul sat in the cell, looping through time, while the world moved on.

He knew what he had to say to the Wednesday him, before the Thursday memories fragmented into a fritter of frustration. He made the call, the only number on the phone that worked.

"I've just remembered," Paul said. "Stay away from Mr. Browne. I got busted after visiting him. He's dirty." But he was too late, as the sound of an old Love and Rockets tune, *The Bubblemen Are Coming*, burst through from the other end of the phone.

The battery strength was almost gone. The clock ticked back to Wednesday.

🐈

I took a tram to the city, got off at Collins Street, walked a block to Bourke, then headed east and took a dank alleyway into Chinatown. Mousy hairs would stand out in this part of town, and I couldn't see any anywhere.

Above the Phuc Lan Tran restaurant existed a discreet internet cafe. I browsed for flights online, unsure how I'd pay by cash, but it only confirmed that dear sweet Cameron hadn't been lying to me. There were no flights to Queensland. Even northern New South Wales was a no fly zone. I bought up a meteorological forecast displaying a thick bruise of weather smothering the north-eastern coast of the country. I checked the news headlines. Big storm warnings. New sedition laws passed in the northern states. Capital punishment approved. Riots in the border towns. Police-enforced curfews.

My phone rang.

For a second, the line echoed with hundreds of different voices stuttering "...meitsmeitsm..." though the crackle of an electrical storm before collapsing into my voice. "The file come through?"

"Yeah, but I can't get a flight to Brisbane. Weather's gone crazy."

"Take an overnight train. Charter a plane. Kidnap someone. Hire a fucking car! Just get up here."

"I can't drive a car!"

"What? But I can. How can you be different?"

"How can you even be calling me! More importantly, if I did get up there, they're talking of closing the borders due to rioting over the new sedition laws. What if they close them?"

"Uh, look, I dunno. I don't think they did, but I'm not sure. How long until Thursday? I'll know when it's Thursday."

"Thursday! That's cutting it short! How long does it take to drive up? How'd you get up there if there are no flights?"

"Good point. I came up in an armoured bus, chained to the seat. There was a pretty cool Arab guy. Probably how I got past the border problem."

"So what are you saying? I've got to get arrested now as that's the only way I'm getting to Brisbane? And then I'll be executed. Like you? You should have just left me alone and it would have happened anyway."

"But you wouldn't have a *temporal displacement field* because you didn't have the seventh file!"

"You've already built the temporal displacement field, you idiot, and you're using it. It would happen."

"Ah, see, that's where you're wrong. I didn't build it. You do."

"That makes no sense at all! Then how can you be using it?"

My phone cut out, as a man with mousy hair walked into the café and took an unoccupied seat. He stared at me, through me, for a second, then fiddled with his mouse.

I couldn't risk examining the seventh file here. The screen was too small to read it on the Blackberry and I needed to get a print out. Somewhere safe, somewhere close to home — Mr. Browne's. He knew how to drive, too.

Mr. Browne squatted in a derelict warehouse near the wharves at Spotswood. He'd successfully diverted all necessary utilities from the local grids and if anywhere was going to be safe, it would be here. Unless someone knew I came here to dissent every couple of months, but I buried that deep in a part of the brain I didn't like to use anymore.

Mr. Browne, resplendent in an orange kaftan, opened the grill to his home. Incense wafted out, something pungent and too sweet, most likely to cover the stink of what he claimed was cat piss.

"Paul? Geez, man, what are you doing, uh, no, I mean, ah, nice to see you, come in, come in."

I followed him into the section of the warehouse he called The Studio, where a table, piled with screens, circuit boards and wires, leant haphazardly against a wall. He sank into a beaten leather cavity he referred to as The Chair, and bid me sit on its arm. He removed his *Lennons* to clean them with the sleeve of his kaftan.

"Not sure about your new look, man." Mr. Browne perched the *Lennons* back on his nose. "Makes you look a little straight."

I frowned. "Huh? I'm in my work clothes."

"Hey, whatever," he said. "What can I do you for?"

I handed him my Blackberry. "You know how to use one of these?"

Mr. Browne chuckled softly, running his fingers through his goatee.

"Everyone's got one of these. This is tiny — is it the latest model? I'll give you fifty bucks."

"It's mine; I'm not selling it. Can you print out an email for me? Secure cable, no outside connections."

"Sure." Mr. Browne fiddled with a stack of wires nesting on the table within arm's reach. "You could've done this at home."

"I think ASIO are on to me."

Mr. Browne leapt out of The Chair faster than his imaginary cats. He flicked through a series of CCTV cameras stationed around his warehouse.

"You got a nerve coming here."

"No one knows I'm here! I was careful. The *Terrorist Handbook* has seven files, not six. On that baby is the magic seventh."

"There's only six. Got a copy if you want it."

"I gave you that copy. Print out the email, see for yourself."

"Sure."

A printer whirred to life somewhere nearby.

"How long to drive to Brisbane?" I asked.

"Two days hard, one day with two drivers. You want some chai? Special chai?"

I nodded. Mr. Browne disappeared behind a tumble of pre-1980 IBM servers into the section of the room where hot water dripped. I hunted down the printer and leafed through the first few pages of a chapter entitled 'Defensive Strategies and Escape Plans'. It resembled the rest of the *Terrorist Handbook* — badly formatted and hard to read in some comic/Arabic half-breed font. The contents page listed sections on how to shop for and build cloaking barriers, polarity reversers, light-sabres, FTL drives, hangover pills, ansibles, sea monkeys, replicators, x-ray glasses, and — thank Christ, because the list was getting long — temporal displacement fields. Marks I, II, II, IV and IV.

"Where is three?" I yelled.

Mr. Browne emerged, chewing on a fat, homemade cigar with two cups of chai steaming in his hands. "Take it easy. Here, get your chops around this." He placed a cup near the printer.

I thrust the contents page in his face. "Fucking terrorists! Error prone, unreliable, non-proofreading, mother fucking bastards!"

Mr. Browne managed to sip a mouthful of chai past the smouldering cigar lodged between his teeth. "Interesting." He held the page up to the light. "I've never seen this font before. My printer's a dot matrix, *it can't have* printed this. This font isn't installed." He handed me back the page, sucked big on the cigar, and exhaled blue smoke. "What is it? And from where?"

"From...um...you're not going to believe this."

Easing himself into The Chair, Mr. Browne tapped The Arm. I perched and over several cups of chai told him about my last few days. Mr. Browne smiled and nodded a lot, muttered "interesting" in all the right pauses, then passed out. Not surprisingly, he'd laced the chai with a tad too much hashish.

I followed suit shortly after.

Thursday — Special Ammunition
for Projectile Weapons

I awoke in the glow of multiple monitors. Mr. Browne snored softly in The Chair.

My phone rang. Me.

Mr. Browne jerked awake as I answered, his eyes wide behind the lenses of his *Lennons*.

"I've just remembered," my voice said. "Stay away from Mr. Browne. I got busted after visiting him. He's dirty."

I made eye contact with Mr. Browne. His face was expressionless, stone. He'd heard my voice on the other end of the line. He knew. And I knew.

"Dirty in a clean way?" I asked.

"Look at the colour of his beard."

Mr. Browne tried to cover it with his hand, but not before I saw the mousy colour.

"Who's that?" He asked, almost calmly.

Red lights flashed around the warehouse interior. An old Love and Rockets tune, *The Bubblemen Are Coming*, began to play.

I grabbed at the sheaf of paper making up the seventh file, while Mr. Browne channelled through the CCTV screens.

"I knew you weren't that smart," he said through clenched teeth. "You were followed!"

"I never thought they'd get to you." Where the Hell was my Blackberry? Had he already secreted it away?

A sudden tearing of metal, and the grill and roller door at the entrance of the warehouse buckled in. Bolts ripped from the wall. The door shrieked across the concrete in a shower of sparks. The lights went out. The power cut. A massive spotlight turned its eye on us, freezing us in its glare. "Don't move and you won't be hurt," barked a loud-speaker voice.

And somewhere further away, a distant, tinny sound: "Swallow your phone!"

I lifted the phone towards my face, the voice getting louder.

"Swallow your fucking phone!"

Boots stomped. Police strobes strobed.

Behind me, Mr. Browne stumbled into the IBM servers. They crashed down around him as he yelped, scrabbling along on what sounded like his hands and knees. The smell of piss was strong.

I wouldn't be able to swallow the phone. It was too big.

Somewhere, behind the spotlights: "Tear gas the cunts."

I pushed the phone into my mouth. It fitted nicely, about as thick and wide as my tongue and maybe half the length. It tasted salty.

Canisters clattered, followed by a hissing sound.

"Hit them if you want," said the spotlight.

I tried to swallow, but the phone was going nowhere. And I hadn't even seen the ingredients for any of the temporal displacement fields.

A black silhouette appeared in front of the spotlight.

"This one's mine," it said.

Something cracked my head, filling it with an extremely bright light that snuffed out even faster.

And that was Thursday.

Friday — Rockets and Cannons

I felt nauseous; my head ached and, disquietingly, so did my rectum.

I sat chained to the rails of the seat in front of me, as the armoured bus roared along the highway delivering me to, I presumed, Brisbane. The windows had been sealed and painted black, though air-con kept the interior cool. Two cops sat up the front. Besides myself, six other men were in the back enjoying the ride. Four of them were of Middle Eastern descent, one was Mr. Browne, and the other was the armed police escort. They all stared at a plasma screen playing *Red Dawn*, mounted at the front of the bus. A young Patrick Swayze, teary eyed and AK-47 wielding, was saying goodbye to his father.

I retched.

One of the men turned to me. He smiled, his teeth white in a forest of black beard. "*As-Salaam Aleikum*. The sleeper awakes. I am called Azam."

The remaining Middle Eastern men turned to look at me, each breaking out into broad smiles. Mr. Browne and the cop didn't budge, absorbed in Charlie Sheen letting a few shells loose at the commies storming the school.

I retched again.

"We have been waiting for you," said Azam. "You've only missed *Pearl Harbour* and *Armageddon*, so far. That Ben Asslick is a wonderful talent!"

I regurgitated my phone into my lap. The clock read 22:45.

"Coming up is *Independence Day*. That Will Smith is a

wonderful talent," said Azam. "Ah, you have the phone."

"*Inshallah*," whispered the other men.

"Guys! Guys!" The cop gesticulated excitedly at the screen. "You gotta see this bit. Cool!"

Both Charlie and Patrick, grinning with manicured pearly whites, were letting loose a few shells at a Russian helicopter.

How the Hell was I going to use my phone?

Azam removed his handcuffs and plucked an aluminium-can lockpick from the depths of his beard. He leant over the aisle and picked the lock on my cuffs. He hid the lockpick back in his beard and slipped his handcuffs back on. "Please, make the calls, but don't let him know you are free."

I pointed to his beard then the cuffs. "You made that? From the *Terrorist Handbook*?"

Azam shook his head sadly. "Ah, yes. The government planted that on my computer. Luckily, it was of some use before they decided to eradicate me to Brisbane."

"You mean extradite."

Azam laughed softly. "No."

The cop woohooed as the screen filled with explosions. "See? See?" He thrust his fingers at us. "That's what you boys got coming!"

Azam smiled at me. "But he doesn't know that we have you."

"*Inshallah!*"

Mr. Browne stared at me, his face full of hate. "He's no hero. He's just a wanker." Then he reburied himself in the glory of *Red Dawn*.

"Where's my Blackberry, then?" I asked.

Mr. Browne scowled, but kept his face fixed towards the screen.

"Do you know of the seventh file, Azam?"

Azam smiled and nodded. "No. There are only six."

"No, no, there's sev— look it doesn't matter. Do you know how to build a temporal displacement device? A Mark III?"

"Why, you, Mr. Haines, are just that device."

"*Inshallah!*"

"No, he's not. He's a wanker."

"Me? How?"

"Everyone knows this." Azam chuckled again. "It is just the beginning."

"*Inshallah!*"

"I don't understand."

"The world is an apple, my friend. And when the apple with the perfect skin and colour has a rotten core, then it is up to the worm to reveal the truth of that apple."

Apples? I shook my head in dismay. "What does that mean?"

"We are all worms in the eyes of God, Mr. Haines." Azam pointed at the screen. "Oh, look, *The Sands of Iwo Jima*. I love this film. That John Wayne is a wonderful talent."

I discreetly used my phone.

"Where have you been? I've been trying to get hold of you for hours! At least, I think it's been hours. Time's a bit screwed up."

"The good news is I'm on my way to Brisbane," I said. "The bad news is—"

"—you're in the divvy van under arrest. You're not too good at this, are you?" My voiced sighed on the other end of the line. "I guess we're on track, though. Did you build the temporal displacement device?"

On screen, John Wayne forced himself onto the token woman in the film, who struggled at first, but then gave in passionately to his kisses.

"No."

"Jesus, if you want a job done properly you have to do—"

"For a guy who should know all the answers, you haven't been too shit hot yourself."

"Listen. The other prisoner will help you; he helped me."

"Which prisoner? One of the four Arabic-looking guys or Mr. Browne?"

"Nah, there's only one Arab — Mr. Browne? What? He wasn't there when I came up. It's Friday, right? Four Arabs? Something's different."

"That's a good sign, yeah? It means we're making a difference. We're going to change our immediate future, right?"

"I can't hear you," my voice said. "You're breaking up."

The bus rocked sideways for a second as a gust of wind buffeted against it. Thunder roared above the sound of on-screen machine guns. Real thunder. Rain hammered at the metal, drowning out anything the movie produced.

"Oh, shit." I said. "We must be in northern New South Wales or nearing the Queensland border."

"Are you there? Hello? You keep breaking up.

Ar...f...batt—"

The plasma screen blacked out.

"Aw, for fuck's sake," whined the cop. "Now what are we gonna do for the next six hours?"

The bus slowed to a calculated crawl as the storm battered against us, the rain an incessant thundering tattoo that made it impossible to talk and pounded coherent thought from the skull. And, somehow, through all that noise, I heard a word from near the front of the bus.

"Wanker."

I think Mr. Browne was screaming it.

Saturday — Pyrotechnica Errata

Saturday rolled over and the bus rolled on through the storm. We stopped before dawn at a Police-owned McDonald's in a pokey town called Murwillumbah just south of the Queensland border. Normally that would mean we'd be in Brisbane in an hour or so, but as the lightning flicked the countryside and the gales thrashed the palm trees, I wasn't sure we'd get there by evening. The telecom towers near the restaurant sparked and sizzled, providing entertainment not dissimilar from the on-board movies.

Mr. Browne munched at a McOz on the opposite side of the table. He refused to make eye contact. Azam and his friends were hiding utensils in their beards while the cops sat around smoking, doing lines and drinking Coke. I offered Mr. Browne my share of lukewarm chips. He took a handful.

One eye regarded me for a split second before

focusing back on escaping the maze on the Happy Meal fun page.

"The fact that we're both in this position means we're both innocent," I said.

"You set me up," Mr. Browne mumbled between a slab of beetroot and sugared bun. "You could still be setting me up."

Hoping the towers would do their job, I handed him my phone. "Call me."

Reluctantly, he did so.

"It's picking up interference from the storm. Sounds like hundreds of voices...oh, hold on, I'm through. No, it's Mr. Browne here...you set me up...no, no, well, maybe...yeah, I thought it was good...what's that? Nah...I've never heard of a temporal displacement field. Where'd you get the seventh—?"

He handed me back the phone. "It cut out." He grabbed some more chips and shovelled them into his mouth. "Maybe I believe you."

"I need to figure out how to make that field before we get to Brisbane."

"Or what?"

"Or...the world will end. Or something like that."

Mr. Browne chuckled through his chewed burger. "I think maybe you will end."

"Do you know why they're sending us to Brisbane, Mr. Browne?"

"To try to execute us for sedition, treason, terrorism, growing beards, whatever. Of course, I know. I'm smarter than you."

"Well, then, you're going to die too!"

Mr. Browne put down his burger, removed his

Lennons, and polished the lenses. "I don't think so, Mr. Haines. There's a loophole in the legislation and I intend on exploiting it."

"But the me already in tomorrow's Brisbane is going to be executed!"

Mr. Browne adjusted his *Lennons.* "Like I said, I'm smarter than you."

Chuckling, he flicked a piece of gristle from his patty at me. "Dead meat."

Loophole? Could that explain the me in tomorrow? Could time be so easily confused?

Sunday — Useful Pyrochemistry

The cops managed to fix the plasma screen and commenced showing *Air Force One.*

We were nearing the detention centre set up at Griffith University, high up on the hill, and prone to lightning strike.

Azam and his friends prayed loudly. Mr. Browne pretended to sleep.

The cop kept woohooing explosions, gunshots and punches. I felt sick, my head was spinning, and my prison uniform clung to my skin. The battery power on my phone was playing up, cycling between full and empty. The storm had even strengthened in its ferocity.

I was going to die. And for nothing. I blamed it on the other me, the one with the knowledge of the future, knowing the mistakes for me not to make. He was useless!

The bus braked to a halt. The doors whooshed open and cops jackbooted inside, truncheons ready.

"Good luck," said Azam, his beard thick and radiant, full of hidden treasures.

"*Inshallah!*"

The only beard I had was a pubic one, so I slipped the phone down into my pants, hoping we weren't searched again. We were dragged out into the pelting rain. The wind tore at my legs and I staggered, pulled along by the chains of the man in front. The air sizzled and spat, the stink of ozone rippling from slashes in the sky. A squat brick building loomed ahead, surrounded by battered, foaming gum trees, and, as we approached, a bolt struck the corrugated iron roof in a brief cascade of sparks.

Inside that building was the other me.

Thunder boomed, the ground trembling beneath, around, over, shuddering through my intestines and roti-ed my brain into a thin, unleavened layer of fear.

I stopped, pulling hard on the chains, slowing the men in front.

"Keep moving, slaphead." The cop raised his truncheon. "Ya know I'd hate to have to hit ya."

"I can't go in there! If I do, we'll all die. The universe will end!"

The cop laughed and tapped me gently enough on the nose to make my eyes water. "Really?"

"Yes. You're not going to believe this, but I'm already inside the building trapped in a tempor — ungh!"

He smashed the truncheon across the side of my head. An eardrum burst, and the hollows of my skull filled with a roaring static.

"You're right. I'm not going to believe you," said the cop. "Get moving, cunt."

And I stumbled forward, dragged by the chains and pulled by something more inevitable than gravity.

Destiny.

I realised, at some point between being forced down that long humid hallway lined with cell doors and being forced through one of them, I had started screaming. And doing a little bit of wee in my pants.

Destiny indeed.

Expecting a sudden sucking infinite implosion, I was surprised to find myself, mobile phone in hand, sitting calmly in the middle of a hard single bed watching me enter the room in a flurry of tears and jabbing truncheons.

And everybody vanished, leaving only me.

I could no longer hear the storm outside. Silence.

"This hasn't quite worked," my mouth moved and my voice said. "I think the storm is part of the problem. We might be causing it."

"Am I inside me?" I asked.

"Did you make a Temporal Displacement Field Mark III?"

"I don't think so. I was told that I am the Temporal Displacement field."

"Is there only two of us in here? In this body?"

"I think so...bloody loopholes. Do you think that means...?"

"Yes, we need three of us for a Mark III field. Or at least three..."

My head hurt.

I stared at the ebbing battery power on the phone. The clock settings cycled rapidly though the hours of each day. It flicked over to last Monday.

Something not quite right here. Too many people on the bus. No, not enough people. Shouldn't I, no, we, know more now we were united? Aaagh! I'd been hit on the side of the head, muddling things up.

I was supposed to ring someone. Who? I brought up the last person called. I laughed. I laughed. It was me. I was supposed to call and warn me to get up here, to get to Brisbane. I pressed send. Send. The worm had turned.

Send. I heard my voice on the other end of the line pick up. "Hello?"

"Paul, it's me," I said.

What day was it?

Everybody, every day, all day —
Defensive Strategies and Escape Plans

I'd been having another bad week at the tax office when I received the phone call. "Hi, it's me," said a familiar, elderly woman's voice. "You downloading cum shots under someone else's account?"

I killed the remote session to Gary's PC and glanced around the office, expecting to see someone peering over a partition. The arthritis flared in my knuckles.

Paul walked past on the way to his desk, smiling his vapid-mousy-haired smile. I gave him my best little-old-lady smile in return, before sitting back down.

"How'd you know that?" I whispered.

"Because, Marlene, I'm you! Now listen..."

Traffic was bad for a Tuesday. And this conversation was getting worse.

"I'm a Kiwi. What about me?" asked the suit with mousy hair from the backseat of my cab.

I thrust my hand into the air. "Ah, for fucken! That's European. New Zealand, Australian, Greek, France, England. We're all European." I glared at him in the rear view mirror again. "Look at the face! Look at the eyes!"

"People can forge passports, even European passports."

I shook my head sadly. When would these dopey fucks learn? "I don't think so, mate."

When he got out of the cab I called him a fucken idiot, just loud enough for him to not be sure I said it. As I pulled back out into the traffic, my phone rang...

I got off at Kensington station, still furious that sleaze with the mousy hair had groped me when the train braked. That was fucking sexual assault! I'd fuck with him first before I pressed charges though. I flipped through the photos on my phone, pausing at the one of his driver's license. This would be useful. Good resolution too. A guy in Delhi I knew could use this to help me out. Maybe take a little money from this sleaze's account. Cancel a few services he might be using. Put a warning on his passport.

Then my phone rang. "Hi, it's me..."

"What about via Auckland? Or Wellington? Suva?" said the man with mousy hair.

I smiled politely. "That would be quite expensive, sir. You must be desperate. Would you like me to check?"

"Please."

This was weird. It had to be a problem with the computers. "I'm sorry, sir. There's a note here saying all flights into Queensland have been disrupted due to severe storm warnings. These are expected to pass by late Sunday evening."

The man stared at me for a second, his face paling, before he shot out of his chair and ran for the exit.

My phone rang. "Cameron?"

I took another sip of chai as Paul blathered about his latest dull idea for a novel. He'd cut and dyed his hair into a tidy mousy look. Like an ASIO twat. Ooh, that chai! A bit too much hashish. Even for me.

Paul's voice slurred and his eyes drooped as he talked about some imaginary seventh file on his, sorry, my new Blackberry. I chuckled when he finally slumped from The Arm of The Chair and collapsed in a contented huddle at my feet. Too easy. I withdrew the Blackberry from the folds of my kaftan and it immediately rang.

I flicked uneasily through the CCTV as I answered the Blackberry.

"Adam? It's me," said a familiar voice.

I was known as Mr. Browne. No one called me Adam anymore. No one except ...myself.

"You've got to get to Brisbane, fast."

Slice of Life — A Spot of Liver

Outside, at the letterbox, I hear screaming coming from inside my house. Granted it's muffled, but I shouldn't be hearing a thing.

"Not good, not good," I mutter to myself.

I pull a couple of bank statements from the letterbox, and wander back up the path towards the front door. I hear another scream.

The first letter from the bank is advising me they will be raising the interest rate on my mortgage by a quarter of a percent. So much for the Reserve Bank. They held interest rates this month. What fucking use are they then, if the banks simply ignore them? The second letter is from the bank advising me they will be raising the interest rate by a quarter of a percent. I guess they need to, seeing they're doing twice as much work as they should be. Useless cunts. It's eating up my pay rise though, pushing me a little closer to the borderline than I'd like to be.

I toss the statements on the couch and wander over to the cellar door. Smarmy, the former real-estate agent once named Mark, seems to have quietened down. I can't hear a thing. I think about getting the keys, unlocking the first door, then opening the tumblers, having a quick peek inside, but I don't want to surprise the poor bastard or let him harbour any false hopes.

And I've already fed him his breakfast. The once-fat motherfucker is shedding the kilos nicely.

I've got plans for this sorry morsel of a man.

The human liver is an amazing organ. It is both the largest internal organ and the largest gland in the human body. It weighs in at a delicious 1.5 kilograms on average, is triangular in shape and is of a soft, pinkish-brown consistency that almost melts on the tongue. It lies to the right of the stomach, overlying the gallbladder (one of those tasty yet obsolete organs that has been hanging around in our bodies from the evolutionary soiree to which they weren't invited), and sits packed away nicely in the upper abdomen. It produces bile to detoxify the body, synthesises glucose, cholesterol and insulin, breaks down ammonia and haemoglobin, and can be baked, broiled or fried, or made into pate or sausages. It's particularly good with onions.

But all of that is not what makes the liver so amazing. It is one of the few internal organs capable of complete regeneration. Chop half of that meat out and in three months time, it's back to its normal size doing its normal job.

Fantastic! I've figured out how many lobes (and which ones), I can slice off the liver without killing Smarmy. It's a slow process, sure, for a good quality piece of liver, but a renewable source of meat is a fuck of a lot easier to achieve than trying to hunt down and capture my next meal.

Smarmy.

Might start calling him Prometheus.

And I the vulture sent by the gods to punish him and peck out his liver for eternity.

I log onto one of the many sites favoured by German cannibals and browse the forums. I'm looking for a doctor, med school, former SS, I don't care. If he's on here, and legit, then I've a business proposal to offer.

From the sound of the muffled screaming, I gather Prometheus has woken. I take a deep breath. And to think, I paid those useless fuckers to soundproof that room, too. It makes you angry, let me tell you.

"Only you can hear him," says a voice from the couch.

It's Vogon. First time I've seen in him a couple of weeks. Apparently, he'd had to check in with his supervisors re: the coming of the mothership and the first wave. I was getting dubious and reckoned the cunt was stalling me.

He had taken on the form of a body that looked familiar, though I couldn't place it.

"What do you mean?" I ask.

"You're a little paranoid, is all, Haines." His face hasn't settled on a particular visage as yet, instead he flicks through myriad main courses we have enjoyed over the last five years. "When you become attuned to a different sort of life, and the lives of those dependent upon you, you can become deeply sensitised to their needs."

His face stops on a younger version of my face. A you-didn't-know-I-could-do-this grin plasters across his cheeks. Cheeky fuck. And very clever for a creature that *says* he can't physically interact with this world. I didn't know he had ingested any of my DNA, so I'm wondering how he's pulling this off. I then realise it's my naked body he is mimicking on the couch. Only slightly flabbier. And with a smaller cock.

Vogon manages to flick on the TV (and I'm fucked if I know how he does this, but he always rambles about frequencies and radiowaves and I don't understand a single word of it). He cycles through the channels before saying, "It's a bit like the bond between mothers, even fathers, and their children. They know when others don't that something is wrong and needing attention, looking after, a little bit of love. I wouldn't worry about it, nobody else will hear him."

Two arms with thin-fingered hands and painted nails sprout from one of the thighs. The head of one of the early whores protrudes from the other thigh. The hands wrap around Vogon's cock, which vacillates between a thick black foreskinned beast, a long thin sturdy circumcised rod, and the wee cock he is pretending is mine. The head blindly bobs forward (he's forgotten to include her eyes), the chapped lips eventually allowed to swallow the ever-changing penis and Vogon giggles.

"Any news on the invasion plan?"

"Nope." He giggles again and simulates a fart while holding the head firm so it can't escape. "Hey, you wanna put on Shriekback's *Big Night Music*? I feel like being seductive."

"You're full of shit." I send a message to a potential conspirator on the forum about setting up an intensive care unit in my basement and sign it *The Vulture*. "And you're a compulsive liar."

"Yeah, but I bet you can't suck yourself off."

Sometimes I fucking hate Vogon.

One of my favourite recipes for liver is a simple one. Liver and Onions.

Simple but classic. One my mum taught me. And hard to fuck up unless you end up cooking the liver through too early instead of browning it. Ends up too tough, and you've cooked all the juice out of the juiciest organ in the body.

I've even decantered a bottle of 1998 Penfolds Grange that I'd swiped from the office liquor cabinet. I'd left enough clues to incriminate Fitzy at work, just in case it gets noticed before I return the bottle re-corked and filled with some Western Australian cleanskin I keep for such occasions. It's pretty fucking exciting really — I haven't had a Grange before.

I flick on some Jesus and Mary Chain and turn it up loud so that inconsiderate motherfucker squatting in my basement doesn't interrupt my cooking time.

Unfortunately, I'm not using a fresh liver, but one I've had in the freezer for about six months. One I've prepared earlier, so to speak. Never as good as a fresh one, and far less nutritious too, but I prefer the taste to that of a beef, lamb or chicken liver. They just don't have enough gusto.

I coat the liver in flour and set it aside. The frying pan is bubbling with a touch of butter and I throw in three slices of bacon, halved, to brown. The smell of the bacon fat hits me immediately and I salivate, and I'm almost back in Mum's kitchen hovering around the stove. I remove the bacon to drain on paper towels and add half a cup of sliced onions to the sizzling bacon fat in the pan. When the onions become translucent, I drop the liver into the pan. It'll only take a minute or two for each side, just enough to leave it pink and wet, so it can then simmer and soften with the pepper and tarragon beef broth I'm making up.

The doorbell rings.

Fuck.

First thing I'm thinking about is Smarmy. Someone knows.

My hand hovers over the frypan with the tongs. See, I need to turn the liver over shortly or I'll fuck this up.

The doorbell rings again, but I decide to ignore it. I can blame the loud music if it turned out to be important. I flick the liver over gently, blood already seeping to the surface of the flesh.

The doorbell rings again, just as the song stops.

"I know you're in there, Paul. I can hear you!"

Oh, fuck fuck fuck fuck.

I stand there dumbstruck, my eyes scanning the

room furiously for anything incriminating, anything she can use, anything she might borrow, break or steal.

She starts pounding on the door. "Paul! Hurry up, boy!"

I open the door, tongs in hand, not wanting this to be happening, but it is and she's standing there next to a large battered suitcase.

"Ho Ho!" Vogon yells from somewhere behind me, an instant before *Snakedriver* blasts out of the speakers.

"Mum. What are you doing here?"

"Just had a feeling you might need me." She wraps her arms around me and plants a kiss on my lips. "And I brought you a present. You got anything to drink? Hmmm. What's burning?"

Fuck. Smoke rises from the frypan. And double-fuck.

My mother is in her late fifties and looks good for her age. The weight is starting to show, but not badly, and she likes to think she's living some spiritual healthy life out in Daylesford munching on all the other gray carpets that live out that way. Hasn't had too good a word to say about men since Dad left her about ten years ago for the "young slut", but that hasn't stopped her from coming on her visits to the city when she gets this feeling-you-might-need-me business. What that really means is she's lodging down at my place for a week's free accommodation while she gets her fill of young Turk and Lebanese cock because she's needing a break from all that bitter lesbian pussy entrenched in those rolling hills. And you don't come in your own nest with forbidden meats in a town the size of Daylesford. She also claims she is not an alcoholic and I guess that's mostly true as she only ever drinks other people's alcohol.

Like mine for instance.

Mum sits on the couch, her legs crossed beneath a long blue flowery dress, sipping on a glass of Merlot. I'd hidden the decanter. Vogon stood in the shadows of the curtains near the TV, his silhouette rippling and reforming.

She points to a small carry bag she has placed on the coffee table.

"Go on, open it."

I unzip the bag and pull out a shiny chrome motor and a bundle of sturdy plastic attachments. I wouldn't want this anywhere near my arse. It looks like it could chew through flesh no problem at all. I have a horrible flash of a minced and battered clitoris in my mind, my mother's minced and battered clitoris. She'd love this fucking thing.

"It's a juicer," she says. "A cold-press masticating juicer. Gets up to forty percent more nutrients out of fruit and vegetables and that's a fact."

"I dunno, Mum, it's not really my scene. I'm a bit of a meat man, you know."

She snorts derisively. "What? Like your father? Off with the bummer boys."

"Eh?"

"Never mind." She drains her glass and wobbles it at

me. "Can make peanut butter. Sausages too. Even juice that liver you were cooking up. Do you how many nutrients in that lovely cut of meat you're killing as soon as you cook the thing? You could juice it and drink it down easy. Great for your health, build up that immune system of yours."

"I'm not sick, Mum." I refill her glass with the last of the Merlot.

"Sure, sure, you've got the arrogance of youth talking here. What are you? Thirty-three, thirty-four?"

"I'm thirty-two."

"Yes. I knew that."

"Your mum's hot", says Vogon.

I stare in disbelief at him. "I didn't hear that."

"Neither did I," says Mum. She's staring at Vogon, or at least where Vogon is standing. It's not possible that she can hear or see him. He is my envoy, and my envoy only. This he has also promised.

"What?" I ask her.

She stares at me, her eyes blue and clear, throws back the contents of the glass and stands up. For a minute I think she is going to walk around the table towards Vogon and lead him off to the spare bedroom, because after all, Vogon is turning out to be fucking liar or at least a vendor of unfulfilled promises the longer our relationship goes on.

Instead she walks to the cellar door and taps her glass on it gently.

"This where you keep the good stuff?'

"No."

"What's in here then?"

"Nothing."

"I'm going to fuck her," says Vogon.

We both look in his direction.

Mum taps the glass again. "Well, I want something stronger than this Merlot pisswater. It's too young and too soft."

"Isn't that how you like your men? Sorry, boys?"

"Don't be cheeky, Paul, you'll end up like your father if you're not careful. And I like them young and hard, not soft."

I hunt out a five-year old bottle of peppery Shiraz and pop the cork. It's going to be a long week.

At least, I hope it's only a week.

Vogon appears at the end of my bed just as I'm beginning the first of my evening wanks.

"What?"

"I sense you're a tad annoyed with me."

"Whatever, Vogon."

"I'm not full of shit. I'm not a compulsive liar. I have some exciting news for you."

I put my unexcited cock away and sit up. "I've heard all this before."

"Seriously. I'm meeting with one my supervisors at the abandoned warehouse in Spotswood tomorrow night. You've been invited. We're ready to meet you, brief you on your role in the first wave."

I don't want to believe him, he's fucked me over before. But my heart is racing, and my palms are sweating off the lubricants I have applied.

"Spotswood?"

Vogon nods. "I know it's the other side of town, but it's easy to get our ship into the bay there, better now since we convinced the council to dredge it out."

"Spotswood," I repeat, trying to affect disinterest. "That's a long way..."

"Two trains easy. Take the Lilydale, change at Flinders onto the Williamstown line and get off at Spotswood. Great pub near the station. Mostly real titties too, which is rare these days. Shouldn't take more than an hour and a half to get there, then maybe ten minutes to the warehouse."

"You'll come with me?"

"Sure. Well, I'll pick you up at Spotswood station. Don't think I can be bothered with the public transport. I got better ways to travel."

My cock is getting excited, which means so am I. I don't want Vogon to know how I feel about this though. I've been waiting over three fucking years for this next step.

"When?"

He gives me a horrid wink, all fluttering stolen eyelashes on oversized flaps of skin. "Tomorrow night, Hainsey boy. You need to be at Spotswood by 7:30pm, my good friend."

He disappears.

I have an extra wank than is normal to try to dissipate the impending excitement.

Mum's making a soup from zucchini, celery and green beans.

"It's great for detoxing the liver," she says. "You should have some before you go out."

"Nah, and how'd you know I was going out?"

She appraises me for a second, in that cruel, cutting way she does.

"You're all dressed up. Didn't think it was for me."

"Yeah, well, just some business stuff really. I should be back by..." I realise I have no idea how long this will take. What if I don't have to come back at all? And then there's Prometheus. "Uh, back by midnight, give or take."

I notice she is wearing lip gloss and has applied a thin layer of foundation to her cheeks. "Are you going out, too?"

"No, just a quiet night in tonight. Do you have any Absinthe perhaps?"

"Some gin and some cognac." I point to her face, indicating her makeup.

"You look like you're planning on some Turkish kebab tonight."

Mum laughs, stirring a ladle through the thick green broth. "No, just practicing tonight. Got a Middle Eastern smorgasbord lined up tomorrow evening, though."

I don't point out the Swedishness of that statement to her, or that a soufra is perhaps more appropriate. I check that my decanter of Grange is still there, and get out three bottles of recent vintages, a tempranillo and a sangiovese from the King Valley, and a youngish durif from up Rutherglen way, all good Victorian stock. She shouldn't be able to get through all this, but you can never tell with my mother. I put out a cognac just in case. I don't want her to go looking. For anything. I'm not comfortable with leaving her in my house at all, but I've been waiting too long for this rendezvous.

I leave her cooking the soup and head down to the station. I thought Vogon would have made another appearance, perhaps some encouragement or direction, or whatever the fuck an envoy for his species is supposed to do.

The train ride is dull and uneventful, but it doesn't bother me. My stomach flutters. My mouth is dry. Palms wet. Cock too hard. This is it. This is fucking it! That useless cunt of an alien has finally come through with the goods. I can hardly wait.

But I do. At Spotswood station, in the dark, in the cold. A drunk lies in his piss in the cubicle amongst old newspapers. Vogon is not here. Cunt.

At 7:50pm I cross the road to the King Charles Tavern offering a ten dollar special on a pot of beer, a parma, and a tittie show. He'll be in here for sure. He can't help himself. I buy a beer and scan the beaten down blokes perched around their tables waiting for the next piece of meat to gyrate out onto the small brightly lit stage. I'm dressed too flash for this place and I expect someone to take a dislike to that fairly soon. I can't see Vogon anywhere, but the pussy isn't waltzing around on stage yet, so that doesn't necessarily mean he's not here.

I'm halfway through the swill in my second beer, admiring the haunches of a hollow-eyed teenage girl when I overhear a grizzled fat bloke old enough to be her grandfather croak, "I'm going to fuck her."

Vogon.

He's not here. He was never here. He was never going to be here.

"I'm going to fuck her," says Vogon.

The lip gloss on her lips. My mother's lips.

Oh, that motherfuckering cunt.

This is not on, no way. I'm out the door of the pub, sprinting towards the Spotswood train station. The rumble of carriages approach like thunder tearing the night apart.

I'm going to make it in time.

The art of the hunt is in the element of surprise.

I pause at my front door, key poised in front of the lock. I press my ear against the cold wood, listening to the murmurings of my house.

The seductive beats of Shriekback's *Big Night Music* lay a backdrop for my mother's pitched laughter. She gasps, a sharp sucking of air and larynx.

A deeper giggle, a mixed up mess of a concoction of borrowed throats and pilfered voices.

Vogon.

I turn the keys, throw open the door and stare accusingly at my mother sprawled on the couch in a room flickeringly lit by scented candles, an amorphous figure hunched between her legs eating furiously.

But it's not quite like that I realise.

She sprawls on the couch, dress hitched to her thighs,

legs apart, but there is no one else in the room. She stares at me insolently, daring me to say something, anything.

I have a horrible feeling I've just caught my mother masturbating.

She places one of the thicker appendages from the juicer on the coffee table and picks up a glass of dark red wine. I note, with a pureed swell of disgust, contempt and fury, that the decanter is also on the coffee table. Empty.

"You're home early," she says. "I saved you some."

She indicates a second glass of wine, poured, ready to be consumed, then pulls up the pair of black lace knickers that had been warming her ankles.

I sit down in the chair opposite her, confused. "I thought that...I thought...could you see..."

"What, my love?" She sips the wine. It stains her lips deep red.

"Nothing." I reach for my wine. I can smell something in the room, something rich, masked by the scented candles. I swirl the wine, noting the thick legs sliding down the inside of the glass.

"Do you like *foie gras*?" she asks. "It is the gastronomical peak in liver delicacies."

I'm suddenly nervous. "I've never had it."

Mum runs her pink tongue over her teeth. "There's nothing like it, so rich and buttery, so delicate. Oh, those filthy Frenchmen." She laughs softly, her mind elsewhere, before her eyes sharpen on mine.

"But you need to make a choice. You can't have both. The best *foie gras* is the entire fattened liver, not just the lobes. Very hard to get, even in France. And it is the fat melting in the pan that gives it such a sweet buttery taste!"

Alarm bells are ringing. Screaming. This does not smell like a 1998 Penfolds Grange in this glass.

"Gavage, Paul, gavage. It's French for force-feeding. Passing a tube through the nose into the oesophagus will often suffice. Gavage. Have you considered this?"

The liquid in the glass is coppery and stringent. On the kitchen bench is the juicer, bloodied and shining in the candlelight. Fibrous pulp litters the bench top.

"Fresh liver or *foie gras*, my darling. You can't have them both. The fattened liver develops a certain delectable bacteria that is not particularly good for the host long term, but, my God, it enhances the flavour of the *foie gras* tenfold. There's nothing else like it."

The cellar door is ajar. My basement. My freezer.

She's managed to pick the locks. The tumblers tumbled, the vault door still open. Oh Jesus fucking Christ! She's still sprawled on the couch, talking, but I can't hear a word.

Oh my poor Prometheus!

I'm too scared to go in, to see if he's still there. She could have raided the freezer, defrosted a good chunk of meat before juicing it. She could have done that.

"Mum! What have you been up to?"

She gulps at the dark liquid in the glass before replying. "Ha! You sound just like your father did. Do you have life insurance?"

She closes the vault door and spins the tumbler, takes me by the arm and gently leads me to the couch.

"Now, have you something to tell me? Are you in trouble? Interest rates are making things tough for a lot of people and I have a fair idea of how much a place like this would cost. Especially for renovations. I have plenty of money. I'd like to help."

I sit numbly. She presses the glass of raw liver juice into my hand.

Vogon. He told her the combination. It had to be him. And what the fuck was that about insurance money? The alarm bells are turning into neon signs spelling things I don't want to read. Multi-layered, life-long lies coalescing into truths. "Where's Dad living these days?"

She forces the glass towards my lips with her fingers.

"Drink up," she says. "It's good for you."

Publication History

'Slice of Life' first appeared in *Dark Animus* #2, 2003.

'The Devil in Mr. Pussy (or How I Found God Inside My 'Wife)' in *c0ck*, 2006

'Mnemophonic' in *Doorways for the Dispossessed*, 2006.

'This is the End, Harry, Good Night!' in *NFG* #2, 2004.

'(It's Not Like) The Good Old Days' in *Ideomancer*, (originally titled 'www. rebirth.@#$%'), 2003.

'Going Down with Jennifer Aniston's Breasts' in *Ripples* #5, 2006.

'The Punjab's Gift' in *Story House*, 2005.

'Failed Experiments from the Frontier: The Pumpkin' in *Andromeda Spaceways Inflight Magazine* #37, 2008.

'Slice of Life — Cooking for the Heart' in *Lullaby Hearse* #4, 2004.

'Inducing' in *Orb* #7, 2007.

'Lifelike and Josephine' in *Agog! Ripping Reads*, 2006.

'Yum Cha' in *Antipodean SF* #48, 2002.

'A Tale of the Interferers: Necromancing the Bones' in *Dark Animus* #10/11, 2007.

'Shot in Loralai' in *NFG* #1, 2003.

'Doof Doof Doof' in *Dark Animus* #7, 2004.

'Where is Brisbane and How Many Times Do I Get There?' in *Fantastical Journeys to Brisbane*, 2007.

'Slice of Life — A Spot of Liver' is previously unpublished.

About the Author

Paul Haines is one of the leading authors in dark fiction working in Australia and New Zealand today. His work has often been described as deeply disturbing and soaked in black humour, with an uncanny ability to take the reader into the mind of many an unsavoury character. He has won over a dozen awards for his short story writing and is currently working on completing his first two novels. Raised in New Zealand, he now lives nestled between the beach and the bush near Melbourne, Australia, with his wife and daughter.

Available Now:

HOW TO MAKE MONSTERS
by GARY McMAHON

Since the dawn of mankind, we have always made our own monsters: the terrors of capitalism and corruption, the things between the cracks, the ghosts of self...terrible beasts of desire, debt, regret, racism...of family ties, and the things that get in the way of our aspirations...the familiar monsters of our own faces, of tradition, rejection, and the darkness that lives deep inside our own hearts...

Can you identify the component parts of your own monster?

Can you afford to pay the dreadful price of its construction?

Available Now:

VOICES edited by
MARK S. DENIZ & AMANDA PILLAR

In every room, there is a story.

In this hotel, the stories run to the wicked and macabre.

Well crafted psychological and supernatural horror offerings await you, each written by a master storyteller. Whether you are looking to be shocked, disturbed or outright frightened, *Voices* will have something to titillate your nerves and make your hair stand up on end. Leave the lights on and brew a strong cup of tea, the voices in the room plan on keeping you up all night.

Available Now:

DEAD SOULS
edited by MARK S. DENIZ

Before God created light, there was darkness. Even after He illuminated the world, there were shadows — shadows that allowed the darkness to fester and infect the unwary.

The tales found within *Dead Souls* explore the recesses of the soul; those people and creatures that could not escape the shadows. From the inherent cruelness of humanity to malevolent forces, *Dead Souls* explores the depths of humanity as a lesson to the ignorant, the naive and the unsuspecting.

God created light, but it is a temporary grace that will ultimately fail us, for the darkness is stronger and our souls...are truly dead.

Available Now:

THE PHANTOM QUEEN AWAKES
edited by Mark S. Deniz & Amanda Pillar

The Phantom Queen, goddess of death, love and war, returns to strike fear into the hearts of mortals in the anthology, *The Phantom Queen Awakes*.

Meet a washerwoman on the shores of the river; cleaning the clothes of the soon-to-be-dead; try to bargain with the capricious goddess of war; hear the songs of the dead as they cry for justice; walk with heroes of the past

Revisit the world of the Celts; a land of mystical beauty, avarice, lust and war through stories told by Katharine Kerr, C.E. Murphy, Elaine Cunningham and Anya Bast, among many other talented authors.

Available Now:

GRANTS PASS
edited by Amanda Pillar & Jennifer Brozek

Humanity was decimated by bio-terrorism; three engineered plagues were let loose on the world. Barely anyone has survived.

Just a year before the collapse, Grants Pass, Oregon, USA, was publicly labelled as a place of sanctuary in a whimsical online, "what if" post. Now, it has become one of the last known refuges, and the hope, of mankind.

Would you go to Grants Pass based on the words of someone you've never met?

Available Now:

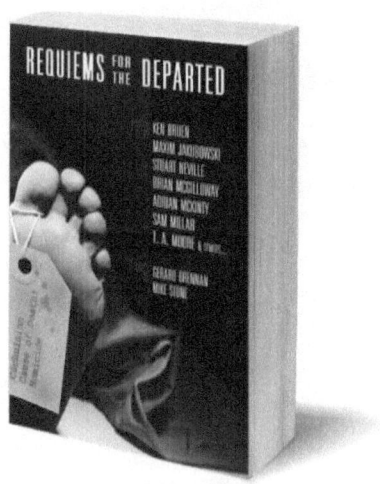

REQUIEMS FOR THE DEPARTED
edited by Gerard Brennan & Mike Stone

Requiems for the Departed contains seventeen short stories, inspired by Irish mythology, from some of the finest contemporary writers in the business.

Watch the children of Conchobar return to their mischievous ways, meet ancient Celtic royalty, and follow druids and banshees as they are set loose in the new Irish underbelly, murder and mayhem on their minds.

Featuring top shelf tales by Ken Bruen, Maxim Jakubowski, Stuart Neville, Brian McGilloway, Adrian McKinty, Sam Millar, John Grant, Garry Kilworth, T.A. Moore and many more.

Available Now:

SCENES FROM THE SECOND STOREY
edited by Amanda Pillar & Pete Kempshall

Scenes from the Second Storey is an anthology that pays homage to the album, *Scenes from the Second Storey*, by The God Machine. Quirky, dark, insightful and sometimes downright disturbing, these tales reflect the emotions and images our authors experienced when they heard 'their' song from *Scenes from the Second Storey*.

In *Scenes*, you will meet a girl struggling to find cleanliness in a world full of corruption with Kaaron Warren; follow the twisted mental pathways of the egocentric with Robert Hood; watch two men search for enlightenment down a dark path with Paul Haines; and dance with a girl struggling to find her role within society with Cat Sparks.

Available Now:

CREEPING IN REPTILE FLESH
by Robert Hood

A detective discovers he knows much more than he suspects...A seemingly normal pool of water becomes a doorway for monstrous things, horrible things, hungry for human flesh...A doctor and his "patient" discover that the location of the soul isn't in the brain, but in the heart...

This collection by Robert Hood, Australia's master of the macabre, offers 15 short stories to tantalise your mind and tempt your appetite. From rotting food to rotting corpses, this collection is vividly thought out madness, with Hood's mastermind at its core. Leave your lights on for this one — all of them.

Available Now:

THE WHISPER JAR
by Carole Lanham

Some secrets are kept in jars — others, in books. Some are left forgotten in musty rooms — others, created in old barns. Some are brought about by destiny — others, born in blood.

Secrets — they are the hidden heart of this collection. In these pages, you will encounter a Blood Digger who bonds two children irrevocably together; a young woman who learns of her destiny through the random selection of a Bible verse; and a boy whose life begins to reflect the stories he reads...

Most importantly, though, if someone should ever happen to offer you a Jilly Jally Butter Mint, just say "No!"